THE CRYSTAL PRISON

BOOK TWO OF
THE DEPTFORD MICE TRILOGY

ROBIN JARVIS

A PETER GLASSMAN BOOK
SEASTAR BOOKS
NEW YORK

FOR THE REST OF MY FAMILY,

WHO NOW LIVE WITHOUT

THE LIGHT OF MY FATHER

SeaStar Books
A division of North-South Books Inc.

First published in Great Britain in 1989 by
Macdonald Young Books Limited. All rights reserved.
Published simultaneously in Canada by North-South Books,
an imprint of Nord-Süd Verlag AG, Gossau Zürich, Switzerland.

Library of Congress Cataloging-in-Publication Data is available.

The text for this book is set in 11-point Walbaum Book.

ISBN 1-58717-107-4 (reinforced trade binding)
1 3 5 7 9 RT 10 8 6 4 2

Printed in U.S.A.

For more information about our books, and the authors and artists who create them,
visit our web site: www.northsouth.com

Reprinted by arrangement with North-South Books, Inc.

CONTENTS

THE DEPTFORD MICE

Audrey Brown

Tends to dream. She likes to look her best and wears lace and ribbons. Audrey cannot hold her tongue in an argument and often says more than she should.

Arthur Brown

Fat and jolly, Arthur likes a fight but always comes off worse.

Gwen Brown

Caring mother of Arthur and Audrey. Her love for her family binds it together and keeps it strong.

Arabel Chitter

Silly old gossip who gets on the nerves of everyone in the Skirtings.

Oswald Chitter

Arabel's son is an albino runt. Oswald is very weak and is not allowed to join in some of the rougher games.

Piccadilly

A cheeky young mouse from the city, Piccadilly has no parents and is very independent.

Thomas Triton

A retired midshipmouse. Thomas is a heroic old salt—he does not suffer fools gladly.

Madame Akkikuyu

A black rat from Morocco. She used to tell fortunes until her mind was broken in the chamber of Jupiter.

Kempe

A traveling trader mouse—he journeys far and wide selling his goods and singing lewd songs.

The Starwife

A venerable old squirrel who lives under the Greenwich Observatory. Her motives are good, but her methods are cruel.

THE FENNYWOLDERS

William Scuttle or "Twit"

A simple fieldmouse who has been visiting his mother's kin. Twit is a cheerful fieldmouse who looks on the bright side.

Elijah and Gladwin Scuttle

Twit's parents. Gladwin is Mrs. Chitter's sister, but ran away from Deptford as a youngster, when she found Elijah injured in the garden.

Isaac Nettle

A staunch Green Mouser. He is a bitter, grim figure, but many of the fieldmice listen to his ravings.

Jenkin Nettle

A jolly mouse who suffers at the paws of his father.

Alison Sedge

A country beauty who flirts with all the boys. She is vain and loves to preen herself.

Young Whortle, Samuel Gorse, Todkin, Hodge, and Figgy Bottom

Five young friends who delight in climbing the cornstalks and seeking adventure.

Mahooot

A wicked barn owl who loves mouse for supper.

Mr. Woodruffe

A very sensible mouse who has been elected to the honorable position of The King of the Field.

Nicodemus

Mysterious spirit of the fields who is trying to get free from limbo.

The Green Mouse

A magical figure in mouse mythology. He is the essence of all growing things, whose power is greatest in the summer.

THE DARK PORTAL

The Crystal Prison *is the second book in the story of the Deptford Mice, which began with* The Dark Portal. *In Book One, Audrey and Arthur Brown, two innocent town mice, are drawn into the sewers beneath the streets of Deptford in search of Audrey's mousebrass–a magical charm given to her by the Green Mouse, the mystical spirit of spring. Deep within the underground tunnels, the two mice discover the nightmare realm of Jupiter, the unseen but terrifying lord of the rats.*

Audrey and Arthur are helped by a number of characters: Oswald, a sickly albino mouse often mistaken for a rat; Twit, Oswald's cousin and a simple country mouse; Piccadilly, a cheeky young mouse from the city; and Madame Akkikuyu, a black rat who ekes out a living peddling potions and telling phoney fortunes.

The Deptford Mice discover that Jupiter is concocting a terrible plan–to release the Black Death upon London once again. However, with the help of the Green Mouse, the mice confound Jupiter's plot and lure him out of his lair. To their horror, they discover that Jupiter is not a rat at all, but a monstrous cat, grown bloated and evil by years of hatred in the sewers.

Audrey throws her mousebrass into Jupiter's face; it explodes and sends the giant cat tumbling into the deep sewer water. As he struggles to save himself, the souls of his many victims rise out of the waves and drag him down to a watery death.

PROLOGUE

SMOKE OVER DEPTFORD

It was a hot day in Deptford. A terrible stench hung over the housing estates, and increased as the sun rose higher in the sky. It was strongest on a building site near the river. There the air was thick and poisonous. The builders themselves choked and covered their faces with their handkerchiefs.

At the edge of the site next to the river wall was an untidy pile of yellowing newspapers. They lay in a moldering heap amongst the loose bricks and spreading nettles. It was here that the stink began.

One of the builders came trudging up. His worn, tough boots waded through the weeds and paused at the newspaper mound. A scuffed toe tentatively nudged some of them aside and a dark cloud of angry, buzzing flies flew out. Revealed beneath the papers was the rotting body of a horrific giant cat.

* * *

Jupiter was dead. The evil lord of the rats had met his end weeks before in the deep, dark sewer water. His immense body had sunk to the muddy bottom, where underwater currents pulled and swayed his corpse this way and that. Slowly he rolled out of the altar chamber and through a submerged archway.

Into the tunnels he had drifted, turning over and over in the water. One minute his grisly unseeing eyes would be staring at the arched ceiling above and the next glaring down into the cold dark depths. As he rolled over in this way his great jaws lolled open, lending him the illusion of life. Like a snarling demon he turned. But he was dead. For some days Jupiter bobbed up and down in the sewer passages until stronger forces gripped him and, suddenly, with a rush of water he was flushed out into the River Thames. The gulls and other birds left him well alone, and for a while all fish abandoned that stretch of the river.

One night nature took a hand in ridding the river of the dreadful carcass. A terrible storm blew up: the wind and the rain lashed down from the sky, and the river became swollen and crashed against its walls with shuddering violence.

On one such surging wave was the corpse of Jupiter, carried along until with a thundering smash the wave smote the wall and the cat's body was hurled over onto the building site.

* * *

The builder who had found him hurried away quickly but soon returned dragging behind him a great shovel caked in cement. With a grunt he lifted the sagging corpse into the air. Jupiter's massive claws dangled limply over the sides of the shovel and what was left of his striped ginger fur blazed ruddily in the sunlight.

Surrounded by the thick buzzing cloud, the builder stepped carefully over to the site bonfire and tossed Jupiter into its heart.

The flames licked over the cat greedily. For a while the fire glowed purple and then with one final splutter there was nothing left of the once mighty lord of the sewers.

Only a thick dark smoke that had risen from the flames remained, and this stayed hanging stubbornly in the air over Deptford for two days, until a summer breeze blew it away on the third morning.

CHAPTER ONE

THE SUMMONS

Oswald was ill. As soon as the white mouse had returned from the sewers he had felt unwell. When the small group of mice who had confronted the terrifying Jupiter had emerged from the Grill and climbed the cellar steps, Oswald's legs had given way and sturdy Thomas Triton had carried him the rest of the way. Although the albino coughed and spluttered, no one realized how serious his condition would become.

For weeks he had stayed in bed. At first the mice thought he had merely caught a cold, and his mother Mrs. Chitter had fussed and scolded him over it. But the cold did not improve and his lungs had become inflamed so that when he coughed the pain made him cry. Steadily he grew weaker. Mrs. Chitter tended to him day and night, and made herself ill in the process, until she too became a poor reflection of what she had once been.

Oswald's father, Jacob Chitter, had moved his favorite chair into his son's room next to his bed. He held his son's paw throughout, shaking his head sadly. Oswald was slipping away;

bit by painful bit the white mouse became more frail. Then one day Mrs. Chitter could take no more. As she was carrying away the soup that Oswald had been unable to swallow, the bowl fell from her paws and she fell heavily to the floor–soup and tears everywhere.

From then on Gwen Brown took charge of Oswald and his mother while Twit, the fieldmouse, looked after his uncle, Mr. Chitter.

All was silent in the Skirtings. The empty old house was filled with quiet prayers for the Chitter family. All the mice helped as much as they could: those on the Landings forgot their snobbery and offered food and blankets. Gwen Brown's own children, Arthur and Audrey, collected all the donations and messages of goodwill, and it was the job of a gray city mouse, called Piccadilly, to keep everyone informed of Oswald's condition.

All the mice owed a great deal to this small group of friends. It was they who had finally rid them of the menace of Jupiter, and all their lives were now easier. No more did they have to dread the cellar and the strange Grill, which was the entrance to the dark, sinister rat world. All the cruel rats had been killed or scattered and a mouse could sleep soundly at night, fearing no sudden attacks or raids. Only the older mice still looked at the cellar doubtfully and would not pass beyond its great door.

So, when they had been told of Jupiter's fall–and when they finally believed it–there was tremendous excitement and they had cheered the brave deeds of these mice. But now the youngest of the heroes was dying.

* * *

Piccadilly swept the hair out of his eyes and got out of bed. The sunlight shone on the city mouse and warmed him all over, but he hardly noticed it. For the moment, he was sharing a room with Arthur, and Audrey was sleeping in her mother's bed, as Gwen was at the Chitters' all the time now.

"Arthur," Piccadilly whispered to the snoring bundle, "wake up." He shook his friend gently.

The plump mouse on the bed blinked and drew his paw over his eyes. "How is he?" he asked directly.

Piccadilly shook his head. "I've just got up–how was he last night when you left him?"

"Bad!" Arthur swung himself off the bed and stood in the sunlight as was his custom. He stared at the clear blue sky outside. "Mother doesn't think it will be long now." He sighed and looked across to Piccadilly. "Will you stay here, afterward?"

The gray mouse sniffed a little. "No, I've made up my mind to stay just until . . ." He coughed. "Then I'm off–back to the city."

"We'll miss you, you know," said Arthur. "I won't know what to do around here when you've gone. I think Twit's decided to leave as well . . . afterward." Arthur turned back to examine the summer sky and then remarked casually, "I think Audrey will miss you most, though."

Piccadilly looked up curiously. "She's never said anything."

"Well you know what she's like: too stubborn to say anything! I know my sister, and believe you me, she likes you a lot."

"Well, I wish she'd tell me."

"Oh, I think she will when it suits her." Arthur stretched himself and rubbed his ears. "He doesn't even take the milk anymore, you know. Mother can't get him to drink it and if he does, it won't stay down. Maybe he would be better off . . ." his voice trailed away miserably.

"I'm dreading it," murmured Piccadilly. "These past few days he's sunk lower an' lower–I don't know what keeps him going."

Arthur touched him lightly on the shoulder. "Let's go and find out."

Audrey was already up and waiting for them. She had not bothered to tie the ribbon in her hair as she usually did and it hung in soft chestnut waves behind her ears.

Outside the Chitters' door they stopped, and Arthur glanced nervously at the others before knocking. They waited anxiously as shuffling steps approached on the other side of the curtain.

The curtain was drawn aside, and the small features of Twit greeted them solemnly. He looked back into the room, nodded, then stepped out and let the curtain fall back behind him.

"He's still with us," he whispered. "'Twere touch 'n go for a while last night: thought we'd lost 'im twice." The fieldmouse bit his lip. "Your mum's all in; she's 'ad a tirin' time of it. What with 'im and Mrs. Chitter, she's fit to drop."

"I'll tell her to lie down for a bit." Arthur nodded.

"And I'll take over," added Audrey. "You look like you could do with a rest as well, Twit."

"Well, Mr. Chitter, he just sits an' mopes, his wife an' son bein' so bad. I can't do anything with 'im." Twit wiped his brimming eyes. "Heck we tried–me an' your mum, but all three of 'em are slidin' downhill fast. I really think this be the last day–no, I knows it. None of 'em'll see the sunset." Big tears ran down the fieldmouse's little face. He was exhausted and felt that all his efforts had been a waste of time–this branch of his family was about to wither and die.

Audrey bent down and kissed Twit's forehead. "Hush," she soothed. "Piccadilly, put Twit in Arthur's bed. I'll wake you if anything happens," she reassured the fieldmouse.

"Thank 'ee," Twit stammered through a yawn, and he followed Piccadilly back to the Browns' home.

Arthur turned to his sister. "Right," he said. "I'll tackle Mother, you see to the Chitters. I'll come and help once Mother's gone to bed." Gingerly he pulled back the curtain.

It was dark beyond: the daylight had been blocked out for Oswald's sake.

Arabel Chitter's bric-a-brac was well dusted, her pieces of china ornament, bits of sparkling brooches, and neatly folded lace shawls and headscarves had all been seen to by Gwen Brown. Mrs. Chitter had always been house-proud and if things were not "just so" she would fret.

Arthur and Audrey slowly made their way to Oswald's room. Arthur coughed quietly and their mother came out to them.

"Hello, dears," she breathed wearily. Dark circles ringed her brown eyes and her tail dragged sadly behind her. "No ribbon today, Audrey?" she asked, stroking her daughter's hair. "And you, Arthur, have you had breakfast?"

"Have you, Mother?" He took her paw in his. "No, I didn't think so. Come on, you're going to get some sleep." He would hear no protests and Gwen Brown was too tired to make any.

"Audrey, promise me you'll wake me if . . ." was all she managed.

"I promise, Mother."

"Yes, good girl. Now, come, Arthur, show me to my bed or I'll drop down here."

Audrey watched them leave, then breathed deeply and went inside.

Illness has a smell all of its own and it is unmistakable. Sweet and cloying, it lingers in a sickroom, waiting for the patient to recover or fail. Audrey had grown accustomed to this smell by now, though it frightened her to enter the room.

It was a small space almost filled by the bed in which Oswald lay. Beside him on a chair was Mr. Chitter, his head bent in sleep. He was a meek mouse, devoted to his wife and son, but this had broken him.

Oswald was quite still. His face was gaunt and drained, paler now than ever before. His eyelids were closed lightly over his dim pink eyes. His fair albino hair was stuck close to his head and his whiskers drooped mournfully. The blankets were pulled up under his chin, but one of his frail paws was wrapped inside his father's.

Audrey felt Oswald's forehead: it was hot and damp. A fever was consuming his last energies, burning away whatever hope there had been for him. Sorrowfully she picked up a bowl from the floor. It contained clean water and a cloth, and with them she began to cool his brow.

Next to Oswald's bed, on the wall, was a garland of dried hawthorn leaves, which he had saved from the spring ceremony and preserved carefully. He had adored the celebrations and was impatient for the following year, when he too would come of age and be entitled to enter the mysterious chambers of summer and winter to receive his mousebrass. To Audrey it seemed long ago that she had taken hers from the very paws of the Green Mouse. She thought of him now, the mystical spirit of life and growing things. How often she had prayed to him to spare Oswald! Now it looked as if nothing could save him.

There was a small table near her and on it were some slices of raw onion. Mrs. Chitter believed this would draw out the illness from her son, and out of respect for her wishes Gwen Brown made sure that the onion was fresh every day. Audrey only regarded this superstition as one more addition to the eerie smell of illness.

A movement on the pillow drew her attention back to the patient.

Oswald's eyes opened slowly. For a while he gazed at the ceiling, then gradually he focused on Audrey. She smiled at him warmly.

"Good morning, Oswald," she said.

The albino raised his eyebrows feebly and tried to speak. It was a low, barely audible whisper and Audrey strained to hear him.

"What sort . . . of day is it . . . outside?" His sad eyes pierced

her heart and she struggled to remain reassuring when all the time she wanted to run from him sobbing. She could not get over the feeling that it was mainly due to her that Oswald was so ill.

"It's beautiful, Oswald," she said huskily. "You never saw such a morning! The sky is as blue as a forget-me-not and the sun is so bright and lovely."

A ghost of a smile touched Oswald's haggard cheeks. He closed his eyes. "You never did get your mousebrass back," he murmured.

"Yes, I did, for a short while. You were so brave, getting it for me amongst all those horrible rats."

"I don't think I shall ever get my . . . brass now," he continued mildly. "I wonder what it would . . . have been."

"The sign of utmost bravery," sobbed Audrey. She held her paw over her face.

"I'm so sorry, Oswald," she cried. "This is all my fault."

"No, it had to be done . . . Jupiter had to be destroyed. Not your fault if . . . if I wasn't up to it."

"Don't, please! Just rest. Would you like some milk?" But Oswald had already fallen into a black swoon. Audrey cried silently.

A gentle, polite knock sounded. She dried her eyes and left the sickroom, pausing on the way to the main entrance to look in on Mrs. Chitter, who lay asleep in another room. Arabel's silvery head was old and shriveled. It was startling to see it against the crisp whiteness of the pillows. But at least she was asleep and not fretting. Audrey crept away and made for the entrance.

"Oh, it's young Miss Audrey!" Sturdy Thomas Triton looked faintly surprised to see her when she drew the curtain back. "I was expectin' your mother, but if you aren't the very one, anyway." The midshipmouse pulled off his hat and asked gravely, "How's the lad this morn?"

"No better, I'm afraid–we don't think he'll last much longer. Mother's resting just now: she and Twit have been up all night."

"Aye," muttered Thomas grimly, then he furrowed his spiky white brows and considered Audrey steadily with his wise, dark eyes. "'Tis a sore thing to bear–losing a friend," and an odd far-off expression stole over him, "'specially if you think it's all your fault. That's a mighty burden, lass! Don't take it on yourself–guilt and grief aren't easy fellows to cart 'round with yer, believe you me."

Audrey turned away quickly. Thomas's insight was too unnerving and she cringed from it. "Would you like to see him?" she managed at last.

Thomas fidgeted with his hat, rolling it over in his strong paws. "Lead on, I'll look on the boy once more."

When they came to the sickroom he hesitated at the doorway and changed his mind. "Nay, I'll not enter. I've glimpsed the lad and that's enough. I've seen too many go down with fever to want to witness it again. He were a brave sort whatever he may have said to the contrary. A loss to us all. I see the father has not moved–is the mother still abed?" Audrey nodded. "That's bad! A whole family wiped out by sickness and grief. Well, how's little Twit bearing up?"

"Oh, you know Twit. He always tries to be bright and jolly. You never know what he's thinking deep down."

"Yes, you're right there. I like that fieldmouse–reminds me of someone I knew once–best friend I ever had. Twit's mighty fond of his cousin there–it'll be a tragic blow to his little heart."

A soft footfall behind them made them both turn sharply–but it was only Arthur.

"Hullo Mr. Triton," he said politely. "Audrey, I've managed to put Mother to bed and she's asleep now, but I think Piccadilly's having trouble with Twit–he needs to rest, but won't settle. He can't stop worrying!"

"Right, I'll get him out of that," said Thomas firmly, and he fixed his hat back on his head. “Come with me, miss, and you milladdo, stay here. I’ll see to my young matey.” The midshipmouse strode from the Chitters’ home with Audrey following.

“Mr. Triton,” she said, catching up with him. “What did you mean before when you saw me and said I was the very one?”

“It wasn’t just to see poor Oswald that I came,” he explained as they entered the Browns’ home, “but to see you as well.”

“Me?” asked Audrey, puzzled. She had not spoken to the midshipmouse very much during the brief times that he had visited the Skirtings, and she wondered what he was up to.

“Aye, lass,” he continued. “I’ve a message for you.”

She looked blank as Thomas Triton charged into Arthur and Piccadilly’s bedroom.

The city mouse was trying to get Twit to stay in bed. He had heated him some milk and honey, but the fieldmouse would not rest. When Thomas barged in Twit grinned in spite of himself.

“How do!” he said.

“Ahoy there, matey,” Thomas said sternly. “What you doin’, lyin’ in yer bunk on a day like this?” The midshipmouse winked a startled Piccadilly into silence. “Get up, lad, there’s folk to see!”

“But he’s only just gone to bed,” exclaimed Audrey.

Without turning around to look at her, Thomas said, “You, miss, had better make yourself presentable. What has happened to your hair?”

“I . . . I didn’t put my ribbon in,” stammered Audrey.

“Then chop chop, lass. Go do whatever you do do to make a good impression. Someone wants to see you.”

“Who’s that then, Thomas?” asked Twit, curiosity banishing the weary lines around his eyes.

The midshipmouse feigned astonishment. “Why, the Starwife, lad–didn’t I say?”

Twit’s eyes shone with excitement. “What? Her that lives in

Greenwich under those funny buildings I saw when the bats flew me over?"

"Aye, matey. First thing this morning, when it was still dark, I had a message from herself delivered by one of her younger jumpy squirrels–took me a long time to calm him down. They are a watery lot! Well the gist of the story is," Thomas now turned to Audrey, "that the Starwife wants to see you, Miss Brown, and she won't be kept waitin'. I've come to fetch you, and milladdo here is welcome to join us."

For a second Twit's heart leaped, but when he thought of Oswald it sank down deeper and lower than ever. Sadly he shook his head. "I can't come, Thomas. Oswald won't see the end of the day–my place is here."

The midshipmouse put his paw on Twit's shoulder. "Lad, I promise you we'll be back for that time. If Oswald leaves us, I swear you'll be at his side."

Twit blinked. He trusted his seafaring friend so much, yet how could he be so certain? Thomas's eyes bore into him and under their solemn gaze the little fieldmouse felt sure that he was right.

"I'll just go an' have a quick swill," Twit said, running out of the bedroom.

Audrey stared at Thomas and began to say something when a stern command from him sent her dashing off to find her ribbon.

Thomas Triton sighed and smiled at Piccadilly. "I'll not keep them away long. The easiest bit's been done–I've got them to go. Your job's not as simple. Pray to the Green Mouse that the Chitter lad hangs on till we return!"

CHAPTER TWO

THE STARWIFE

Thomas Triton led a flustered Audrey and Twit across the hall. Through the cellar door they slipped and jumped down the stone steps beyond. Thomas strode through the cellar gloom to the Grill.

Wrought in iron with twirling leaf patterns, this had always been an object of fear and dread. And, indeed, when Jupiter the terrible god of the rats had been alive it had possessed strange powers.

Now Audrey shivered as she stood before it, recalling how she had been dragged through the Grill by an evil band of rats. Twit backed away from it slightly. He remembered the horrible effect that the black enchantments had had upon Arthur. Only Thomas dared to touch the Grill.

With a hearty laugh he looked at the others. "Jupiter is dead," he reminded them. "Whatever forces were lurking in or beyond this grating are long gone." As if to prove it, he banged an iron leaf with his fist. "The spells are as cold and lifeless as the mangy moggy who made them." The midshipmouse chuckled and squeezed himself through the rusted gap in the Grill.

"This is the quickest way to Greenwich," he said, popping up on the other side. Audrey and Twit still hesitated, so Thomas pulled a silly face. It looked so ridiculous that they couldn't help laughing. Perhaps the Grill was an ordinary metal grating after all. Audrey and Twit crawled through the gap and joined Thomas.

Down into the sewers they went. Although it was a hot summer day in the outside world, here it was chill and damp. Audrey had forgotten how bleak it all was. So many ugly memories were kindled by everything around her; the musty, stale smell of the dark running water, the slippery slime on the ledges, and the weird echoes, which floated through the old air. Around every corner there was a dark memory.

Thomas sensed her unease and remarked casually, "I use the sewers quite a bit now. I never get lost, me. I can find my way home on a black foggy night with no moon and my hat over my eyes." Twit chuckled softly, and Audrey was grateful to the midshipmouse; he took her mind off things.

"Now there ain't no more rats down 'ere," Twit piped up, "there's no danger of us gettin' peeled, is there, Thomas?"

"'S right, matey."

"But won't others arrive and take over where Jupiter's rats left off?" Audrey asked, doubtfully looking over her shoulder.

"No, rats are mostly cowardly," answered Thomas. "Only the fear of Jupiter gave them a false sort of courage. Ask that city mouse–he'll tell you how cringy they are in the city. You just have to cuff 'em about the head if they start gettin' uppity."

Audrey felt relieved. Like Twit she found the midshipmouse to be a comforting figure. He was so sure of himself that it rubbed off onto everyone he was with. Audrey's thoughts returned to Oswald lying in his bed. She shook her head to dispel that image and tried to think of something else. "Tell me about the Starwife, please, Mr. Triton," she asked.

"She'm the grand dame of the squirrels," put in Twit.

"Yes, but what can she want of me?" asked Audrey, baffled. "I'd never heard of her before."

"Maybe," said Thomas, "but she's obviously heard of you. Somehow the name Audrey Brown has reached her ancient ears. Rumors spread quickly–she must have heard about Jupiter's downfall and wants to know all the details of it."

"Yes, but you were there as well Mr. Triton. You could have told her, surely?"

"True, I was there on the altar when that old monster was sent to his watery grave–but you did the sendin' remember, and it was your mousebrass that toppled him."

"What shall I tell her then?" Audrey asked nervously.

Thomas whirled around. "Why the truth, lass, and nothing but that! Don't go addin' bits or leavin' stuff out, or your ears'll ring for weeks after. It's plain speaking in the Starwife's drays and chambers–and that only when you're spoken to."

"Have you seen her then, Mr. Triton?" pressed Audrey, desperate to know as much as possible about the strange personage she was about to meet.

"That I have," he replied cautiously. "When I first came and settled around here I was summoned to meet her." Thomas grew grave and added, "There were matters that I needed to talk to her about." He stroked his white whiskers and cleared his throat. "I've been hurled around by tempests on angry, foaming seas and nearly got drowned twice, but I don't mind telling you that I've never been so skittish as when I went to her drays. And I was shakin' even worse when I came out of them!"

Twit whistled softly. He couldn't imagine sturdy Thomas being afraid of anything. What a creature this Starwife must be! "What did she do to you, Thomas?" he asked wide-eyed.

"Well, I went in there, knees-a-knockin'. I'd heard many a strange tale of the Greenwich Starwife, and only an idiot would go into her chambers unabashed. Well, down some tunnels I was took and there behind a fancy curtain was the Starwife. Oh, she saw right through me, knew everything about me–what I'd done, what I hoped to do–uncanny that was. I think I made a right tomfool of myself in front of her. She weren't impressed with her new neighbor at all. Still, I came away feeling better, but I ain't clapped eyes on her since."

"And this morning you got a message from her about me," added Audrey.

"Yes, that surprised me no end." Thomas paused and looked at Audrey. "In fact, it's so rare an occurrence that I'd be careful, if I were you, Miss Brown."

Audrey was worried. She imagined the Starwife to be as bad as the rats. Her thoughts must have showed plainly on her face, for Thomas added, "Oh, she won't eat you, but the Starwife has motives of her own. She never does nothing for nothing. Sometimes she can be as subtle as Jupiter himself, and that's what I'm puzzled about. So I say again just watch yourself."

"You don't encourage me, Mr. Triton. I'm not sure if I'm looking forward to this. I'd rather go back to the Skirtings."

"Too late for that, miss. Here we are now."

They had come to the end of the sewer journey and a small passage lay before them, at the end of which bright sunlight streamed through the holes in a grate.

Thomas led them down it and they followed him to the outside world.

The mice stood outside Greenwich Park. Before them the green lawns stretched away up to the observatory hill. The sweet scent of freshly mowed grass tingled their noses.

Twit breathed it in deeply. "Oh," he sighed, "that do lighten me heart."

The fieldmouse leaped into the mounds of drying grass cuttings. Gurgling with delight he burrowed down into the soft damp darkness where the fragrances tugged at his memories and visions of home swam before him. Snug in the grass cave, Twit's tiny eyes sparkled. The city was no place for him–he belonged to the open fields where corn swayed high above and ripened slowly in the sun until it burned with golden splendor.

The grass rustled above his head and the harsh dazzle of midday broke around him.

"Come on, matey!" Thomas laughed, parting the cuttings. "Not far to the Starwife now."

Twit scrambled out of the mound, wiping his forehead with a clump of the sweetest, dampest grass. Audrey smiled at him as he rubbed it into his hair.

"Luvverly," he exclaimed, "I feel bright and breezy now." She had to agree: the fresh, clean scent of the grass cleansed her nose of the smell of the sickroom.

"We better catch up with Mr. Triton," Audrey suggested. "Just look how he's marching off."

"I'm thinkin' old Thomas ain't happy about meetin' that there Starwife again."

"Well, I don't want to meet her a first time. She sounds like a right old battle-ax. I'm telling you, Twit, no matter who she is, I'm in no mood for a bad-tempered old squirrel."

"Oh, I am," cried Twit. "Anything to be out of those dark rooms for a while."

They ran after Thomas, skirting around the tangled roots of the large trees. Gradually the three mice made their way up the hill.

Thomas's brows were knitted together in concentration. They avoided the paths and kept on the grass, obeying their instincts of survival–out of sight, out of danger.

The farther up the hill they went the more thoughtful and quiet Thomas became. By the time they were halfway up he was positively frowning, and his tail switched to and fro irritably. Audrey caught his mood and stayed silent. Only Twit chirped up now and again, gasping at the view and remembering when the bats had flown him over this very hill.

Presently the Observatory buildings drew near. How high they were with their onion-shaped domes and solid walls! They sat proudly on top of the hill, fringed by railings and thick rhododendron bushes.

"Look," called Twit suddenly. "In those bushes there. No, it's gone now."

"What was it?" asked Audrey.

"A squirrel," explained the fieldmouse. "It were watchin' us–didn't half give me a shock. There it was a-starin' straight at me–gray as ash then *poof*! It darted away as speedy as anything."

"How long do you think it had been watching us?" asked Audrey, slightly unnerved. She had never seen a squirrel before.

Thomas glared into the bushes. "They've been keeping an eye on us ever since we stepped into the park. Thought they were being clever, but I spotted them a-spying and jumping from branch to branch over our heads. Let them scurry and keep her informed of our progress. Like a spider in a wide web she is, gathering news–you'd be surprised at what she hears," he added grimly.

Audrey twisted the lace of her skirt between her fingers. "Mr. Triton," she began nervously, "I don't want to see her now. Please can we go back?"

"No, lass," Thomas sighed, shaking his head. "She has summoned you and you've come this far. Don't let an old jaded rover like me frighten you now. Courtesy must be kept and you never know–maybe the old boot's mellowed since last I saw her."

Twit giggled at Thomas's description of the Starwife. "I can't wait," he babbled excitedly.

"Right ho, matey," said Thomas, "let's take the cat by the whiskers." The midshipmouse ducked under a railing and scampered up the bush-covered bank. Audrey and Twit followed.

Thomas Triton stooped and sat down in the mossy shade of the dark-leaved rhododendrons.

"What are you doing?" asked Audrey in surprise. "I thought we were going to find the Starwife."

"We've come as far as we can on our own," said Thomas solemnly. "I'm waiting for our escort."

Twit blinked and peered around them. The shadows under the thick bushes were deep. "I don't see no ones," he whispered. "Where is this escort, Thomas?"

"Oh, they're here," replied the midshipmouse dryly. "I'm just waiting for them to find their guts and show themselves."

Above their heads amongst the leathery leaves nervous coughs were stifled.

Audrey glanced up. "What are they doing?" she murmured fearfully.

Thomas stretched and yawned, then he lay back and rested his head on the spongy moss. "This is where we have to wait till one of them plucks up enough nerve to come down and lead us farther. Could be hours."

"But we can't wait too long, Thomas," urged Twit, thinking of Oswald.

The midshipmouse eyed Twit for a moment. "You're right, matey. I'll not be idle while the Chitter lad's fadin' fast." He sprang to his feet, then in one swift movement snatched a small stone off the ground and flung it into the air.

Up shot the stone into the canopy of rhododendron. A surprised yell came from the leaves. Thomas jumped nimbly to one side, and with a crash of twigs, a gray lump dropped to the ground.

"Oh, oh!" cried the furry bundle in panic.

"Peace, squire!" calmed Thomas. "We have no time for your

formalities today. Forgive me for speeding up the proceedings."

Twit stared at the terrified squirrel before them. It was young and its tail was strong and bushy. The squirrel's face was small, but his large black eyes seemed to be popping out of his head. He looked at the three mice in fright.

Thomas waited for him to find his voice, making no effort to conceal his impatience during the squirrel's stammerings.

"But . . . but . . ." the squirrel began, "three . . . there are three of you–we . . . I . . . thought there would be only two." He regarded Twit uneasily.

"This is my good young matey William Scuttle," Thomas roared in a voice that made the squirrel shrink away. "Where I go, he goes." He laid his paw firmly on the fieldmouse's shoulder.

"She won't like this . . . she won't like this–not at all, no."

"That's enough!" rapped Thomas. "I'll face whatever squalls she throws my way, but we'll not sit here becalmed by your dithering. Lead us and have done."

"The . . . the girl first," instructed the squirrel timidly. "The mouse-maiden is to follow me."

Audrey nearly laughed at the anxious gray figure, which hesitated and twitched before her, but she remembered her manners and tried to remain serious. She stepped in line behind her escort.

"Good . . . good," he muttered, and with a jerk of his tail he bounded through the bushes. The mice followed him as quickly as they could.

Into the leafy clumps they ran and there, in the shadows, were a dozen other squirrels all fluttering and trembling with fright. Their escort was laying into them as the mice approached.

"Why didn't you?" he scolded the others crossly. "Leaving me all alone to deal with them."

"Well, we weren't to know," they answered meekly. "But you did so very well, Piers," some added. "Sshh, here they are now." They fell back as the mice entered.

"Ermm . . . this way," the escort said shakily, and he set off again.

The crowd of squirrels watched them leave and they turned to one another tut-tutting. "She won't like that will she? Three of them, I ask you. He ought to have said something. The look that little fellow gave you . . . little savages they are . . . makes me shiver all over. Who's going to tell her then? Don't be soft–you know she doesn't need us to tell her anything, she has her own ways of finding things out."

Audrey followed the escort's bushy tail as it bobbed before her. Through lanes of leaves it led her, under arches of twining roots and past startled squirrel sentries who disappeared in a flash of gray. The bushes grew thicker overhead and no daylight filtered down. Suddenly a great oak tree appeared at the end of the green tunnel and the escort vanished down a dark cleft in the trunk.

Audrey paused, wondering how far down the drop was. She braced herself and with her eyes closed tightly leaped into the black hole.

Down she plunged until she landed with a soft jolt on a bundle of dry leaves and ferns. Audrey rolled to one side as Twit came down, whistling and laughing.

"It smells in here," sniffed Audrey.

"Only oak wood and leaf mold," said Twit, staggering to his feet.

They were in the base of the old oak's trunk, hollowed out by years of squirrel labor. Small wooden bowls hung on the walls and these were filled with burning oils. The light they gave off was silver and flickering, illuminating the smooth worn oak with gentle, dancing waves.

"It's as cold as the sewers down here." Audrey shivered.

Twit sat beside her and brushed the leaves off her back. “I have heard some in my field at home as do call squirrels tree rats,” he whispered.

A muffled crash and a mariner’s curse announced Thomas’s arrival.

“I’d forgotten about that drop,” he muttered, rubbing his back. “Where’s that nervy chap gone to now?”

“I don’t know,” said Audrey. “There are some openings over there–are they the roots of this tree?”

“Aye, we are in the heart of the squirrel domain and here the Starwife lives, but there were Starwives before this oak was an acorn and before this very hill was made. The Starwives go back a long way.”

Just then the escort came bounding back. “What are you waiting for? Come, come,” he implored, “she is impatient. Hurry now!” He scurried away down one of the openings.

Audrey and Twit set off after him. “I wish I’d brought some rum with me,” murmured Thomas to himself.

Down the narrow passages the mice followed the squirrel. Deep into the earth they seemed to be going. After a short while Audrey noticed something other than the silver lights twinkling ahead. It was a richly embroidered banner hung across the width of the passage. The background was a dark blue and over it was stitched a field of twinkling stars that reflected the light of the lamps around them. As Audrey examined the stars more closely she saw that the silver thread of which they were made was in fact tarnished by great age.

The escort paused and bowed before the banner.

The three mice waited apprehensively. Audrey and Twit stared at each other and wondered what lay beyond this elaborate partition.

A strong, impatient voice snapped from the other side. “Bring them in, Piers–stop dawdling, boy!”

The squirrel jumped in fright. “Oh, madam, forgive me!”

He clutched one corner of the banner and popped his head through as he drew it aside. "By your leave, madam, may I introduce . . ."

"Show in the midshipmouse first!" commanded the voice.

The squirrel looked back at Thomas and said, "Come through when I announce you."

Thomas grinned at Twit. "Battle stations!" he remarked wryly, dragging the hat from his head.

"By your leave, madam," the squirrel had begun again, "may I introduce to you, midshipmouse Thomas Triton."

"Triton," called the other, sharp voice, "come in here."

Thomas scowled as he straightened the red kerchief around his neck and strode through the banner.

Audrey held on to Twit's paw as they waited for their turn.

With a rising dislike for the voice she presumed was the Starwife's, Audrey tried to keep calm.

"So, seafarer," said the voice on the other side of the banner. "It has been a long time since last I saw you in my chamber."

"Yes, ma'am," came Thomas's awkward reply, "too long."

"The fly has kept away from the web as best he might. But now you could say that the old boot is on the other foot."

Audrey gasped. How did the Starwife know that Thomas had compared her to a spider and an old boot? Whatever her sources, it was unkind and downright rude of her to taunt Thomas with his own words. Audrey felt herself becoming angry.

The midshipmouse was coughing to cover his embarrassment. He was a mouse of action, not words, and the respect he had for the Starwife and his own code of honor would not allow him to answer back.

"I hear you've settled down in your retirement at last," the voice began once more. "No more nightmares to haunt you?"

"No, ma'am, not since my last visit when you were kind

enough to give me those powders. That particular ghost has been laid to rest."

"It should be so. Though wounds of the heart and mind are the hardest to heal. You seem to be on the right path at last."

"I have taken your advice, ma'am, and not taken to the water once in all these years."

"Let it be so always, Thomas or . . ." the Starwife's voice dropped to a whisper and Audrey could not catch what she was saying. She considered all that she had heard. Evidently there was something in Thomas's past that he had not spoken about.

A loud sharp knock brought her up quickly. The escort peered around the banner.

"Bring in the fieldmouse," called the Starwife sternly. "I'll teach him to tag along when he's not invited."

Twit looked at Audrey in dismay. "She ain't magic is she?" he asked. "I don't want her to turn me into no frog or stuff like that."

"You stand up to her," Audrey told him. "Don't let her walk all over you."

"Master William Stutter!" announced the escort. "Scuttle!" corrected Twit angrily as he pushed past. Audrey tried to glimpse what was beyond the banner, but the escort pulled it across and tutted loudly.

"The very idea!" he said tersely.

"So, country mouse," greeted the Starwife coldly. "You have come to visit me have you?"

"If it pleases you, your ladyship," Twit's small voice piped up.

"It pleases me not at all," she snapped back. "Who are you to presume a welcome in my chamber? A lowly fieldmouse before the Starwife!"

"Now look 'ere, missus," Twit protested.

Audrey was very angry. How dare that old battle-ax pick on little Twit like that? After all he had been through lately he deserved more than to be shouted at by that rude creature. She stood tight-lipped, her temper flaring.

"Please, ma'am," came Thomas's voice, "it's my fault. I brought the lad–he needed the break. Times are bad in the Skirtings."

"Silence, Thomas," ordered the Starwife. "I know of the Chitters and their son. True the lad needed a rest from those dark rooms but what of you, midshipmouse?"

"Ma'am?"

"I sense a strong bond has grown between you and young Scuttle. I find myself wondering why–a lone wanderer such as you taking friends on board at your time of life. Who do you see in him, Thomas?"

"Ma'am, please . . ."

"I see you walk a dangerous rope, midshipmouse. Reality and memory ought never to entwine so closely! Beware your dreams and forget what has passed."

"I try, ma'am."

"Enough! Piers–fetch the girl." The loud knocking began again.

Audrey prepared herself and the escort pulled back the banner. "Follow me, please," he said stiffly.

Audrey smoothed her lace collar and stepped into the Starwife's chamber.

After the cramped tunnel it was like walking out into the open, for it was so spacious. Suspended from the ceiling above were hundreds of small shiny objects, colored foils, metal lids, links from silver chains, and polished pieces of glass. All were hung in a certain order, and for a moment, Audrey thought their pattern familiar but could not place it until she realized that, like the banner, they represented all the constellations of the heavens.

Below this dangling chart sat the Starwife.

"Miss Audrey Brown!" the escort pronounced.

"Come here, girl. Where I can see you."

Audrey moved toward the Starwife. She was an ancient squirrel perched on a high oaken throne carved with images of twisting leaves and acorns. Audrey had never seen anyone like her before. Age seemed to smother the Starwife. It was a miracle that she could move at all. Her fur was silver and patchy, and her muscles were wasted, falling in useless rolls beneath fragile dry bones. The Starwife's eyes were a dull gray and over one of them was a thin white film like spilled milk.

In her gnarled, crippled paws she held a stick and it was this that Audrey had heard knocking on the wooden floor. The Starwife had sat there with that stick for so many years that it had worn a definite trough in the floor.

Around her neck hung a silver acorn, the symbol of her knowledge and wisdom.

Behind the throned figure Audrey could see a deep darkness, which the lamps were unable to illuminate, except for now and again when a silver flash shone out brilliantly. It was curious, but before she had a chance to look farther, an impatient tapping of the stick brought her attention back to the Starwife.

"How do you do?" Audrey asked, dropping into a formal curtsy. The Starwife made no reply, so Audrey repeated herself, a trifle louder than before.

The ancient squirrel shifted on her throne and sucked her almost toothless gums. "I'm half blind, girl, but not deaf yet." She gazed at Audrey with unblinking eyes and sniffed the air.

Audrey did not like the Starwife one little bit. She looked over to where Thomas and Twit were standing and grimaced at them. No way would this squirrel intimidate her. "Rude old battle-ax," she thought to herself. She didn't see why she had to be on her best behavior if the Starwife had no manners of her own.

For several minutes Audrey remained silent and motionless under the continuing stare of the Starwife until the prolonged silence became embarrassing for her. It occurred to her that maybe the squirrel had nodded off like some old mice did in the Skirtings. Once more she thought of Oswald and felt that this was a waste of precious time.

"Excuse me," she began politely, "but we can't stay long, I'm afraid."

The Starwife blinked and opened her mouth. She rose shakily in her throne and her joints cracked like twigs. The stick pounded the floor indignantly. Thomas put his hat over his face and the escort began to stammer idiotically.

The Starwife switched her stare from Audrey to him. "Piers!" she barked, "get out, you imbecile!" The escort looked around uncertainly, but at that moment the Starwife threw her stick at him. It struck him smartly on the nose and he fled howling from the chamber.

The Starwife eased herself gingerly back down onto her throne and gave a wicked chuckle. She relaxed and turned once more to Audrey. "You must think me a rude old battle-ax," she said calmly. Audrey flushed–it obviously wasn't safe to think in front of this creature. "I do have manners, but it's so rare that I find anyone worth practicing them on. You must forgive me, child."

"Why did you send for me?" Audrey asked.

"There are two reasons, Miss Brown. Firstly, I desired to speak to the one who sent Jupiter to his doom. Tell me all you know and all that happened on that glad day."

Audrey breathed deeply, not sure where to begin. Then she recounted all that had happened to her since One-Eyed Jake had dragged her through the Grill up to the time she had thrown her mousebrass at Jupiter. Throughout her tale the Starwife kept silent, nodding her head on occasion as if she understood more than Audrey about the events. When she had finished Audrey stepped back and waited for the other to comment.

"A dark story you have told, Miss Brown, with more horror than you know. There are certain things contained in your nar-

rative that I had no knowledge of. Of course I knew all the time that Jupiter was a cat. I recognized the body he concealed in the darkness behind those burning eyes of his. A two-headed rat monster–rubbish, as I always maintained. But other things do surprise me. That episode in the pagan temple where Jake murdered Fletch, now that is disturbing–Mabb, Hobb, and Bauchan are old gods and it frightens me to think they are but newly worshiped. Who can tell what folly will come of that?" The Starwife raised her head and gazed distractedly at the star maps.

"Your pardon ma'am," said Thomas softly. "You mentioned two reasons for wanting to see Miss Audrey–may we know the second?"

"Oh, I'm sorry, Triton," she replied, and it seemed to Audrey that the Starwife was just a harmless squirrel older than nature had ever intended her to be.

"Fetch me my stick will you, lad," she motioned to Twit. The fieldmouse ran to retrieve it from the floor. He bowed as he presented it to her. The Starwife received it gratefully. "Thank you, lad. It is more than a missile with which I bruise my subjects' stupid heads–I would not be able to walk without it."

"And now," she sighed, turning to Audrey once more, "you shall know the other reason why I brought you here." She banged the stick on the floor loudly and waited for the young squirrel to return.

"Ah, there you are, Piers. Don't be afraid. I promise not to throw it anymore today."

"Did you wish for anything, madam?" asked the squirrel doubtfully.

The Starwife nodded and told him, "Bring in our guest."

Piers disappeared once more.

"It's over a week ago now," she began, "that our sentries spotted someone skulking in our park. The sight of this creature was fearful to behold and all fled before it. Nearer to my realm it drew. I could not get a word of sense from my guards–such a state they were in. 'A gibbering ghost,' they called it. I gave them a clip around the ear and told them they would be the gibbering ghosts if they didn't bring the creature to me." The Starwife allowed a slow smile to spread over her face.

"Did they bring the ghost?" asked Twit breathlessly.

"Oh yes, they did right enough, but it was no ghost. They caught her in their nets and she was in a terrible state."

"She?" asked Audrey in surprise.

The Starwife narrowed her misty eyes. "Yes, her ribs were like roots poking through the soil and her belly was taut as a bark drum. She had not eaten for many days, but she still managed to put up a hearty resistance. Seven of my sentries still have sore heads."

"So who was she?" Audrey broke in. "What did she want?"

"She wanted nothing, but I made her drink some milk and with that some life seemed to return to her dead eyes. I questioned her but could learn very little. In fact, Miss Brown, you have told me more about my guest than she has herself."

"*I* have?" Audrey could not believe it. Slowly a vague suspicion began to dawn on her.

"Yes, for she is known to you–can you not guess? I see you suspect."

Audrey's heart was fluttering with apprehension and dread.

Behind the banner, coming down the passage she could hear Piers returning–his quick, nervous footsteps were unmistakable, but alongside came a clumsy flapping of large ungainly feet and with them there was a voice.

"Go to see squirrel boss lady, oh yes."

Audrey's mouth fell open and she inhaled sharply.

The banner was thrust aside and Piers scampered into the chamber followed by . . . Madame Akkikuyu.

CHAPTER THREE

THE BARGAIN

Audrey backed away as Madame Akkikuyu entered.

Once she had been a beautiful rat maiden, but her looks had faded with the cruel blows life had dealt her. When Audrey had first met her, Madame Akkikuyu had been a fortune-teller who also dabbled with poisonous love potions. But she had always craved genuine magical powers and that is how Jupiter had corrupted her into his service. It was Madame Akkikuyu who had delivered Audrey to him. Even then she had still been a striking figure–her fur a rich, sleek black and her eyes dark and fathomless.

Audrey pitied the fortune-teller now. As Madame Akkikuyu dragged her feet toward them they could plainly see that the rat had nearly starved to death in the past weeks. Her skin hung baggily off her frame and her fur was molting away in ugly patches. Only the tattooed face on her ear looked the same. Around her shoulders she still wore the old spotted shawl, and strapped about her waist she carried her pouches of dried leaves and berries. In one large bag was her crystal ball.

Madame Akkikuyu stumbled up to those gathered around the throne and grinned sheepishly up at the Starwife. With a shock Audrey saw something terrible dancing in the rat's eyes–Madame Akkikuyu had lost her mind.

"Welcome, Akkikuyu," said the Starwife warmly. "There are friends of yours here."

The rat gazed distractedly at the mice. She did not recognize the sturdy one with the red kerchief around his neck, but then she hardly knew anything anymore. Her head was in such a muddle these days, ever since . . . no, she could not remember when. There was a closed door in her head that she could not open and she knew that all the answers were locked behind it . . . and yet for some reason she was afraid to discover the truth.

Her memory was as patchy as her fur. She knew the crystal ball and the pouches of leaves were important to her, but she did not know why. Since these nice squirrels had taken her in she had sat with the crystal in her hands many times and admired it–how the light curved over its perfect round surface and how it soothed her. She regarded it as her most precious belonging.

Occasionally a vivid image of some past time would flit over her eyes and she would snatch at it, then hold it dear without knowing what it was. There was one scene where the sun beat down harshly and there was sand between her toes, and water all around. She felt as though she were traveling a great distance, and when she looked down at her claws they were young.

Two other things she remembered. The first was a rat with one eye who faded into ash. Indeed, in with her herbs she had found an eye patch. It was frustrating not to know what this meant and most nights Madame Akkikuyu wept long, bitter tears.

The last memory was the one that she feared the most. She was in a vast echoing chamber, and in front of her were two candles and, between them, an archway, which she could not force herself to look into. This was the key to unlock that door, but she was terrified to discover what lurked in there.

Madame Akkikuyu looked at Twit–the face of the little field-mouse stirred nothing in the jumble of her memories. Finally she turned to Audrey.

The fortune-teller froze. Yes, she had seen that young mouse before, somewhere. A confused array of images crowded in. Audrey was standing before her, but it seemed as though a ball of fire separated them. This was suddenly swept away and an overwhelming sense of guilt washed over her. As she continued to stare at the mouse her own voice spoke to her from the past. "Mouselet. You, me–run away. Leave dark places, hide and be happy."

A tear rolled down Akkikuyu's sunken cheek–what had happened to that wonderful plan, she wondered? That was what she wanted now, to go away and have peace in a quiet spot where the sun shone. Swallowing the lump in her throat she said, "Mouselet, Akkikuyu know you. Why did we not go to distant places and sleep in summer sunlight?"

Audrey felt uncomfortable. She knew why. The rat had been taking her to Jupiter when this idea had first gripped her. Akkikuyu had weighed up all the unhappiness she had suffered and would have escaped with her when Morgan, Jupiter's henchrat, had interrupted them and Madame Akkikuyu had been forced to carry out her orders. Audrey had felt sorry for the rat even then but all the more so now. She could not answer her question.

The Starwife tapped her stick and all looked to her. "Akkikuyu," she began, "you have been my guest for nine days now and are free to remain, yet I sense that there is a yearning in you and you feel you are unable to stay here."

The fortune-teller bowed her head. "Oh, wise boss lady, you see into Akkikuyu's heart." She closed her eyes and clasped her claws in front of her as though in prayer. "You so kind to Akkikuyu. You give food and shelter when others throw stones. Akkikuyu never forget you, sweet bushy one, but mouselet and me, we special–she and I promised. We go away together–we friends."

Audrey spluttered and lifted her head, but the glitter she saw in the Starwife's eyes silenced any outcry she might have made.

Gently the old squirrel held out one arthritic paw to the fortune-teller.

The rat took it, careful not to hold too tightly. The Starwife bent down and patted the rat's claw.

"Peace, Akkikuyu," she said. "You shall go with your friend, but first you must make ready. The day after tomorrow you will leave. Go now to your room and prepare."

Madame Akkikuyu wept with joy and moved to embrace Audrey. The mouse backed away, horrified.

"Hurry, Akkikuyu," cut in the Starwife. "Run along now. There is much to do."

"Yes, yes, Akkikuyu go at once," chuckled the rat gleefully as she ran from the chamber.

When she had left, Audrey turned on the Starwife angrily. "That was the cruellest thing I've ever seen," she stormed. "Why did you build her hopes up like that?"

The Starwife sat back in the throne and heaved a sigh. "What is it I have done wrongly, girl? I merely told her a fact."

"But what will happen when she finds out that I'm not going anywhere with her?"

The stick began to tap the ground slowly. "She will not find out any such thing, for one simple reason–you are going with her."

Audrey laughed. "Not on your life."

The stick crashed down. "Silence!" raged the Starwife. "I will not be spoken to in such a manner. I have told Akkikuyu, now I am telling you. You and she will depart the day after tomorrow."

Thomas Triton stepped up beside Audrey and put his paw on her arm. "Take care, miss," he whispered. "She can make you do anything she wants."

Audrey glared at the old squirrel. Was this the real reason she had been summoned? Or was this a punishment for her rudeness before? One thing was certain, however. Nothing would make her go anywhere with Madame Akkikuyu.

Thomas spoke to the old squirrel. "Ma'am," he began politely. "Where are they to go, the rat and this girl? And how are they to get there?"

The Starwife pointed her stick at Twit. "This lad does not belong around here," she said. "He knows it and was about to go home before his cousin fell ill. What better place for Akkikuyu than a remote field to spend the rest of her days in?"

"You have to be joking!" Audrey remarked, shaking her head in disbelief.

"Never was I more serious," the old squirrel replied, a deadly tone in her voice. "The day after tomorrow you, young Scuttle, and Akkikuyu will leave."

Suddenly, Twit piped up, "But I can't go yet, missus–poor Oswald . . ."

"The Chitter boy will die before this day is out," she said flatly.

The fieldmouse cried out in dismay.

"Silence!" the Starwife demanded. "You thought so yourself, remember. Late this afternoon the Chitter lad will reach the crisis point and pass away."

Twit sobbed uncontrollably. "How do you know? He might not."

"This I have seen," snapped the Starwife irritably. "Look behind my throne. Behold the Starglass!"

The mice peered around the carved oak throne and there,

as tall as three mice, was a flat disk of black, polished glass set in a carved wooden frame. It was this that Audrey had glimpsed before. Over its surface silver flashes flickered and in its midnight depths swirled a multitude of vague and distant images.

"It is my life," explained the Starwife quietly, "and it has been the life of every Starwife before me. Our most precious and most powerful possession. With it I have looked into the heart of the rat Akkikuyu and found no evil. That is why she must be taken away from this place. She must not remember what happened in the sewers and never must you mention the name Jupiter to her–it would unhinge her totally. There is only this one chance of redemption for her–are you the one to deny her this, child?"

Audrey thought for a while. Finally she said, "I am truly sorry for her–but why must I go?"

"Because she will feel safe with you. Somewhere in her mind you have become linked with this notion of safety in the sun. Only you can lead her away. She will go with no one else." The Starwife stared intently at Audrey as if willing her to accept the heavy burden she was offering.

Audrey looked at Thomas, but he was staring at his feet. She wondered what he was thinking. Had he known about this? No, he had suspected none of this–she was sure of that.

Twit was drying his eyes and saying, "Why must we go so soon? We won't have time for . . ."

"I think one day is sufficient for the necessary arrangements to be made and undertaken," the Starwife replied coldly.

"What about Mr. and Mrs. Chitter?" pleaded Twit. "They'll need me to help them get over . . . it all."

An icy glint appeared in the old squirrel's eyes. "They will not need any comfort after tonight," she said darkly. Twit choked and buried his head in his hands.

Audrey felt cold. She stared grimly at the Starwife. How could anyone be so unfeeling? She put her arm around Twit's shoulder and spoke softly. "Don't you listen to her. I'm not going anywhere with that rat–no one can make me do anything I don't want to." Thomas raised his eyes but said nothing.

"So, you still refuse," the Starwife remarked dryly.

"I do. There's no way I would ever do anything for you now."

The Starwife tapped her stick and called for Piers. The young squirrel had been waiting silently at the entrance of the chamber. Now he jumped to attention.

"Madam?" he asked eagerly.

"Fetch it, Piers."

The young squirrel became agitated and flustered. "But my lady," he whined. "You know the consequences, my lady."

"I said fetch it!" she roared, the stick pounding on the floor. "There is more to this than you know."

Piers bowed and dashed off through the banner.

The Starwife tilted her head and smiled at Audrey triumphantly. "So, there is nothing I can do to make you take Akkikuyu away?" she almost chuckled as she said it.

"Nothing," answered Audrey firmly. She eyed the Starwife warily. Who could tell what she might try next?

Piers came bounding back. In his paws he carried a small cloth bag tied tightly at the neck. "I have it, madam," he puffed.

The Starwife's smile disappeared and for a moment she looked sad and dejected. "Thank you, Piers," she said as he handed it over. He stopped to kiss her paw. "Help me down now," she asked. "Mr. Triton, could you take one arm and Piers the other?"

The midshipmouse rushed to help. Carefully they eased the Starwife off the great chair. Her face screwed up as her old bones creaked and the stiff, dry joints ground together noisily.

"Thank you," she said to both of them when finally she stood on the floor.

"I curse this old body of mine–it grows worse with every winter."

"That is because you do not sleep properly, madam," said Piers unexpectedly.

"There is too much to attend to–how can I sleep? Now, the Starglass. Come along, young Scuttle, it needs the relative."

She hobbled slowly with her stick to the rear of the throne until she stood before the Starglass. There she leaned on the stick heavily and eyed Twit solemnly.

"Stand in front of me, lad," she told him, "and take this in your paws." She gave him the cloth bag and placed her own paws on his shoulders. "Now, hold your arms out straight–that's right."

"No, Twit," said Audrey violently. She had watched them curiously and now she was afraid of what the Starwife might do to him. "Don't trust her!"

"Ignore her, boy," rapped the Starwife crossly. "Do as you're told!"

Twit looked from Audrey to the Starwife. What was he to do? Was the old squirrel going to turn him into something dreadful after all? Audrey's face was anxious and frightened; the Starwife's was set and stern. But what about Thomas, his friend and hero, what did he think?

"What'll I do, Thomas?" asked the fieldmouse.

The midshipmouse gave him a smile and reassured him. "It'll be all right, matey–I know what she's doin'. She won't hurt you."

"That's good enough fer me," said Twit, greatly relieved. "Don't worry, Audrey, Thomas says there ain't nothin' to fear." Audrey hoped he was right, but then she noticed Piers turning away, a troubled look on his face.

"Go ahead, missus," called Twit, holding out his arms as straight as he could.

Before the Starglass stood the two figures, mouse and squirrel. The Starwife whispered under her breath and the silver lamps on the walls grew dim and went out. Only the flashes over the black glass lit the chamber now and as the Starwife chanted the light grew brighter.

Twit opened his eyes wide as he witnessed the strange squirrel magic happening before him.

From the depths of the dark glass he saw the night sky–only the stars shone a hundred times brighter. Presently the light from them gleamed stronger and the stars drew nearer. Twit gasped. It seemed as if the whole sky was about him now. In a blaze of blue and silver the stars leaped out of the glass and whirled all around. The chamber had vanished, and only he and the Starwife were left amid the burning heavens.

Twit heard the Starwife's voice calling into the sky and felt her old paws on his shoulders. Suddenly the bag in his paws grew heavy and all the starlight seemed to be sucked down into it. At the same time he felt two sharp pains in his shoulders as the Starwife gripped too tightly.

Twit stifled a cry of surprise as a fierce tingling sensation shot down his arms, as if a thousand ants were crawling over them, stinging as they went. The tingle traveled to his paws and then seemed to enter the bag.

"Enough!" cried the Starwife. "It is done." She released Twit and blew on her paws as if to warm them. Then she groped for her stick.

Twit blinked. He was back in the chamber again and the lamps were lit once more, but the Starglass was dark and impenetrable. He shook himself and whistled softly.

Piers ran forward and took the Starwife by the arm. She seemed feebler than before, and older–if that was possible.

Audrey did not understand what had happened. She had heard the old squirrel mumbling strange words and seen Twit's face light up in awe, but then a bright flash had dazzled her. It seemed to have come from the bag, but she was not sure. Now the Starwife was breathing hard and clinging onto Piers.

When she had regained her breath, the Starwife turned to Audrey and said, "Before, I told you to take Akkikuyu away to young Scuttle's field. Well, now I am asking you. Will you take her?" Her voice was cracked and hoarse, she seemed to have no strength left in her at all.

Despite herself, Audrey felt sorry for her, but still she said, "I've told you, nothing will make me go."

"So you said–I remember. Well, girl, what if the life of your friend Oswald depended on it?"

"That's unfair. Oswald's ill–nothing can save him."

The Starwife interrupted with a fierce striking of her stick. "Wrong!" she shouted. "What is now in that bag can restore his health."

Twit looked at the bag in his paws. "Really, missus?" A broad grin spread across his face.

"I don't believe you," said Audrey cautiously.

The Starwife sighed, too tired to reply.

"Oh, it's perfectly true," Piers remarked, speaking for her, "and it costs dear."

Thomas Triton nodded. "It'll do what they say, lass."

Audrey began to believe them. "That's marvelous," she said happily, "Oswald will be well again."

Piers had been trying to get the Starwife back to the throne but she pushed him away from her and pointed the stick furiously at Audrey. "If!" she cried.

Audrey did not understand.

"You may take that bag away with you and cure your friend and his parents only if . . ."

Then she knew. "You mean if I agree to take Akkikuyu away."

The Starwife nodded. The triumph was plain on her face.

"So if I said no, even now you wouldn't let us take that bag away with us?"

"The bag would be useless. The bargain must be kept or the Chitters will perish."

"But I made no such bargain," Audrey protested urgently.

The Starwife regarded her coldly. "I made the bargain, child–I always do."

Audrey thought of poor Oswald lying in his bed perilously close to death. Then she saw Twit's little face turned expectantly to her. "I have no choice, then," she said. "The day after tomorrow I will take Akkikuyu to Twit's field."

"I knew you would," replied the Starwife. "Piers, show them out, the audience is at an end."

"But, madam, let me help you into your throne first."

"Get out, you fool–if I weren't so tired I'd throw this at you again," she snapped, waving the stick menacingly.

"This way, please!" Piers called from the other side of the banner.

Thomas bowed before the Starwife. "May we meet again," he said to her.

"You stay in your ship and leave me alone," she answered shortly.

"Thank 'ee, missus." Twit laughed when he stood before her. "This bag do make me so happy. I be fair burstin'."

"Get out, you country simpleton," said the Starwife. But she had a smile on her face as she said it.

When it was her turn to say good-bye Audrey looked at the old squirrel with intense resentment. She was glad to be leaving at last. Thomas had been right. The Starwife never did anything for nothing. She had known all along that Audrey would agree eventually. "Remember, child," she said, "the bargain will keep. If you cure him this afternoon but later refuse to go with Akkikuyu then the fever will return and strike him down once more. This bargain is for life, girl. As long as Akkikuyu lives you must remain with her."

It was a chilling prospect and Audrey felt a cold dread grip her heart as she realized the doom that the Starwife had decreed for her. She shivered. "You are cruel," she said, though wanting to say more. "Why is that fake fortune-teller so important to you? She's only a rat after all."

The Starwife looked steadily into her eyes. "And does that make a difference, child?" she asked with scorn. "To me you are just a mouse–and a very rude mouse at that."

"Well . . ." Audrey stammered.

"Well, nothing. Listen to me. I have seen in the Starglass an important future for Akkikuyu. Exactly what that may be I cannot be certain, but I do know that she will make two choices in her life. Her decisions will undoubtedly affect us all. It may seem harsh to you, but I want you to be with her all the time–good may come of it. I pray so anyway." She closed her eyes wearily and waved the mouse away from her. "Now leave me. I am too drained–you have been an expensive guest to entertain." The Starwife turned her back and laboriously limped to the great oak chair.

Audrey left the chamber deep in thought, but as the banner swept down behind her the Starwife raised an eyebrow and said softly to herself, "Can she be the one?"

In the passage Twit was asking Piers, "What does I do with this bag?"

"Steep it in hot water and when it is cool enough make him drink, then call his name three times. Remember, you must never open the bag."

"Oh, I won't!" Twit was nearly back to his old self. Hope was filling his little chest and that was all that mattered.

Audrey caught up with them. "But Oswald can't bring himself to drink anything," she reminded Twit.

"He will drink this," said Piers haughtily. So saying, the young squirrel led them up through tunnels they had not seen before, along winding passages with the light of the silver lamps glimmering about them. Soon the soft lights became mingled with a brighter radiance. It was the sparkle of sunlight streaming through green leaves.

"There it is!" said Piers, halting suddenly. "I will go no farther. Once you pass through those leaves you will find yourselves in the park once more. I presume you will be able to find your way from there?" he added sarcastically.

"Oh, I think we can manage it," put in Thomas.

"Well, go straight back to your holes," retorted Piers pompously. "You will be watched."

"By your ferocious sentries, no doubt." Thomas arched his brows and a flicker of a smile wandered over his face.

"Indeed," said Piers, greatly agitated. "They are there to make sure you leave in an orderly fashion–we don't want riffraff cluttering up our park."

Thomas laughed heartily. "And what would your brave lads do if we did leave in a disorderly fashion–pelt us with daisies?" Twit joined in the laughter.

The young squirrel pursed his lips and eyed them disdainfully. When he was able to be heard he loftily told Thomas, "When you have finished with the bag, you, midshipmouse, must return it to us. Tonight at the latest. Now good day to you!" he dismissed them curtly.

The mice made their way to the opening and crawled out between the leaves. As Audrey stepped out into the sunlight, she turned to see Piers for one last time. For a moment she blinked blindly as her eyes adjusted to the brightness and then, through the leafy gateway, and partly hidden in the comparative darkness of the tunnel she saw the squirrel watching them intently. What a strange race they were, these bushy-tailed creatures, running around in a constant state of nervous fluster–all except the Starwife, of course. Audrey shivered in spite of the afternoon heat as she thought of the old half-blind animal seated on her throne in the heart of the hill, weaving her cruel webs for everyone.

"He's making sure we go quietly," whispered Thomas in Audrey's ear. "Let's go back to the Skirtings and leave this hill far behind us."

Audrey continued to stare moodily through the leaves. "I hate squirrels," she decided, and pulled such a grim face that Piers scurried farther into the shade.

"Come, lass," Thomas told her, "we've a pleasant task ahead of us."

"Yes," agreed Twit, "we're off to make Oswald well again."

Audrey finally tore herself away from the leaf-covered entrance but hesitated before following the others. She looked at how happy Twit was and felt guilty because she was unable to join him. It should have been a time of celebration for them all, but the Starwife had denied her that. The day after tomorrow she would have to leave with that awful Madame Akkikuyu and set off for a horrible field in the faraway country.

"I don't want to leave Deptford!" she cried to herself.

CHAPTER FOUR

A DRAFT OF STARLIGHT

In the Skirtings, Oswald's condition was failing fast. His face had a deathly pallor and his temperature was soaring. Sweat beaded his forehead and ran glistening down his hollow cheeks.

Arthur watched him fearfully. "Go and rouse Mother," he told Piccadilly quickly. "I think this is it." The two mice exchanged hurried, meaningful glances, then the gray city mouse dashed out of the sickroom.

Arthur knelt beside his stricken friend. "Oh, Oswald." He sighed sadly. He took the albino's frail, hot paw in his own and waited.

Shortly, the muffled sound of hushed voices came to Arthur's ears. Evidently, curious mice anxious for news were gathering outside the Chitters' home. There was soon quite a commotion and Arthur could hear Piccadilly's voice above the clamoring queries.

"Put a lid on it and let Mrs. Brown through there. I'm sorry we can't tell you more. Blimey!" Piccadilly's exasperated voice floundered amongst the good-natured and well-intentioned questions.

Arthur smiled grimly to himself at Piccadilly's situation–coping with gossipy, fussing housemice was something he had not encountered in the city.

The outer curtain was drawn aside and Gwen Brown squeezed in. She had escaped the prying neighbors, although a covered bowl had been thrust into her arms. She shook herself and entered the sickroom.

"Piccadilly told me he's worse," she said, moving quickly to Oswald's bedside. She felt the albino's brow and studied his face. "Yes, this is the crisis," she sighed. Gwen turned to her son and drew him to her. "I'm afraid he hasn't the strength to fight it. This will be the end. How is Mr. Chitter?"

They both looked at the figure asleep on the chair. Jacob Chitter was pale and weak–he appeared as ill as Oswald.

"I looked in on Mrs. Chitter before," whispered Arthur. "She's as bad as he is."

"Yes," nodded Gwen. "The lives of this family are all tied together. As Oswald fades–so do they. It's so terrible." She laid the covered bowl, which she had been carrying, on the low table next to the pieces of raw onion.

"More ointment from Mrs. Coltfoot?" guessed Arthur. "A bit late for that now."

"Let's not presume the end before it's come," breathed his mother. "We must continue as before. Audrey and I will see to Mrs. Chitter, you see to . . ." She paused and puckered her brow as Arthur bit his lip. "Arthur?" she asked. "I haven't seen Audrey since I woke up . . . and Twit wasn't in his bed when I looked in on him. Where are they?"

Arthur gritted his teeth, then took a long deep breath while he shuffled his feet awkwardly.

"Arthur!" demanded his mother sternly.

"Well you had just gone to sleep, so we didn't like to disturb you," he began earnestly.

"Who's we?"

"Well, us and Mr. Triton."

"Mr. Triton!" Gwen Brown exclaimed. "What did he want?"

"He took Audrey and Twit to Greenwich," said Arthur nervously.

"To Greenwich? Oh, Arthur, what's got into the old fool's head? And why did you let them go? I'm surprised at Twit–up and leaving like that."

Arthur waved his arms and tried to calm her down. "But it wasn't like that! He promised they'd be back in time and Twit needed to get away for a bit. Mr. Triton can be very persuasive, you know," he added lamely.

"Oh, I'm sorry I snapped, Arthur." Gwen smiled apologetically. "I do remember Mr. Triton's way–he's a forceful one, there's no denying. I suppose they didn't have time to think what they were doing when he arrived. But why take Twit and Audrey to Greenwich? Audrey hardly knows him, for one thing, and it isn't like her to be interested in boats and such."

"Oh, didn't I say?" put in Arthur quickly. "Mr. Triton brought a message from someone called the Starwife. She apparently wanted to speak with Audrey."

Gwen Brown was taken aback. "The Starwife! Let me see now . . . yes, I do seem to have heard of her. Oh, dear–what can she want with our Audrey? I don't like it, Arthur. If I had been awake I would not have allowed her to go. Just wait till I see that midshipmouse–I'll bend his ear for him."

The afternoon crept by. The hot sun veered west and the evening clouds gathered lightly about the horizon.

In the hall of the old house many mice were gathered: Algy Coltfoot and his mother, the two Raddle spinsters, flirty Miss Poot, and many more had mustered together to see how the Chitters were faring. It was as if some instinct had told them that the end was near for that family. A dark shadow lay over all their hearts.

Poor Piccadilly was getting impatient with them all. They kept badgering him for information and they evidently considered his bulletins too few and scanty in detail. Just when the city mouse felt like punching a couple of stupid, nosey heads, Master Oldnose, disturbed by the row, strode out of his rooms and waded through the crowd.

"Now then, now then!" He clapped his paws and looked around crossly.

Master Oldnose had been the tutor of most of the mice present, and their memories of him with his ears white with anger awoke their old respect for him. Voices were hushed and silence fell.

Master Oldnose eyed everyone severely–even those mice who were older than him respected him and held their tongues. Besides his school duties, Master Oldnose was the mousebrass maker and that was a position of great honor.

Now he surveyed them all and waited until he was satisfied.

Piccadilly flicked the hair out of his eyes.

"Ta, mister, they were gettin' out of hand."

Master Oldnose bristled at being called "mister" by this uncouth and obviously ignorant city mouse but decided to pass over it. "You, boy," he addressed Piccadilly. "What is the meaning of this riotous gathering? Explain yourself." He stood with his paws clasped firmly behind his back and rocked slightly on his heels awaiting a reply.

"It's the Chitters, mister. Oswald's in what Mrs. Brown calls 'the crisis' and she an' Arthur are doin' their level best for 'em, but this lot aren't happy with just knowin' that and won't shift."

"I see." Master Oldnose glared at the crowd as if they were children. "Go about your business–there is nothing more for you to learn here."

The mice stirred and mumbled feebly, and the two old maids fluttered shyly and hid their mouths behind nervous paws. Algy coughed and put on his most stubborn face. Nobody moved away.

"Tough luck, mister." Piccadilly grinned cheekily. "I thought you had 'em then."

"We only want to know how they are," said a small voice. It was Tom Cockle. "We owe the lad a lot, you see, and well–I've been stewin' all day, not knowin' how he was doin', so I come here, and blow me if there wasn't a blessed crowd already."

"That's right," broke in Mrs. Coltfoot. "Algy an' me were terrible restless–poor Oswald, I had an awful feeling about today." Murmurs of agreement ran through the crowd.

"We're not doin' any harm," continued Tom. "We're sorry if we were a bit rowdy, but we're not budgin'."

Even the Raddle spinsters nodded. Master Oldnose sighed. He could see that today he would not be obeyed. Indeed, *he* had been sitting in his workroom unable to concentrate on the unfinished mousebrasses before him. He was quite prepared to remain with the others now and wait for news. Everyone expected the curtain to be pulled to one side at any moment and to see Gwen Brown's tearful face appear and relate grave, tragic words. All eyes were fixed on the curtain and even Piccadilly was forced to turn and stare at it glumly.

The evening drew closer. Outside, the day was still warm and the sun had not yet disappeared, but no mouse took any notice.

Eventually, the mice on the Landings crept down the stairway and stood, silent and depressed, with the Skirtings' folk. Time stole by–only the breathing of many mice disturbed the blanketing stillness.

All at once, confusion broke out. Cries of alarm rippled through the crowd. Piccadilly looked around. The Raddle spinsters, as usual, had the same expression on their faces. Even in panic they were identical. No one seemed to know what was happening. Master Oldnose scowled. The disturbance seemed to emanate from the back of the crowd near the cellar door. He gulped and wondered with dread what had crept out of that dark place. Something was forcing its way through the assembled mice. Master Oldnose drew back in fear.

"Out of my way!" shouted a gruff voice. "Let me through there!"

Piccadilly managed a smile–he knew that voice.

"Hey! Avast there." A blue woolen hat bobbed into view amongst the sea of startled mice.

Master Oldnose was relieved, but glowered as he saw Thomas Triton emerge from the crowd. "Mr. Triton," he declared, "what means this rude interruption?"

Master Oldnose was not fond of the midshipmouse, for on the few occasions they had met, Thomas had flagrantly disregarded his authority.

"Evenin', Nosey!" greeted Thomas cheerily.

Master Oldnose's mouth dropped open as he watched the midshipmouse barge past him. Thomas ruffled Piccadilly's hair on his way then nipped behind the Chitters' curtain.

Excited whoops then came from the crowd. "How do, Algy! Hello, Algy's mum!" called a small but unmistakable voice. It was Twit, finding it more difficult to get through the crowd than the midshipmouse had done.

Master Oldnose came out of his sulk and looked up quickly.

"What you got in that bag, Twit?" asked Tom Cockle.

"Oh, you'll see, Tom, you'll see." Twit blundered out of the assembled mice, carrying the Starwife's bag as high as his little arms could manage.

"Hello, William," said Master Oldnose warmly. "Are you feelin' well, boy?"

"The best I ever did!" And as if to prove it Twit burst into a fit of joyful laughter.

The crowd thought he had gone potty and sighed and tutted

with disapproval. Audrey had been following Twit unnoticed by everyone, but now she stepped out and took his paw.

"He really is fine," she explained to them all, and hurried the still giggling fieldmouse into the Chitters' rooms.

"Audrey?" Piccadilly stopped her. "What *is* going on? Why were you so long and why is Twit acting so barmy?"

"He's just happy because Oswald is going to get well," she answered.

Piccadilly looked at her doubtfully. "Come off it," he whispered. "There's no way to save him now."

"Oh yes there is," said Audrey in a strange, somber voice. "There's *one* way to save him." She turned suddenly and ran through the curtain.

The city mouse stared after her. He could have sworn he had seen tears in Audrey's eyes. But if Oswald was going to be cured, why was she so unhappy?

In Oswald's sickroom excitement charged the air. Thomas had told Gwen Brown about the Starwife's bag and she was already boiling some water.

Oswald lay still and silent on the bed like a broken statue of cold marble. He was unaware of everyone around him. He felt so weak that even breathing seemed a dreadful labor. It was as if he had been falling down a deep black well: gradually the light at the top had grown fainter and more distant, until he accepted that there was no way out for him. Down he sank into the blackest night imaginable. He could hear nothing but the darkness filling his ears and closing in around him. How easy it was to sleep and forget everything, all he had known and all he had been–to be one with the rich velvet blackness.

Mrs. Brown came into the sickroom carrying a bowl of hot steaming water. Twit was about to drop the bag in when he hesitated. Was this a cruel trick of the Starwife? He glanced around at his friends and at once drew heart from Thomas's wise, whiskered face. The bag plopped into the bowl.

At once the steam snaked higher and filled the sickroom completely. All who breathed it in felt refreshed and tingles ran all the way down their tails.

A silver light began to shine in the room. In his chair Jacob Chitter stirred in his sleep. Small stars gleamed through the steam and once again Twit felt as if he was swept up into the bright heavens. Only this time Oswald was next to him and there seemed to be music everywhere. As he looked at his cousin the fieldmouse gasped. For a moment it seemed as if he could see the Starwife lying in his place, but the vision was snatched away and Twit could see that it was indeed Oswald lying there.

"The water is cooler now," said Gwen. "Twit, dear, see if he will drink it."

Twit took the bowl from her and knelt beside Oswald. He used one paw to raise his cousin's head and tilted the bowl slightly with the other.

At first the water simply touched Oswald's lips and trickled down onto the pillows.

"Come on, cuz," cried Twit urgently. "Drink it!" Everyone held their breath and watched. More of the precious water spilled onto the pillows. The albino looked dead.

Twit's paw trembled as he feared they were too late. The pillow was very wet now and there was not much left in the bowl. Thomas lowered his eyes and removed his hat. Mrs. Brown buried her face in her paws.

"Oh, Oswald," the little fieldmouse cried. "Oswald, Oswald." Twit's little heart was breaking. And then Oswald's lips moved.

"Look!" yelled Twit. "He be drinkin'." Oswald swallowed the liquid and then opened one eye feebly. He gazed at them all and managed a smile.

"Hooray!" shouted Twit, skipping around the room. "Hooray!" He took Mrs. Brown's paw and dragged her into the dance.

Thomas stepped up to Audrey and said softly to her, "I'll be off to Greenwich later to return the bag. No doubt I'll be told details of your departure. She won't leave anything to chance–everything will be planned and organized."

"Mr. Triton, I have to go, don't I?" said Audrey. "I am the price of all this, aren't I?"

He nodded regretfully. "Alas, miss, I'm afraid you are. Forgive me for taking you to her. I am truly sorry."

Audrey smiled at him. "It isn't your fault, Mr. Triton–she would have done it with or without you."

They were interrupted by an impatient knocking on the wall. Everyone paused and listened.

"Where's my milk? What's all that noise? Can you hear me, Jacob?" Mrs. Chitter was in fine form by the sound of her.

Jacob Chitter jumped to attention in his chair. "Yes, dear. Of course, dear, I . . ." he paused suddenly as he noticed his son smiling up at him. "Oh, Oswald," he said, and burst into tears.

Gwen Brown led the others out of the sickroom. Thomas hung back and collected the small cloth bag.

On the way out to the hall Gwen looked in on Mrs. Chitter. She was sitting up in bed fussing with her hair. "Oh, Gwen what is going on in there?" she asked. "What does my husband think he's doing, the old fool?"

"Arabel," cried Mrs. Brown. "Oswald is better! It's all over now."

Mrs. Chitter dabbed her eyes and gave thanks to the Green Mouse. "Well if that isn't the best news I've ever heard," she sobbed. "You see, Gwen, I told you those pieces of onion would do the trick."

In the hall Thomas was telling an awestruck crowd about Oswald's recovery. For a short time they simply blinked at the midshipmouse–not sure if they had heard him properly and then with one voice they cheered.

"My word!" exclaimed Master Oldnose.

"Let's celebrate," called Tom Cockle.

Audrey felt miserable and dragged her feet back home. Arthur was munching away in the kitchen and getting crumbs everywhere.

"Isn't it terrific?" he mumbled, with his mouth full.

"Oh yes, Arthur, I couldn't be happier for the Chitters." Her voice fell and she sat down heavily.

Arthur swallowed and licked the crumbs around his mouth, forgetting the ones clinging to his whiskers. "What's the matter?" he asked seriously, sensing his sister's mood.

"Didn't Mr. Triton tell you?" she asked wearily.

Arthur sat down beside her and said fearfully, "Tell us what? You're all right, aren't you? You're not coming down with what Oswald had, are you?"

"Oh no, Arthur–nothing like that. My fate's much worse than that," she said morosely. "It's the miracle cure of the Starwife."

"That was amazing wasn't it–really magic stuff that was."

Audrey stared at him steadily. "It had . . . conditions, Arthur. We could only take the cure *if* I agreed to go with Twit to his field the day after tomorrow *and* . . . take Madame Akkikuyu with me."

"Audrey! That's terrible. I thought that ratwoman was dead." Arthur thought deeply for a moment then brightened. "But Oswald is cured now–they can't make you go if you back out now, can they?"

"I'm afraid so. Oswald and his family will fall sick again if I don't stick to it."

Arthur put his arm around her. "Don't worry, Sis," he soothed. "I'll come with you. I promise. How long do you think it will take to get there and back?"

"But that's just it." Audrey wept. "I shan't be coming back–I've got to stay with Akkikuyu forever."

Arthur gasped. "But that's dreadful. Oh, how shall we tell Mother?"

"I don't know," sobbed Audrey.

"My dears!" Mrs. Brown was standing in the doorway, tears falling down her cheeks–she had heard it all.

She wrapped her arms around Audrey and kissed her. "There must be a way," she whimpered. "Oh, what would your father do if he were here?"

An apologetic cough sounded behind them. "Forgive me, good lady," said Thomas self-consciously. "I came to tell you about the party the rest of your Skirtings' folk are arranging, but I see you are busy. Excuse me."

"No wait, please," called Gwen desperately. "Mr. Triton, you seem to know this Starwife better than us. Is there any way she would release Audrey from this horrible bargain?"

Thomas's eyes were grave beneath his frosty white brows. "No, ma'am. I'm sorry, but the Starwife clings to a bargain like a limpet to a stone. She does not make idle threats either: that family will surely perish if Miss Audrey does not go." The midshipmouse fumbled with the cloth bag in his paws. "I must leave now," he said, tugging the edge of his hat. "I have to return this, you see. No doubt you will see me in the morning if I guess rightly about the messages I'll find waiting for me." He turned and left the Skirtings and began the journey back to Greenwich.

"If it's all right with you, Mother," ventured Arthur, "I'd like to go with Audrey to make sure she's safe."

"I don't need looking after," said Audrey indignantly. "Just you stay here with Mother!"

"Listen, silly," argued her brother crossly. "I can go with you, make sure you settle in, then come back and tell Mother how you're doing."

"Oh," said Audrey–she could see the sense in that.

So could Mrs. Brown. "That's a very good idea, Arthur," she said, and hugged them both tightly.

Meanwhile, Algy Coltfoot and Tom Cockle had brought out their instruments–whisker fiddle and bark drum–and soon the strains of a melody came floating in through the hall.

Gwen Brown made her children wash the tearstains from their faces. "It may sound silly of me," she said, "but I don't feel as though you'll be away too long. Let's regard this evening as a sort of grand going-away party. We'll all be together again soon, you see."

Audrey and Arthur agreed–for her sake–though in their own hearts they doubted her. Audrey went to fetch her tail bells, which she had not worn for weeks. She felt that tonight was a good occasion to wear them once more.

In the hall the other mice had not been idle. To celebrate the Chitters' return to health, food had been brought out and decorations festooned the walls. Algy and Tom played "The Summer Jig" and their audience danced and clapped heartily. Between tunes Mr. Cockle slipped out a bowl of his own berrybrew and quaffed it down happily, hoping his wife wouldn't see. Mrs. Coltfoot was being congratulated on the success of her ointment, and the Raddle spinsters were tittering on the stairs as usual.

Into this mirth came Twit. He was immediately grabbed and hauled into the dancing–until someone called for him to play on his reed pipe. The fieldmouse darted away to fetch it.

It was a joyful chaos of noise and laughter. Soon the tensions of the last weeks were forgotten–forgotten by everyone except Audrey.

Perhaps this is the last time I shall wear bells on my tail or have a ribbon in my hair, she thought. With a rat for company I shan't need to look nice.

"Come on, Audrey," said Arthur, suddenly interrupting her thoughts. "There's some terrific food here. Mrs. Cockle and Mrs. Coltfoot have been busy." Arthur dragged his sister over to a crowded area where a cloth had been spread on the floor and laid with biscuits, cheeses, soft grain buns, jam rings, and a large bowl of Mrs. Coltfoot's own specialty–Hawthorn Blossom Cup. Gwen Brown was chatting mildly to Biddy Cockle.

"Here she is," Arthur told his mother. "I found her over there all dreamy and sorry for herself."

Gwen linked her arm in her daughter's. "Try to be happy, my love," she said. "It'll be all right, you'll see!"

"Where's Piccadilly?" asked Audrey suddenly. It occurred to her that he knew nothing of the bargain. Perhaps he would come with them to Twit's field–it might not be so bad after all if the cheeky city mouse came too.

"Piccadilly was over there before with the dancers," said Mrs. Brown, relieved that Audrey had snapped out of herself.

Audrey left her mother behind and went in search of the gray mouse. The musicians were now playing "Cowslips Folly," a lively dance in which a ring of boy mice rushed around a central circle of girl mice and chose a partner from them. Audrey hovered at the edge of the dancing. She saw Piccadilly choose Nel Poot three times. Miss Poot was evidently enjoying all the attention and she was brazen enough to wave at Audrey!

At first Audrey was amused–everyone knew how dotty Nel Poot was. But when Piccadilly chose her a fourth time the smile twitched off Audrey's face and her foot began to tap bad temperedly. What did Piccadilly think he was doing?

"Cowslips Folly" ceased and the musical trio went to see if there was any food left. Audrey watched the dancers break up, but before she could turn away, Piccadilly caught her glance, excused himself from Nel, and sauntered over.

"Did you want somethin'?" he asked her. "Only Miss Poot thought you were trying to get my attention."

Audrey answered casually. "Yes, I did as a matter of fact. I just wanted to say good-bye to you and take this opportunity to thank you for all you have done for me and my family."

"You gone soft in the head?" Piccadilly laughed. "What you on about?"

"I'm leaving," said Audrey, enjoying the moment. "Arthur and I are going with Twit to his field on a visit."

Piccadilly's face fell and his shoulders drooped sadly. Audrey bit her lip and cursed her stupid tongue.

"I see," he managed. "I hope you have a nice time," he muttered, staring at the ground miserably. "When was all this decided?"

"Oh we decided as soon as Oswald got better," she said. "We're going the day after tomorrow. You can come and wave us off if you like." How could she be so cruel, she wondered. Had the Starwife put a spell on her too?

Piccadilly raised his head as if stung. He stared at Audrey incredulously, then with anger said, "Sorry, ducks, but I'm goin' back to the city tomorrow."

"Oh," gasped Audrey.

"Well, Whitey's better now, ain't he, and there's nothin' to keep me here is there?"

"I suppose not," said Audrey in a small voice. She wanted to tell him of the terrible bargain that she had to keep–surely he would not think she was cruel then. "Piccadilly . . ." she began.

"Listen to that," he said, cocking one ear to the band. "That's the Suitors' Dance and I promised Miss Poot." The city mouse left her and Audrey's eyes pricked with wretched tears.

The rest of the evening swept by merrily. Nobody noticed Audrey slipping away to her room with her paws over her eyes.

Slowly the party broke up. Those from the Landings yawned and made their way up the stairs. The Raddle sisters tittered at Tom Cockle, who was sound asleep and snoring loudly with an empty bowl of berrybrew at his side. Biddy Cockle scolded and shook him, then with some help from Algy, Tom Cockle staggered home singing at the top of his voice

about a mouse called Gertie. Biddy was not amused and made him sleep in the spare room for three days afterward.

Eventually, Piccadilly was left alone in the hall. “I must go tomorrow,” he told himself miserably. “Back to the grit and grime of the city.” He bowed his head and wept silently beneath the crescent summer moon.

CHAPTER FIVE

A MEETING AT MIDNIGHT

It was not yet dawn. The grayness of night lingered reluctantly in corners and doorways. Somewhere, behind the tall tower blocks and council estates the sun rose slowly over the hidden horizon and the night shadows shrank deep into the earth for the rest of the day.

Piccadilly quietly rose from his bed and put on his belt. He checked to see that everything was where it should be: small knife–yes, that was there–mousebrass–yes, the belt was looped through it securely–and finally, biscuit supply–well, the leather pouch was there, but it was empty. He wondered if Mrs. Brown would mind if he took some of her biscuits. It might take a long time to walk back to the city. Piccadilly frowned–it would seem like stealing to take without asking, but he wanted to slip away without any fuss–maybe he ought to leave a note. He crept into the Browns' kitchen.

The biscuits were next to the crackers, so Piccadilly took two of each, broke them into small pieces and slipped them into his pouch. He looked around for a bit of paper to write on. Then he wondered what he could write–it needed a long explanation to tell Mrs. Brown why he was going, but how could he put into words all that he felt?

In the end, Piccadilly simply wrote: *"Have gon back to the city. Thank you for having me. Have took some biskitts hope you don't mind–Piccadilly."*

He was not very good at writing. Long ago he had neglected his schooling for more exciting adventures. Now he regarded his handiwork with some doubt. Would anyone read his note? His handwriting was unsteady and he had pressed too hard with the pencil. He pulled a wry face. "I bet Audrey can read an' write perfect," he grumbled to himself.

Outside the house a sparrow began to sing to the new day. Piccadilly looked up quickly. It had taken longer than he had intended to write that note. Now he had no time to spare. He propped the piece of paper on the table, tiptoed out of the Browns' home, and passed through the cellar doorway. Quickly he scrambled down the cellar steps and through the Grill into the sewers.

The morning stretched and shook itself. The clouds were few and wispy–it was going to be another blazing June day.

When Audrey woke, her mother handed the note to her. She read it quietly and with dismay. "Has he really gone?" she asked.

"Yes, love," said her mother. "Arthur has looked everywhere."

"Oh, it's all my fault," was all Audrey was able to say.

She ate her breakfast dismally as she thought about Piccadilly. Her heart told her that she was the reason he had gone off without a word. When Arthur came in she avoided his accusing eyes and went to start her packing.

Arthur was unhappy too. He had begun to consider Piccadilly as his best friend and he guessed that Audrey had something to do with his abrupt departure. It was about time she stopped playing games with everyone. Ever since poor old Piccadilly had arrived she had used him, made him feel guilty for surviving the horrors of the rats when their father had not. She had sent him into peril with Oswald down into the rat-infested sewers to look for her mousebrass and had never really apologized for that. She really was a silly lump. To cheer himself up Arthur went with his mother to see the Chitters.

In the sickroom even the air felt healthier. The sickly smell had gone completely. Oswald was propped up in bed with a great smile on his face as Twit told him funny stories. Mrs. Chitter was up and about, chiding and tutting, finding dust where there was none and rearranging all her ornaments. She herded Gwen Brown into the kitchen, where she demanded to know all the latest doings of everyone in the Skirtings.

Arthur sat himself on the end of the bed next to Twit and waited for a tale to end. Idly he looked about the room. Something was missing, something that had seemed such a fixture that now it was gone he couldn't think what it could be. Oswald saw his puzzled expression and laughed.

"Father's gone to bed finally," he said. "It does seem odd without him in here, doesn't it? I wanted to get up today, but Mother wouldn't let me. She says I'll be here for at least two weeks–or until she's satisfied with my health."

"You'm in bed forever then," giggled Twit, holding his feet and rocking backward.

"Twit says he's going home tomorrow and that you and Audrey are going too–I'm so jealous, Arthur. I wish I could go too."

Arthur caught a quick, cautionary glance from the fieldmouse and understood that Oswald had not been told about the Starwife's bargain.

"Still . . ." continued the albino, "I suppose my hayfever

would have driven me crazy in the country. I can't wait for you to come back and tell me all your adventures."

"I will," said Arthur.

"Of course we shall all miss cousin Twit, but he says he might come visiting again. I'm going to be terribly bored all alone here, but I suppose I should count myself lucky, really."

A knock sounded outside and the patter of Mrs. Chitter's feet accompanied by the clucking of her tongue came to them as she went to see who it was. There were some muffled words, which the three friends were unable to catch, but presently Arthur's mother popped her head into the sickroom.

"Arthur dear and Twit, could you step out here for a moment, please?"

Soon Oswald was left alone to stare at the table covered in raw onion.

Outside Twit and Arthur found Thomas Triton. He grinned warmly at the fieldmouse and began.

"I've come from the Starwife," he said. "Plans are slightly changed. You leave tonight–seems the old dame can't get none of her folk to escort the ratwoman down to the river in the daylight, so tonight it is."

"Oh, dear," sighed Mrs. Brown. "Arthur, fetch Audrey–she has to hear this."

"Wait, lad, I already told the lass. I went there first y'see, thinkin' you'd all be there like," the midshipmouse explained. "Seems there's a merchant chappy the Starwife's persuaded to take you to my young matey's field."

"A merchant mouse?" asked Twit.

"Aye, lad, he's a sort of peddler–sells and trades things. Well, it seems he knows everywhere along the river, stocks up in Greenwich, then takes his goods 'round to out-of-the-way places."

"Well, I ain't never seen him afore in my field," said Twit.

Mrs. Brown had been frowning deeply. Now she suddenly said, "Would this peddler be Mr. Kempe?"

Thomas looked surprised. "Why yes, ma'am, that it is–how do you know of him?"

"Why, he comes here in the autumn to see Master Oldnose on mousebrass business. Yes, he seems respectable enough. . . . I think I'll feel a lot happier knowing my children are in his paws."

Thomas agreed. "Just so, ma'am. Well, as for tonight, I shall lead milladdo here and your two children down to Greenwich Pier where Kempe will meet us. There we shall all wait until the rat arrives with those fidgety squirrels."

"About what time will this be, Mr. Triton?" asked Gwen.

"Midnight, if it pleases you, ma'am."

"Oh, Mr. Triton, it does not please me–not at all. Still there is much to be done. Arthur, come with me. Are you packed yet, Twit?"

"Bless me. I clean forgot about that," admitted the fieldmouse.

* * *

The rippling river was dark, and cool air drifted lazily up from its shimmering surface. It was a clear, clean night pricked all over by brilliant stars. Greenwich Pier huddled over the lapping water like a tired old lady. Its timbers were creaky, its ironwork rusted, and yellow paint flaked and fell from it like tears. Daily trips departed from the pier to see the landmarks of London from the river, and in the summer many crowded the benches and ice-cream stands. But now it was still and dark, its gates were closed, and the visitors had all deserted the pier for gaudier delights.

The only sound was the water breaking gently against the

supports and slopping around a broken wooden jetty nearby.

There were no lights on the pier at night, all was dim and gray–a place of alarming shadow.

Audrey held on to her mother's paw. They had come through the sewers once more, led again by the midshipmouse. She watched Arthur and Twit run ahead to explore the deep pools of darkness and shuddered. She was cold, but her mother had knitted her a yellow shawl and she pulled it tightly over her shoulders.

All the mice were carrying bags packed with provisions, blankets, and personal treasures. Audrey's arms ached with the weight of hers and she was glad when Thomas said it was not much farther. Somewhere, in amongst the folded clothes, was a dried hawthorn blossom. Oswald had given it to her when she said good-bye to him that evening–it was one of those he had saved from the Spring festival.

Gwen Brown was savoring every moment with her children, storing up the sound of their voices for when she was alone.

Twit and Arthur ran ahead once more, swinging their baggage happily. After some moments they came rushing back, their faces aglow with excitement.

"Thomas," squealed Twit eagerly, "there be somethin' up there. We done heard it."

"Yes," joined in Arthur. "Someone's singing." The little group of mice edged forward cautiously. In the shade ahead nothing could be seen, but gradually a voice floated to them on the night air.

It was a merry, hearty sound, first singing, now humming.

Poor Rosie! Poor Rosie!
I'll tell you of poor Rosie,
The tragedy that was Rosie
And why she died so lonely

Coz for all her looks her armpits stank,
The suitors came, but away they shrank
Far away from Rosie,
With their paws tight on their nosey.

Twit spluttered and laughed helplessly as the song continued. Gwen Brown gave Thomas a doubtful look. The midshipmouse shrugged and hid a smile.

"Who is it, Mother?" asked Audrey.

"That is Mr. Kempe," Gwen replied dryly.

Thomas coughed and shouted. "Ahoy, Mr. Kempe! Come out so we may see you! And before your verses become too colorful, remember there are tender ears here."

From the shadows a great clanking noise replaced the song, as if some metal monster had been roused from sleep. Audrey waited with wide eyes wondering what this Mr. Kempe would be like.

"Are you the party bound for Fennywolde?" came the hearty voice.

"That's right," Twit piped up, "that be the name o' my field."

"Why, that sounds like a fieldmouse."

"I be 'un."

The clanking drew nearer and into the dim light stepped one of the strangest figures Audrey had ever seen.

There was a mass of bags, pans, straps, and buckles mounted on a pair of sturdy legs and somewhere amongst all this madness was a furry round face and two small beadlike eyes. It was friendly and welcoming, and Audrey warmed to Kempe immediately–especially as he said, "Bless my goods, two beautiful ladies and I knew nought of it. A curse on my palsied tongue that you should hear it yammering away like that. But 'tis the lot of the lone traveler to sing when he's on his tod. Forgive my verses, dear ladies." The clanking began again as he attempted to bow.

Gwen Brown smiled as she accepted his apology. "You just keep your songs tucked away while my daughter travels with you, Mr. Kempe," she said.

"Oh, please," he protested, "there's no 'Mister,' plain Kempe I am—no titles, no end pieces! Kempe, and that's all."

Audrey was staring in fascination at his bags. Poking through the sides there were glimpses of fine silks and silver lace, and strung around the handles of his pans and around his own neck were beads of every type and variety—pear-shaped droplets done in gold, green leaf patterns threaded on a single hair from a pony's mane, little charms worked in wood and hung on a copper wire, and chains of fine links from which dangled tears of blue glass.

"I'll trade anything for anything," he continued, catching Audrey's eye. "Well, young lady—see anything that tickles you? I see you like fine things, with your ribbon and all that lace. Why, I've got such an array of ribbons in here—enough to make rainbows jealous. Take your pick, and all I ask are those wee bells on your tail."

"But these bells are silver!" Audrey exclaimed. "They're worth more than all your ribbons."

"Alas for sensible girls," he sighed. "Still, you can't blame a mouse for trying."

Thomas chuckled and introduced everyone to the traveler.

"What a fine party we'll be making to be sure, sailing up the river together, leaving the fume of the city behind us. A pity you'll not be joinin' us, Mrs. Brown, but have no fear. I'll keep one eye on my goods and the other on my charges." He turned to Thomas. "And you, Mr. Triton, sir, sorry I am not to have your stout company on board, I bet you know many a worthy tale."

"That I do," replied Thomas, "though not all are comfortable to listen to."

"Still, I'll wager we'd not get bored with you on hand."

"Oh, I don't think you need worry on that score, Kempe, my

boy." Thomas smiled. "Have you met your other traveling companion yet?"

"Why no, that's the truth of it, but I had word from herself what lives up yon hill–the batty old squirrel."

"What did she tell you exactly?" asked Thomas, smiling.

"To be here tonight, at this hour, to guide certain parties to Fennywolde–they being your own good selves and one other, a special lady." He turned to Gwen Brown and confessed. "To be honest I thought my luck was in and you were she–alas, it seems not." He clapped his paws together. "So where is this other of our jolly group?"

Thomas considered Kempe for a moment and said, "Has the Starwife promised you anything for your services?"

"Why no, sir." He seemed surprised. "Why 'tis only a simple task and I'll have the pleasure of it, such fine young fellows a trader never had to journey with! I'd do it for nought . . . but now you mention it, herself made me give my traveler's oath not to change my mind–ain't that funny now?"

"Not really," said Mrs. Brown, "not when you know who this lady is. The Starwife has used you like she has used my daughter–deviously."

Kempe looked at the mice before him and grew concerned at the expressions on their faces. "Why, there you go worrying a body–kindly tell me who this lady is."

But even as he spoke they all heard voices, one loud, the other timid.

Madame Akkikuyu strode onto the pier followed by two squirrels.

"Mouselings!" cried the rat, dropping her many bags and flinging her arms open.

Kempe's face sagged and it seemed as if all his goods drooped as well. Audrey ducked quickly behind her mother, avoiding Akkikuyu's attention.

"We travel at last," the fortune-teller exclaimed triumphantly.

"Off to sun and rest–together forever."

"Why the batty old she-divil," bellowed Kempe, cursing the Starwife and shaking his fist at the two terrified squirrels. "My traveler's oath an' all–for this, this . . . lump of a rat. I be conned outright."

One of the squirrels braved a reply. "The bargain with you must stand," he said, dodging a blow from a pan. "If not, all the river will know of your falseness."

The trader stood still, but his face looked as though it would burst. "A traveler depends on his reputation and the goodwill of others–why, if his traveler's oath is doubted he goes out of business."

"Just so," replied the squirrel smartly.

"A plague on you," called Kempe angrily.

Thomas intervened. "Now look, squire," he said to Akkikuyu's escort. "You've done your delivery, now tell your mistress it's all working well for her. Get you gone before this chap cracks you both one."

The squirrel stroked his tail smugly and glanced casually around for his silent comrade–but he had already run away. That was enough. The squirrel jumped in the air and dashed after him.

"They sure are slippery, Thomas," said Twit.

"So," said Kempe sourly, "here we are with that baggage to join us. A pretty lot we are, to be sure."

"Yes," said Thomas briskly. "And if I'm going to get some sleep tonight I've got to take Mrs. Brown home first. Make your farewells please–it's time to go."

Gwen held Audrey in a desperate embrace. "You will come back, Audrey, my love–I know it."

"I hope so, Mother, I wish I was as sure as you." She tried not to cry, but her eyes were already raw and swollen from Piccadilly's departure.

Gwen turned to her son. "Now, Arthur," she said, "you look

after your sister and come home when you can." She hugged and kissed him, much to his embarrassment.

Thomas Triton turned to Twit. "Well, matey," he said awkwardly, "there's no denyin' I'll miss your cheerful face around here. Ever since you dropped on my ship we've got on famous." He fumbled with a flask that was slung over his shoulder and thrust it into the fieldmouse's paws.

"What is it, Thomas?" asked Twit.

"Just a little something for your journey–and to remember our first meeting by."

"Will you come visitin' one day, Thomas?"

The midshipmouse shook his head. "No, Woodget–not by water, you know I can't go that way again."

"What did you call me then, Thomas? It's me, Twit, remember?"

The midshipmouse looked flustered and apologized for getting muddled. Twit laughed and said it didn't matter. "I reckon I'll be poppin' this way again some time," said Twit. "I bet there's a bundle of stories you've still to tell me."

"Maybe, matey, maybe."

Then Madame Akkikuyu, who up till then had been gazing earnestly up at the stars, hugged Mrs. Brown. Gwen gasped but found nothing to say.

"Oh, mother of my friend, good-bye," Akkikuyu breathed with feeling. "And you old salty mouseling, farewell also."

Thomas cleared his throat and hurriedly waved "Cheerio" before she had a chance to hug him. Then he led Gwen Brown away from the pier.

The three young mice sadly watched them go. "Well," began Kempe. "I'll show you our trusty vessel."

"Are we to leave tonight?" asked Audrey.

"No, missey," said Kempe above the jangle of his goods. "The boat sets off in the morning, but we've got to settle down."

"I shall be near my mousey friend," declared Madame Akkikuyu, stooping to collect her things. Audrey looked at Arthur and grimaced.

Kempe took them farther along the pier to where the river splashed through the planks under their feet. A large tourist cruiser was moored at the edge and it bobbed gently up and down bumping against the pier.

"There she is," said Kempe. "Our transport–well one of them, anyway. Now up this rope here and we'll be on deck."

"Easy," cried Twit, and scampered up the mooring rope in a twinkling.

"Akkikuyu do that also." The fortune-teller hauled herself onto the rope bridge and clumsily made her way along with her thick tail flicking behind her.

"That's right, missus," grinned Kempe. "Don't go fallin' in now–we wouldn't want to lose you!"

It was Arthur's turn next; he stared at the rope warily. "I'm not usually very good at balancing," he admitted. "I can climb, but . . ." he looked despondently at the sloshing water below–it seemed green and cold, and he did not want to land in there.

"Come on now laddie, just don't look down."

From the boat Twit watched them and laughed, "Come on, Arthur. If you spend any time in my field you'll have to learn to climb stalks. But I suppose you'd have to lose some weight first."

"I'm not fat," protested Arthur.

"Course not–you great puddin'."

That settled it. Arthur virtually ran up the rope and began scuffling with the fieldmouse, who was helpless with giggling.

Now it was Audrey's turn, but she stepped onto the rope nimbly and was soon aboard–straight into the welcoming arms of Akkikuyu.

"Clever mouselet. Akkikuyu knew mouselet could do it."

Whistling a quick tune, Kempe ambled up to them, balancing with perfect poise on the rope, his many goods not affecting him whatsoever.

"Now follow me, fellow travelers," he said once he was on deck. They strode over the boards and between wooden benches to where a steep flight of wooden steps plunged darkly down into an invisible blackness.

"Down here," called Kempe, briskly jumping onto the first step.

Silently they all descended. Twit followed Kempe. Then Arthur went, followed by Audrey, and Madame Akkikuyu brought up the rear.

Audrey tried to hurry down the steps as quickly as she could. Close above she could hear the rat's claws clicking as they caught on the steps, and Akkikuyu's croaky muttering breaths. Once the fortune-teller's tail brushed against Audrey's face in the dark and the mouse cried out in alarm, nearly falling off the steps altogether.

"Hush, mouselet," the rat cooed, "only the tail of Akkikuyu–fright not."

When they were all at the bottom of the steps, Kempe lit a small candle and they looked around them.

It was a storage hold. Oil drums and tarpaulins surrounded them, thick black rope snaked across the floor, and a stack of folded wooden chairs was piled precariously in one corner. It smelled strongly of the river and of stagnant, neglected pools.

"This is where we bunk tonight," said Kempe brightly as though he was used to much worse accommodation. "And tomorrow we'll hide here under the tarpaulin out of the way–until we change boats."

"Change boats?" repeated Arthur. "Why? Doesn't this one take us to Twit's field?"

"Bless you, laddie, no. Whatever made you think it did? I'm sure I said. Never mind. No, three vessels will bear us on our way. That's the joy of the traveler, hopping from boat to boat.

Knowing which one goes where and when. Why, I know the sailing time of everything along the whole great stretch of Grand Daddy Thames, from the biggest ship to the smallest barge."

They put their bags down and Kempe disentangled himself from his rattling goods. Without them he seemed a much smaller figure.

Madame Akkikuyu hugged her knees and muttered happily to herself.

Audrey did not like the hold: it was stuffy and more like a prison than anything she could imagine. The small flickering candle flame brought no cheer to the gloomy place and the rocking of the boat made her feel sick.

Arthur and Twit sat near Kempe, each lost in his own thoughts. The fieldmouse delved into his little bag and brought out his reed pipe. He put it to his lips and blew absentmindedly. He was thinking of his home and wondering if it had changed in all the months he had been away.

Arthur listened wistfully to the slow, solemn notes from the pipe. He too was thinking of Twit's home. What had Kempe called it–Fennywolde? Strange how Twit had never called it by that name before–it was always "my field" or just simply "back home." Arthur wondered what he and Audrey would find there.

The haunting music stopped and after a short while Twit's little voice gurgled with pleasure. "Good old Thomas!" he cried. He had remembered the little flask, which the midshipmouse had given to him, and pulled the cork out. The exotic smell of rum met his twitching nose.

Kempe was sorting through one of his bags, pulling out scraps of material and stuffing them back again. He hummed quietly to himself–it had been a busy week for the traveling mouse, deals had been made, a good bit of trading done down Tilbury way, and in Greenwich itself earlier that evening he had done a nice little deal with a Norwegian mouse from a ship docked near that old power station. Seven little wooden charms he had got in return for two spoons and a length of buttercup yellow satin. It was these small charms that Kempe was looking for–he was sure he had put them in this bag. Ah–yes, there they were. Kempe fished them out and examined them in the candlelight.

"Oooh," admired Twit, "they'm pretty. Can I see 'em proper?" Kempe inspected the fieldmouse's paws for dirt, then, when he was satisfied, handed the little carvings to him one by one.

All were figures of mice delicately done in boxwood. Every detail was correct down to the suggestion of fur. There were running mice, old wise-looking mice, pretty damsel mice curtsying and dancing, and an angry mouse with a sword in his paw.

"They're terrific," said Arthur, peering over Twit's shoulder.

"To be sure, they're right dandy little things," nodded Kempe. "Chap I traded with says he got them from a holy mouse what lived up in some mountain or other–not that I believed him like, probably knocked them up himself, but I took a fancy to 'em."

"I ain't never seen so neat a bit o' carvin'," said Twit, handing them back. "We never had nothin' like that in my field."

Kempe raised his eyebrows and shrugged. "In Fennywolde–I'm not a bit surprised. I never go there."

"Why not?" asked Arthur.

"Got chased out only time I did go," Kempe replied, shaking his head. "Some pious feller it was, babbling about frippery and vanity."

"What do you mean?" pressed Arthur. "What's wrong with what you sell?"

"Why, nothing! I have the finest selection on all the river. But you see–and begging your pardon, youngster," he said to Twit, "there are some in this world who think we come into it empty-handed and should leave that way, with no decoration or little luxury to cheer us along. And they don't like those of us who deal in these indulgences."

"But I still don't understand why," said Arthur, confused. "What harm can your wares do?"

Kempe raised his hands in a gesture that showed he too had asked that question many times.

It was Twit who answered. Slowly he said, "Because they go against the design of the Green Mouse." He spoke the words as though he was repeating something he had heard many times.

"Twit!" exclaimed Arthur in surprise.

"Staunch Green Mousers," put in Kempe darkly, "fanatics too busy livin' in fear of the Almighty to enjoy his bounty."

Arthur stared at the fieldmouse. "But you never said," he stammered, "I thought your field was a happy place."

"Oh, it is," Twit assured him quickly. "Most of us don't think and reckon things like that. It's only a few what's hot against 'owt different an' such."

"Really?" Arthur was slightly annoyed. "What do you think that few will make of Audrey with her bells and lace?"

"Oh, they won't take to her," agreed Kempe. " 'Specially that pious feller what chased me–if he's still there."

"Oh, he be there all right," confirmed Twit glumly. "Old Isaac still goes into a fume and temper when it comes to the Green Mouse design."

"What do you make of this, Audrey?" asked Arthur, turning around. But his sister was not there–nor was Madame Akkikuyu.

* * *

The night breeze had made Audrey feel better. She hated being cooped up in that dreary, musty hold. She had left everyone engrossed and climbed the steps once more. Audrey leaned against one of the railings along the deck and gazed up at the bright stars. The sloshing of the water and the motion of the boat lulled her senses and the rich green smell of the river was brought to her on the breeze. She closed her eyes and a calm descended on her.

"Mouselet."

Audrey jumped at the sound of that voice behind her. Akkikuyu had followed her from the hold. The rat's black eyes were gleaming.

"The night–she is beautiful. See the stars–how they burn." She raised her claws to the heavens and spun around. "Oh, mouselet," she cried. "Finally we are together and we shall never be parted."

Once more Audrey felt a wave of compassion flow over her. Madame Akkikuyu was really a creature to be pitied. Audrey decided that the Starwife must be right–all the rat's wicked memories had indeed been forgotten. Madame Akkikuyu was little more than a harmless mouse child dressed in a rat's skin.

From the other side of the river a dog howled, breaking the peace of the night.

Akkikuyu traced a wide circle in the air with her claws and drew her breath.

"Wolf sees death and gives warning," she muttered. "Akkikuyu must not linger in dark places–listen to the wolf voice, 'Beware,' he says, 'old Mr. Death walk near.'" She pulled her spotted shawl tighter and kissed her dogtooth pendant. Whatever else she may have forgotten, Akkikuyu's instinctive belief in the supernatural remained.

Turning to Audrey, the rat added, "Akkikuyu have many treasures, mouselet. Things she not understand, powders in pouches, leaf and herb in bundles, secret packets that do smell most strange, and a terrible trophy of a kitty head." She frowned as she looked into the swirling water, as if all her answers lay there. "What they all about? Why for Akkikuyu keep such grislies? Was she doctor to have bowl for pounding and mixing? A darkness is behind Akkikuyu–too black to see." Her voice trailed off as she sighed with regret.

On impulse Audrey said, "Don't worry, leave the past alone–look to the future, Madame Akkikuyu. There will be answers enough for you there."

"Oh, mousey, how good it is for you to be such a friend." The fortune-teller grabbed Audrey and because the mouse pitied her she did not struggle as the other hugged her tightly. Large rat tears ran down Audrey's neck.

Arthur, Twit, and Kempe peered over the top of the steps.

"We've a tidy way to go before we get to Fennywolde," said the traveler slowly. "We had better keep an eye on that Madame there, bad business to be sure. You can wash a rat and comb a rat, but it will still be a rat. You can't trust 'em!"

"We know that," said Arthur.

"What I says is," continued Kempe, "nourish a rat and one day it will bite your head off. Just you watch her when you get to your field, young laddie–rats is always trouble."

* * *

It was much later that night when they had all bedded down in the hold that it really began.

The mice were sleeping soundly. Arthur's soft snores rose and fell with a steady rhythm. Kempe twitched his whiskers as he dreamed of pearls and silks flowing through his trader's paws. Twit, as always, was curled up in a circle, looking for all the world like an addition to Kempe's wooden carvings. Audrey had untied her ribbon and her hair spread around her like a fine network of fairy webs.

Nearby, Akkikuyu grunted as she wandered through her own dark dreams. She was sprawled amongst her bags and sacks, and occasionally her face would screw itself up into an expression of pain and her tail would beat the tarpaulin with heavy, agitated smacks. She rolled over and over, shaking her great head and mumbling to herself.

From somewhere in her dreams a voice seemed to be calling to her: "Akkikuyu! Akkikuyu–are you there?"

In her sleep Madame Akkikuyu groaned aloud. "Yes, I am here," she muttered, as if in answer to the unseen thing of her dreams. "What do you want? Who is it? Leave me alone."

For the rest of the journey along the river the night was to become a time of dread for Madame Akkikuyu–a time when the nameless voice invaded her sleep to call her name unceasingly.

CHAPTER SIX

FENNYWOLDE

The sunlight spread across the growing corn and cast deep charcoal shadows under the elm trees. The field was a large one–a mass of green, rippling like the ocean as the wind played over its surface and murmuring with lovers' whispers as the breeze sighed through it. The corn soaked up the sun, drank its gold, and grew tall.

The field was bordered on one side by a deep ditch that fed a pool at the far end where the hawthorn grew thick and impenetrable. But now the ditch was dry and the mud at the bottom was cracked and studded with sharp stones. Along the side grew the tall elms and one solitary yew, dark giants rearing high over the swaying grasses and stretching into the fierce blue.

To the left of the ditch was a meadow. Too small and difficult to plow, the meadow was rich in the glossy show of buttercups and flowering grasses. An enchanted scent hung over the place–a perfect blending of wild perfumes, so strong that you could almost taste them. Beyond the meadow was a great clump of oaks, fully in leaf, like green clouds come to rest on the earth.

This small land was what the fieldmice called "Fennywolde" or "the land of Fenny"–he being the first mouse to have lived there many years ago. It provided them with everything they needed: an abundant supply of corn, berries from the hawthorn, water from the pool, and brambles for autumn brewing. In the winter the steep banks of the ditch provided excellent shelter, and there were numerous tunnels and passages under the roots of the elms, which had been dug a long time ago by venerable ancestors. Secret holes to hide from the bitter winds and escape the midwinter death, places to spend chill dark days, and spacious halls to store supplies.

During the summer it was usual for the fieldmice to move out of their tunnels and take up residence in the field–to delight in climbing the tall stalks and nibble the ripening corn. So far, however, the inhabitants of Fennywolde had remained in their winter quarters. Only during the day would they dare venture into the field, and woe betide any mouse not safe in the tunnels at dusk. A terror was hunting in the night.

* * *

Alison sauntered through the meadow lazily. She was a beautiful country mouse, her strawberry blond hair hung in two creamy ponytails behind her ears. Her fur, like the fur of all fieldmice was reddish gold, but Alison's held a secret glint that dazzled when it caught the sun. She was a curvy young mousemaid with an impish pout and large brown eyes. Her skirt was of simple cotton stitched around with humble rustic embroidery. At her breast a mousebrass dangled–a sickle moon with a tiny brass bell–the sign of grace and beauty. And this was the trouble. Alison had received the charm a year ago and it had gone straight to her head.

She flirted with the boys, flicking back her hair and flashing her eyes at them, promising sweetness. They had all fallen for her: Todkin, Hodge, Young Whortle, and even skinny Samuel had been victims of her careless, dangerous glances. Those slight tosses of her head and devastating grins had been practiced and scrutinized in the mirror of the still pool where she spent most of her days preening and rehearsing her powers.

The warm afternoon, mingled with the dry rustle of the grasses, was a potent drug. Alison slumped on the ground, face upturned. The seeding grass heads bobbing overhead seemed to be bowing before her beauty. She fanned herself with a buttercup, allowing its rich buttery aura to wrap around her.

"Poor Dimsel," mused Alison in a throaty whisper. "Face like a cow's behind and wit to match." She laughed softly and stretched. "Dear Iris, legs like a redshank and not a curl in her hair." She passed her paw through her own crowning glory and made a mock appeal to the world in general. "But, friends, let us not forget Lily Clover, she has the grace of a swan–but she do stink like a fresh steaming dunghill." They were the names of Alison's rivals and she spoke of them with casual disregard, because today she had decided she had surpassed them all. It was clear in her mind now that she had no equal anywhere.

A bee droned in and out of the clear patch of blue above. "Old Bumble knows." Alison laughed, and her voice rose high and flutey. "He do know it! Bees go to honey and I be the sweetest thing by far." She rolled over and spied a forget-me-not pricking through the grass stems. Reaching out, she plucked it mercilessly. After weaving it into her hair she paraded up and down for her invisible audience. She contemplated whether she should return to the pool to assess the impact of the flower, but then her mouth curled and she set off purposefully.

* * *

Jenkin kicked the hard ground and scratched his head. He was carrying a large bundle of dry wood and felt like throwing it all into the ditch. His friends Hodge and Todkin were in the field practicing their stalk climbing while Samuel and Young Whortle had gone off to quest the oaks beyond the meadow.

Jenkin was tired and fed up–his father made him work hard. "Waste not the hours the good Green gives" was just one of the rules drummed into him.

Suddenly his mousebrass reflected the sun full into his downcast eyes. He dropped the sticks and rubbed them. For a moment he was blinded. It was a brass of life and hope–a sun sign. His father, the local mousebrass maker, had forged it specially with him in mind and was gravely pleased when Jenkin managed to choose it from the sack two springs ago.

"Ho, there! Jolly Jenkin!" came a clear voice suddenly. "Why for you rubbin' your eyes? Do I dazzle so much?"

Jenkin blinked. As his eyes readjusted through the misty haze of light he could just see Alison strolling toward him out of the meadow. Her fur was a fiery gold and there was buttercup dust glittering on her face. In her eyes there were dancing lights.

"Is that you, Alison Sedge?" he ventured, doubting his vision.

"Might be," she answered, staying just within the fringes of the meadow grass. "Then again I might be the goddess come down from the moon to torment you with my beauty."

Jenkin snorted. "Pah! You don't half talk addled sometimes, Alison Sedge. Just you mind my dad don't hear you goin' on like that. He'll tell your folks, he will."

"Pooh." She stepped out onto the hard ground.

Jenkin eyed her again. She had certainly changed in the past year–why, before she had been given that mousebrass they had been firm friends. He had even thought that perhaps . . . He saw her eyebrows arch in that infuriating way of hers. She had guessed what he was thinking about and tossed her head.

"Like my flower?" she asked huskily.

"Look better in the ground," Jenkin replied shyly, turning away from those eyes that held those dangerous lights. "Why don't you go show Hodge?"

"I may," Alison answered mildly. It amused her to flirt with the boys and see how she set them at odds with one another. How easily they could be confounded by a sideways glance or a sweet smile. It was Jenkin, though, whom she enjoyed teasing most. He was so serious and solemn and when he was with his father she reveled in disconcerting him. In fact, if her pride and vanity had not swelled so much she would quite happily have married Jenkin. He was by far the most handsome mouse in Fennywolde. Now, though, she enjoyed dangling him on a string with all the others, tempting and rejecting with soft, mocking laughter.

An impatient voice rang out over the field. "Jenkin! Where are thee, lad?"

He jumped up and hastily retrieved the bundle of sticks. "That be my dad callin' for me." Jenkin began to run to the ditch, past the bare stony stretch and up to the cool shade of the elms.

Isaac Nettle stood stiff and stern outside one of the entrances to the winter quarters. He scowled as his son came panting up to him. He was a lean mouse whose face was always grim and forbidding–no one had heard him laugh since his wife had died. His eyes were steely and solemn, set deep beneath wiry brows in a sour face.

"Where did thee get to?" he snapped. "Idling again, I'll warrant. Come here, boy."

Jenkin set the wood down before his father, watching him warily.

"What's this!" bellowed Isaac. "The wood is green. How am I to burn that! We should choke on smoke!" He grabbed his son by the neck and raised his hard paws to him. "I'll beat sense into thee yet, boy, and with the Green's help I'll cure thee of thine idleness."

Jenkin knew better than to protest. He gritted his teeth and screwed up his face. His father's paw came viciously down on him. Jenkin gasped as he opened his eyes; the blow had been a severe one. The blood pounded in his head and the side of his face throbbed with pain.

Isaac raised his paw again and smacked his son across the head once more. He spared no effort, so that Jenkin sobbed this time. "Thou must learn," exulted his father. He hit him one more time to emphasize his words.

Jenkin staggered on his feet when Isaac had finished. His head was reeling and already he felt a swelling around his eye. In his mouth he tasted the tang of iron and knew that his lip was bleeding. Soon the shock would wear off and he would be left with a dull ache and painful stinging.

"Now what have thee to say?" rumbled Isaac.

"I . . . I thank thee, Father," stammered Jenkin, holding his sore lip.

"We shall pray together," intoned Isaac to his son. "Midsummer scarce a week away and still we live in winter holes. 'Tis a judgment on us all. The Green is angry. There are those in our midst who have offended thee, Lord. Heathen loutishness creeps in. Give your servants strength to drive out the vain pride that you despise. Let us walk free at night once more." He dragged Jenkin inside.

From a safe distance Alison had watched it all. She had flinched as she saw Jenkin suffer those three terrible blows. Everyone in Fennywolde feared Mr. Nettle. His temper was dreadful, but he commanded the authority and respect due to a mousebrass maker. Several times Jenkin had carried the bruises given to him by his father and no one dared do anything about it–indeed Mr. Nettle was not the only staunch Green Mouser in Fennywolde.

Alison walked up to the ditch. She knew that Isaac classed her as one of the offenders in the field. He sermonized at her whenever he saw her. She thought of the miserable night that lay before Jenkin: he would have to kneel on a painfully hard floor next to his father for hours praying to the Green Mouse for deliverance and forgiveness. Alison sighed and told herself that she must make sure to be kind to Jenkin the next time she met him–why, she might even let him kiss her. She chuckled at the notion and looked about her.

The evening was growing old, and clouds of gnats were spinning over the barren stretch of ditch. It was time for her to go home.

She turned on her heel and made for one of the other entrances to the winter quarters.

"Alison Sedge," came a distraught voice. She looked up quickly and noticed a group of six worried mice. A plump harassed mouse bustled over.

"Hello Mrs. Gorse," greeted Alison politely.

The mouse brushed a long wisp of hair out of her red-rimmed eyes and asked, "Have you seen our Samuel?"

Alison shook her head. "Why, no, Mrs. Gorse. I think he went off with Young Whortle this morning."

"Oh, dear," murmured Mrs. Gorse. "I was hoping you might know where they were. Mr. and Mrs. Nep are asking everyone in the shelters. If they don't come back soon . . ."

Alison turned toward the meadow and stared at the grasses intently. It was getting dark and no mouse was safe above ground then.

* * *

Samuel Gorse was close to tears. He held on tightly to his friend and tried to pull himself farther under the oak root.

CHAPTER SIX

It had been a magnificent day. The morning had been so fine that he and Young Whortle Nep had decided against joining Todkin and Hodge in the field and planned an adventure.

"Warty," as Samuel was fond of calling his friend, was always full of terrific ideas. Last year he had built a raft and together they had sailed it along the ditch, fending off imaginary pirates and monsters from the deep. This year, though, the ditch had dried up and they had been forbidden to sail the raft on the still pool as it was too deep.

Young Whortle was older than Samuel, though not as tall. "Right, Sammy," he had said that morning. "If Jenkin's too busy an' Todders an' Hodge are set on climbin' today, then it be up to us to take what thrills the day has to offer."

So they sat down and thought seriously about what they could do. They had already explored the field this year and the ditch promised little in the way of adventure in its parched state. They had been to the pool once or twice, but Alison Sedge was always there teasing them. Alison Sedge had been declared dangerous territory by them both, so the pool was out of the question, with or without the raft.

While the two friends contemplated the day's destination Young Whortle had raised his head and seen the oaks in the hazy distance.

"Aha!" he cried, jumping to his feet and assuming a triumphant pose. "The oaks, Sammy. We shall quest the oaks and see what secrets they keep." So off they went, passing a dejected Jenkin and waving cheerily to him as they entered the meadow.

Now Samuel shivered. Fear chilled him and his teeth began to chatter.

"Sshh!" whispered Young Whortle close by. "It'll hear you."

What a situation they had landed themselves in. All had been going wonderfully. They had charged through the piles of last year's leaves, which still filled the hollows near the oaks, and had played hide-and-seek behind the roots; then Young Whortle had suggested that they attempt a climb.

"Don't go frettin', Sammy," he had said. "We won't pick a difficult tree and we won't go too high–promise."

"But, Warty," Samuel had protested, "shouldn't we be getting along now?"

"Bags of time yet! Sun ain't low enough to think on going back. Come on, give us a leg up."

So up an oak tree they had climbed. It was gnarled, knobbly, and ideal to climb. Footholds were plentiful and there were lots of low branches to run along and swing from.

Then Samuel had noticed the hole.

"What's that up there?" he had asked, pointing higher up the tree trunk. "Looks like some sort of big gap in the bark."

Higher they had clambered. Samuel had been determined not to look down and had kept his eyes strictly on his paws. Eventually, Young Whortle had drawn near to the hole.

"Seems like the tree's hollow here," he had called down.

"Wait for me!" Samuel had pulled himself up to his friend's side. Together they had peeped over the brink of the hole.

Inside all had been dark . . . but their sharp eyes had picked out something in the gloom. Something terrible . . .

Samuel shrieked and nearly fell off the tree. Young Whortle's eyes opened very wide and he gave a funny sort of yelp. Here, in the oak, was the frightful thing that had kept the fieldmice below ground this year–a large and very fearsome barn owl.

It was fast asleep amongst some old straw, but it stirred when the mice gasped in fright. Lazily it opened one eye and puffed out its soft feathery chest.

Quickly Young Whortle and Samuel ran down the tree. They slid and slithered, scraped their knees and broke the skin on their paws scurrying down it.

As Young Whortle jumped from the lowest branch a great

shadow fell on him. Quickly he yanked Samuel to the ground and ducked under one of the roots.

Seconds later sharp talons scored the ground where they had been.

Now here they were, two small frightened fieldmice cowering in terror from a dreadful enemy.

"Be it still up there?" asked Samuel in a tiny voice.

"Aye, Sammy, prob'ly sat on one o' them low branches just a-waitin' for us to make a move."

"Oh, Warty, I'm whacked," whimpered Samuel. "It's gettin' so dark now an' I haven't eaten for ages: just listen to my belly!"

"I hear it an' so can the owl most like. Put your paws over it or somethin'."

"I can't! I be starved."

"So be yon owl, Sammy, an' I don't want to be no bird's breakfast."

Samuel tried to control the growls and rumbles coming from his stomach. He was a thin mouse–"too thin," some said. The likes of Alison even called him "skinny Samuel." His mother was most perturbed by his weight, but no matter how much he ate he never got any fatter. " 'Tis his age," Old Todmore said of him. "Too much energy–he'll plump out afore he's wed." Now the thought that he would make a poor breakfast brought Samuel no comfort at all.

"We can't stay here," he said softly.

Young Whortle patted his friend on the shoulder. "Right," he said decisively. "I got me an idea."

"Smashin'!" Samuel brightened instantly. "I knowed you'd think o' somethin'. What be the plan?"

"Well," Young Whortle kept his voice low in case the owl was listening, "if I throws a stone yonder," he pointed behind them to a patch of ferns and bracken, "it just might fool Hooty up there an' distract him long enough for us to make a dash for them hollows full o' leaves."

"You're barmy!" exclaimed Samuel. "No way will that work. He's crafty he is. He'll spot that trick for sure an' we'll be runnin' straight down his gizzard."

Young Whortle said nothing. Instead he picked up a good paw-sized pebble and threw it for all he was worth. The ferns rustled and swayed as it crashed through them.

"Now!" he hissed, grabbing Samuel by the arm.

The fieldmice darted from under the root. Samuel ran as fast as he could, too terrified to look up in case he saw the owl rushing down to meet them–talons outstretched.

And then they were at the edge of the hollows, and with one leap they dived into the heaps of dry leaves.

"It worked!" Samuel cried. His heart was racing and his ears flushed with excitement.

"I told 'ee we'd have adventures today," said Young Whortle. "Now we'll have to be careful. He won't have liked that trick and it might make him anxious to get us."

"So what now?"

"We tunnel through these here leaves till we're at the point closest to the meadow. Then you just run like crazy."

Samuel gulped nervously, but their first success at owl-foxing heartened him. "Lead on, then," he said.

In the leaves it was easy to believe that it was autumn again. The smell of the dry decay was the very essence of that season. The leaves crackled over and beneath them as they pushed their way through. The sound filled their ears, like the noise of a greedy consuming fire. The mice moved quickly. Like moles they scooped the leaves out of the way with their paws and kicked them backward with their feet. Through the leafy ceiling the owl could be heard hooting irritably. It froze their hearts and made them move faster than ever.

Suddenly there was an explosion of leaves and twilight shone down on them.

"He's dive-bombing us," wailed Samuel. He looked up and

could see the owl soaring above, gaining height for the next dive.

"We'll have to zigzag and hope he misses us," shouted Young Whortle, burying himself in the leaves once more.

Samuel jumped in after him, and they madly dashed from side to side.

The owl tore into the leaves close by and gave an angry hoot at finding his talons empty. "Hooo mooouses, I'll get yoooou!" he bellowed furiously. The owl beat his great wings fiercely and rose high above the treetops. He stared with his great round eyes at the leafy hollow and glided on the night airs, silent as a ghost. There–a movement.

He dropped like a stone. With murderous intent he descended. He'd show them! How dare they wake him then hide and play silly tricks.

The owl skimmed the surface of the hollow with his talons, churning up leaves and twigs in the chaos of his wake.

Samuel and Young Whortle had managed to dodge that onslaught–but only just. Samuel lost the tip of his tail and the pain was terrible. Blood poured out of it and made him feel sick.

Young Whortle was near to panic himself. Both mice were tired now, but the owl had been asleep all day. Young Whortle wished they had stayed under that oak root after all. Even in the dim light he saw how pale Samuel had become, and in horror he noticed his friend's wounded tail. He knew then that they would not survive the next attack; they were exposed and too tired to move fast enough.

An insane idea gripped him suddenly and in a wild frenzy Young Whortle scrabbled amongst the muck of the floor until he found a stout twig.

Samuel was too groggy and near to fainting to question his friend. He watched Young Whortle bite the twig and strip away the bark with his teeth, gnawing like a demented demon. Then high above he saw the dark sinister shape of the owl plummeting toward them.

The owl had licked the blood from his talons and was cackling to himself, eager for the kill. The blood was warm and it tasted wonderful. The first mouse of the night was always the best and he had been unable to find any for months. But now, oho! Two lovely mice for him to swallow.

The cool night air streamed over his flat face as he hurtled down, legs stiff and talons glinting under the light of the first stars.

He had them in his sights–wise of them to stop running. "Ooooh mooouses." He chuckled, licking his beak in anticipation.

"FENNY!" bawled a voice. The owl blinked, and as he bore down on the mice one of them jumped up and drove something sharp into his left leg.

"Oooowww!" screeched the owl, floundering in the air with the shock. He rose up, shaking his head in disbelief. How dare they! The audacity of it! The owl was really furious now. Screaming with rage, he plucked the twig from his leg with one deft movement, spat it out, and glared down. This was serious; insult and injury–that had never happened to him before and he was deadly in his wrath.

"Mooouses!" he cried in a bitter cold voice. "Mahooot will find yooou!"

Young Whortle had wasted no time. As soon as he had wounded the owl he had dragged the wilting Samuel out of the hollow and pulled him toward the meadow.

How they managed he never knew. Samuel had lost a lot of blood and kept swooning. But fear kept them going and suddenly they were in.

Tall grasses surrounded them. Young Whortle knew, however, that it would take more protection than the meadow afforded to save them from a determined owl.

Samuel panted heavily. He felt very weak and his legs were like water. He tried to focus his eyes, but everything was blurred. Young Whortle's voice came to him urgently, calling his name.

"Sammy! Come on, we've made it to the meadow, but Hooty's still after us."

As if in agreement, a frightful screech came down out of the night sky.

Samuel felt himself tugged at roughly. "Leave me, Warty," he mumbled. "Too tired, you go."

"Shut up!" Young Whortle gripped his friend none too gently and shoved him farther into the meadow.

They stumbled and staggered along, flinging themselves to the ground when they felt a shadow pass overhead.

"What's he doing?" Young Whortle asked himself. "Why doesn't he strike? He must know where we are. Why doesn't he get it over with?"

A wicked cackle told him the reason. The owl was tormenting them, letting them know the full meaning of fear before the kill.

"Mooouses," he called, "Mahooot sees yooou." A dark wing swept over the tops of the grass.

Young Whortle bowed his head in defeat. He could run no more and even if he could the owl would snatch him before he made it to the ditch. The dark wing soared over again; this time battering down the grass.

Next time, thought Young Whortle desperately. "This is it, Sammy," he said, "I'm sorry this adventure has ended so badly."

Samuel shook his head feebly. "Not your fault, Warty." He held out a thin, trembling paw and Young Whortle clasped it tightly. Together they waited for the end.

Down came Mahooot, the owl. He smashed through the

grass and landed in front of the fieldmice.

"Ohooo, mooouses!" he said wickedly, narrowing his baleful, round, tawny eyes into evil slits. "Piece by piece will yooou slide dooown." He stepped nearer and opened his sharp beak. "Mahooot learn yooou tooo behave."

The owl shot out a talon and grasped Young Whortle by the shoulder. The small mouse squealed in pain as Mahooot drew him near to his waiting beak.

Samuel felt his friend's paw being dragged out of his own, but he was too far gone to be frightened of the sinister night bird about to feast on them.

Young Whortle saw through his tears the ghastly beak open. He felt the iron grip of the talons squeeze even tighter. The musty breath of the bird swept over him and he swooned. Mahooot sniggered. He was about to pop the fieldmouse's head into his beak when . . .

"Aiee! Aiee!" screamed a strange voice. "Aiee!"

Mahooot blinked and glanced up. Who was that disturbing his breakfast? The owl swiveled his face around but could see nothing. He grunted irritably and turned his attention back to the mouse.

"Aiee!" A stone came flying out of nowhere and stung Mahooot right on the beak.

"Whoooo? Whooo?" he began ferociously. He unfurled his wings but kept a tight hold on Young Whortle.

Great clumping footsteps came rushing toward them. Mahooot twitched with uncertainty–he would take to the air and see who this intruder was. His wings opened out and he began to flap them. He decided to leave the thin mouse behind, this one would do, he could eat it at his leisure in the oak tree.

"Aiee, beaky hooter!" came the voice. "Put down the mouselet!" Into view, crashing through the meadow, came a large ratwoman with a shawl around her shoulders and a bone in her hair. It was Madame Akkikuyu.

Mahooot eyed her doubtfully and rose into the air; he didn't like rats.

"Help!" squeaked Young Whortle, dangling from his talons.

The rat leaped up and grabbed the owl's other leg, bringing him sprawling to the ground with an astounded screech.

Madame Akkikuyu hopped onto Mahooot's back and dealt him a great thump with the bone from her hair. "Let go, feathery one, free mouselet."

The owl twisted under her and scrabbled at the ground in a bewildered frenzy. Another *thwack* hit his head. "Oooow!" he roared.

Madame Akkikuyu laughed out loud, then thrust the bone back in her hair and proceeded to pluck the owl.

Mahooot's screeches were deafening, and he turned his head to snap at the rat.

"Oh no, fowl one." She laughed, giving the slashing beak a swift smack with her claws.

Clouds of soft, pale feathers floated into the air as the raw bare patch on Mahooot's neck grew larger. Madame Akkikuyu began to hoot herself, mocking him as she tore out large clumps of feathers and threw them before the owl for him to see.

Suddenly Young Whortle was free. The talons opened and he staggered over to Samuel, where he fell unconscious.

Mahooot writhed and managed to scramble upright. Madame Akkikuyu clenched her claw and gave him a powerful punch. He staggered backward and she flung her arms around his neck and bit deeply into his shoulder.

That was enough for him. The owl let out one last hoot of pain, shook the rat off his back, and rose shakily off the ground–but not before a hail of stones and twigs battered him as Madame Akkikuyu jumped up and down with glee below.

"Scardee Birdee!" she shouted, sticking out her tongue at the receding dark shape in the sky. The fortune-teller smiled,

then rushed over to the fieldmice and inspected their wounds. "Poor mouseys," she cooed sadly, "very bad they are." She fumbled in one of the pouches that hung around her waist and brought out a broad-leafed herb. With it she dabbed Young Whortle's punctured shoulder and then with some more, bound Samuel's mutilated tail.

Madame Akkikuyu stepped back and sat down with a bump. How had she known what to do? She looked into her pouches and knew the properties of all the herbs in it–most of them were deadly. "Oh, Akkikuyu," she gasped breathlessly. "What memories are you waking?" She looked at Samuel's tail and it seemed to dissolve away, and in its place was a rough rat's tail, stumpy and with an old rag tied at the end. From out of the past a coarse voice said, "Just don't get in my way, witch!"

Madame Akkikuyu shuddered and all her instincts told her not to delve into her past too deeply. Yet she began to wonder, just who was she and why did she carry all these weird objects and powders around with her?

A sound from the real world reached her ears and she broke out of her brooding. The others were coming; already she could see the torches flickering. Silently she waited for them and reflected on the past days.

* * *

The journey to Fennywolde had been uneventful, but it had been so wonderful to be with her friend Audrey, to know that they were going somewhere pleasant in the sunshine. She had not stopped counting her blessings and hugged herself with pleasure.

It had taken three different boats to get this far, and Mr. Kempe had guided them all the way. He had been a little standoffish to her, but she was very grateful to him for taking the trouble to lead them here. This afternoon they had all waved good-bye to him and set foot on dry land once more. From there that funny little fieldmouse, Twit, had led them, pointing out local features and telling amusing stories. Madame Akkikuyu had reveled in the company of her friends. They turned from the river and followed a little stream, which divided and became several small brooks. The one they followed soon became a dry ditch. There they found a crowd of worried-looking mice staring across a meadow.

Someone had gone to fetch Twit's parents and they nearly hugged the breath clear out of him when they saw him. But the celebration had been short-lived. An owl screeched over the meadow and all the mice gasped; some had tears in their eyes. It was explained that two youngsters were missing. Akkikuyu saw the owl circling and knew it was about to strike. To everyone's astonishment she had dropped her bags and stormed into the meadow, calling out a challenge. Yes, what a day it had been–if only the nights were as good. She had come to dread the empty darkness and the fear it brought her.

"Over here!" came the babble of voices. Madame Akkikuyu wrenched herself back to the present and got to her feet.

The meadow was lit by little burning torches carried by a host of fieldmice. They hurried toward her and she threw open her arms in welcome. The mice came and stared at the scene before them with open mouths.

There were the two youngsters lying, dead for all they knew, on the ground, and the peculiar ratwoman was boldly waving her arms about. Covering everything was a layer of downy feathers like a light fall of snow. They gazed at Madame Akkikuyu dumbly, not knowing what to do.

Mrs. Gorse pushed her way to the front and ran to her son's side. She wept over his damaged tail and kissed his forehead.

"He need rest," advised the fortune-teller. "I make broth to heal tomorrow."

Young Whortle's parents came squeezing out of the crowd

and knelt beside their son. Slowly his eyes opened and he managed a weak smile for them. Then he lifted a finger and pointed at the rat.

"She saved us, Dad," he said. "Saved us from the owl she did."

"Thank you," said Mr. Nep gratefully to Madame Akkikuyu.

The crowd cheered until she flushed with pleasure. Then to her great surprise and enduring delight, they picked her up and carried her on their shoulders, although it took eight of the strongest husbands to manage this feat. Others helped to take Young Whortle and Samuel back to the winter quarters.

Arthur and Audrey could not believe their eyes. Here they were, newly arrived in Fennywolde and Madame Akkikuyu was being feted as a heroine. Everything was happening so quickly. They hadn't had a chance to meet Twit's parents yet.

Arthur stood amongst the feathers and shrugged. "I'd never have believed it," he said flatly.

"She is remarkable," said a voice behind them. They turned around and saw a fieldmouse sticking a feather in his hair. "Even my father approved of her," he added. "Oh, sorry, my name's Jenkin. You're the ones who came back with Twit, aren't you?"

"Yes," replied Audrey. She liked the look of this mouse and he had been the first one in Fennywolde to speak to them so far. "I'm Audrey and this is my brother, Arthur. What's been going on here?"

"Oh, an owl's kept us in our winter quarters all year. We daren't go out at night coz he'd catch us an' eat us. But it looks like we've done seen the last of him for a while." Jenkin beamed at them and Audrey noticed an ugly bruise on his ear and that his lip was badly swollen.

"You've been in a fight," she said to him.

Jenkin turned quickly away and said, "We better get goin'– the others are nearly home now." The rows of bobbing torches had dwindled in the distance. "Follow me," he told them, and set off back to the ditch.

"You embarrassed him," Arthur hissed at Audrey, "Why can't you mind your own business?"

"Why should it have embarrassed him?" protested Audrey. "I shouldn't think he's trying to keep the fact a secret. Did you see the state of his bruises?"

"Yes, I did, but I've had worse. Anyway, we must follow him now, I don't want to spend our first night here tramping through the fields lost. Come on."

At the ditch, the fieldmice put Madame Akkikuyu down and the husbands wiped their brows wearily. The fortune-teller gazed about her, enraptured. She could not remember ever feeling like this before–she wanted to burst with joy.

By the time Arthur and Audrey arrived she was speaking: "Owly not come back in hurry, if he do–Akkikuyu bite him again."

There was thunderous applause and some mice cried, "We can move into the field at last!" and "Hooray for the ratlady!"

Then other voices called, "Where be Mr. Woodruffe? He's got to declare the field open." The mice looked at one another and muttered agreement. Hastily a young mouse ran into the shelters to fetch him.

At the Spring Ceremony every year the fieldmice elected a "King of the Field." This year the honor had gone to Mr. Abraham Woodruffe–a well-liked and respected mouse who so far had been unable to enjoy his high office, being stuck in the winter quarters all the time.

The mice waited for him and excited expectation charged the cool night air. Audrey and Arthur sensed their mood and they too grew impatient. Audrey began to fidget and started to look around at the fieldmice. It was the first chance she had had so far to view them properly. There were fat mice, thin mice, some tiny ones with large pink ears and long twitchy tails but no tall mice. Except perhaps . . . yes, on the far side of the crowd Audrey saw a lofty mouse. She stared at him curiously: what a grim face he had! It seemed as if his face never saw a smile. Idly she wondered who he was and then, next to him, she noticed Jenkin, who to her surprise and lasting embarrassment was looking straight at her. Audrey coughed and turned quickly away. She felt her ears burn with her blushes and hoped it would not show under the torchlight.

Audrey tried to compose herself and gazed fixedly ahead, hoping that her ribbon was tied properly. However, she could not resist having a crafty peep around to see if Jenkin was still looking at her.

As casually as she could manage, Audrey turned, but Jenkin was speaking with that tall mouse now. She was amused to find that she was disappointed, and smiled broadly at herself until she saw something that made her cough and turn away again.

A girl mouse was glaring at her–glaring with real hatred in her eyes. Audrey could feel them boring into the back of her neck. She could not think who the girl was and asked herself if she had done anything to deserve it.

"Oh, what the heck!" she said to herself in a low determined whisper and looked back at the girl. Alison Sedge was still eyeing Audrey with a face like thunder. Their eyes met and Miss Brown gave her her most insolent, pretty smile, then turned away.

Suddenly a hush fell on the gathered fieldmice as Mr. Woodruffe stepped out of the winter quarters. He was a jovial mouse and seemed quite ordinary except that on his brow he wore a crown of plaited corn. Mr. Woodruffe raised his paws and began solemnly.

"May the field be blessed and may the goodwill of the Green Mouse follow us therein."

"Amen to that!" called out Isaac Nettle, but he was drowned out by the frantic cheers of everyone else.

Mr. Woodruffe waved his arms for silence and continued. "I have been told of the daring bravery shown 'ere by our guest." He bowed to Madame Akkikuyu. She pointed her foot and managed a curtsy back. "And as 'King of the Field,'" he went on, "it is my pleasure to offer her the freedom of Fennywolde, for surely she is a messenger of the Green Mouse come in our most desperate hour."

There were shouts of agreement from the fieldmice. Arthur and Audrey stared at each other. Isaac Nettle nodded his head gravely.

"And now," shouted Mr. Woodruffe, "you may all enter the field!" He stood aside and the fieldmice scurried past him.

"Make the Hall," they yelled happily.

Soon only Mr. Woodruffe, Madame Akkikuyu, Audrey, and Arthur were left standing by the ditch, and the field was filled was joyous calls and mysterious sounds.

Mr. Woodruffe looked at the Deptford mice and smiled. "So you are Twit's companions. Come, he is below with his folks. I think we can interrupt them now. You look like you could do with a good sleep. The field is no place for you tonight. The work would keep you awake."

"Please, sir," Arthur asked, "what work?"

"Hah, you'll see tomorrow, lad." Mr. Woodruffe turned to Madame Akkikuyu and raised his eyebrows. "Will you join us below, ma'am? We would be most honored."

The fortune-teller grinned at him and came over to give Audrey a big hug.

"Yes, Akkikuyu come, she not leave her friend. First Akkikuyu find bags. You go, I follow."

The three mice left the rat to find her things and entered the winter quarters.

Madame Akkikuyu was left alone in the dark. In her mind she relived the thrilling moments of glory, and the thrill that those cheers gave her. What undreamed wonders there were in the world and how her heart swelled with pride to think that all these mice honored her!

As a tear fell from her furry cheek, Madame Akkikuyu knew that she had never been so happy before. Tonight, she thought, would be a good time to die, while she was happiest. The fortune-teller sniffed. No, with her friend there would be many more times such as this–if not greater. Madame Akkikuyu blew her nose on her shawl, then cast about for her bags.

It was too dark to see them. The sky had clouded over and the moon was hidden. She stooped down and groped for her things. It was so quiet. The noise of the mice in the field had died down or they had moved farther away, out of earshot.

"Akkikuyu!"

Madame Akkikuyu paused and tilted her head to one side.

"Akkikuyu!"

There it was again. A distant, echoing voice calling her name. It had troubled her on the river but no one else seemed to have heard it. Madame Akkikuyu despaired. Tearing at her hair, she shook her head violently. "Leave me!" she wailed. "Go away. Akkikuyu not listen!" And she ran up the side of the ditch and down into the shelters.

CHAPTER SEVEN

THE HALL OF CORN

The sun brimmed over the tops of the oak trees and its dazzling, early rays moved slowly over the meadow, pushing back the gray dawn and creeping toward the field. The corn seemed to stir at the sun's warm touch and stretched as high as it could. Fennywolde awoke.

Audrey rubbed her eyes and gazed sleepily at the low, rough ceiling. She was in a small room in the winter quarters, that part lived in by the Scuttles. The room was bare–there was no decoration on the lumpy earth walls, no flowers, drawings, ornaments–nothing. Only a small tallow candle flickered miserably in one corner and Audrey looked at it thoughtfully. She was sure she had blown that out before she had gone to sleep. Someone must have been in to relight it. Yes, on the floor near her bed was a bowl of water for her to wash in. That was a kind thought and one which Audrey felt she needed.

She dragged herself out of bed and began splashing the drowsiness and grime of the past few days away.

"Is that you awake now, Audrey?" came a friendly voice just

outside the room. "Well, breakfast's ready when you are."

Audrey finished dressing and smoothed the creases out of her lace. She tied a new ribbon in her hair–a parting gift from Kempe, then she slipped her bells onto her tail and went into the breakfast room.

Again it was bleak and bare with only a table in the center and three stools around it. Mrs. Scuttle pattered in carrying a bowl of porridge.

Audrey and Arthur had been surprised when they first saw Mrs. Chitter's sister. She wasn't a bit like that gossipy old fusspot. Gladwin Scuttle was a brown housemouse, as they were. She was slender with short chestnut hair, graying at the crown, and a thin, delicate face. Around her neck she wore a prim starched collar. Audrey thought that she must have been quite lovely when she was younger.

"Where's my brother and Twit?" asked Audrey between mouthfuls.

"Gone out with Elijah," replied Mrs. Scuttle, settling down on a stool and beaming warmly. "Oh, and your . . . er . . . friend, Madame–what was it?"

"Akkikuyu," prompted Audrey, "but she's not exactly my friend, you know."

"Well, I did wonder. I came from Deptford too, remember, and I know how horrible the rats were there. I'd watch her if I were you, wouldn't trust her an inch despite her doings last night."

Audrey wondered about that. "That's what Kempe said, but you know I really do think she's changed. She really is trying her best."

"Hmm," Mrs. Scuttle sounded doubtful. "Still, I suppose I shouldn't judge her too harshly. My William's been telling me all about you and her and . . . ," here she lowered her voice to a faint whisper, " . . . Jupiter."

"Please," begged Audrey, "you mustn't mention that name

to Madame Akkikuyu. She can't remember a thing and it might just be too much for her."

"Oh quite, dear . . . I can keep mum. I don't suppose my sister has learned how yet–no, your smile gives that away. So, Arabel's not changed a bit, I thought William was being too polite when I asked him about her. Still it was good of her to look after him all this time."

Audrey finished her breakfast and then said, "You never did tell me where Madame Akkikuyu had gone."

"Oh yes, why there I go again–forgetting things. I tell you, dear, my head's like a sieve these days. Oh . . . where was I?"

"Madame Akkikuyu."

"Yes, such an odd name. Well, you should have seen how much she ate this morning, and I'm sorry, but her table manners are dreadful. Anyway, after making a right mess she ups and goes outside hauling one of those big bags with her. What does she keep in them, do you know?"

Audrey nodded. "They're her herbs, powders, mixing tins, and other stuff like that."

"Well. William did tell me how she's supposed to be a fortuneteller, I didn't like to ask her myself–I find that sort of thing very frightening."

"Oh, it's all right," assured Audrey. "She doesn't do any of that anymore. I think she just carries that junk around with her out of habit. You don't have to worry, she's not likely to start brewing up spells now."

Mrs. Scuttle put her paws on the table and stared at Audrey. "But my dear! That's precisely what she is doing. That's where everyone's gone. She's making a healing broth, so she says–for Young Whortle Nep and Samuel Gorse."

"What!" spluttered Audrey, aghast. "But she doesn't know how. She'll probably poison them with what's in those bags of hers." She jumped up from the table and ran out of the Scuttles' rooms.

The winter quarters were a series of drab tunnels with family rooms leading off the main passages. There was no decoration anywhere, just the dismal tallow candles flickering on the walls. Up the tunnel Audrey hurried and sped out into the fresh air.

She followed the sound of voices and ran along the top of the ditch overlooking the bare stony stretch. There were all the fieldmice and in the center was Madame Akkikuyu.

Her brewing pot was over a crackling fire and she stirred the bubbling contents with the bone from her hair. Occasionally she delved into one of her pouches and threw some leaves in the boiling mixture.

The fieldmice watched her with keen interest and admiration. Audrey spotted Arthur and Twit and pushed past the others to reach them.

"Mornin', Audrey," greeted Twit brightly.

"Hello," she mumbled. "Arthur, what do you think you're doing letting her do this? It's bound to be poisonous."

"What am I supposed to do?" asked Arthur crossly. "She'd already started by the time we got here."

"But she might poison one of those boys," Audrey said. "I can't let her carry on." She forced her way through the fieldmice to the front.

"My," whistled Twit, "your Audrey ain't one for standin' by."

"That's what worries me," said Arthur.

Audrey went to the fortune-teller's side and tugged her elbow fiercely.

"Mouselet!" cried the rat gleefully. "You sleep well, yes? Akkikuyu look in on you before she go. You sleep like twig." She put her arm around the mouse and Audrey squirmed.

"What are you doing?" she asked. "You don't know what those herbs and powders are for."

Madame Akkikuyu gave a deep fruity laugh. "But, my mouselet, Akkikuyu remember now–leaves make you better, heal wounds. They strong nature magic."

"But they're poisonous," hissed Audrey.

"No, no," tutted the fortune-teller, "some leaves bad, yes, Akkikuyu chuck them, she knows those that heal." She gave the potion one last stir and declared to the fieldmice, "Is ready, come–take to the poorly little ones."

Mrs. Gorse stepped forward and looked apprehensively at the steaming thick broth bubbling away in the pot.

"Come, come," encouraged the rat, beckoning with her claws.

Mrs. Gorse held out a wooden bowl and Madame Akkikuyu scooped some of the potion into it.

"Take to boy, make him drink all. He get better soon."

Audrey rushed over to Mrs. Gorse. "Don't take it to him," she implored, and a murmur of surprise rippled through the fieldmice. "Madame Akkikuyu isn't well herself. She doesn't know what she's put in there, it might make your son worse."

Mrs. Gorse blinked and regarded the bowl with suspicion. The crowd muttered and stirred uneasily.

"Mouselet!" exclaimed the fortune-teller in a shocked tone. "Why you say such fibs? Akkikuyu knows–she not moon calf. Potion good–take to boy," she insisted.

"Well," began Mrs. Gorse uncertainly.

"See," cried Madame Akkikuyu, and she took the bowl from her and drank down the whole lot.

The crowd fell silent and stared at her wide-eyed.

Madame Akkikuyu swilled some of the potion around in her mouth before swallowing. She knitted her brows and Audrey looked up at her, fearfully expecting the rat to keel over or for her claws to drop out. The fortune-teller licked her lips and simply said, "Need salt." She sprinkled some into the pot.

That was enough for the fieldmice. They broke out into a peal of applause.

"But that doesn't prove anything," Audrey tried to make herself heard.

Mrs. Gorse took the bowl again and filled it herself. "Listen, young lady," she said to Audrey, "this Madame Akkikookoo saved my Samuel last night and that's good enough for me. It's wicked of you to say such things about her."

Audrey was speechless. It was no use. Mr. Nep came forward and took a bowl for Young Whortle, giving her a very disagreeable look in the process.

"This potion keep," shouted Madame Akkikuyu. "If mouseys seal it in jar, potion last till spring."

"My Nelly's got jars," said Mr. Nep. "You come with me, missus, we'll see to our boy then root some out for 'ee."

The crowd cheered as Madame Akkikuyu followed Mr. Nep to the shelters. The rat waved regally as she passed by. As the fieldmice dispersed and went into the field, Arthur and Twit came over to Audrey. Arthur was shaking his head.

"A right idiot you made of yourself there, you soft lump," he said. "I've never seen anyone make such an ass of themselves before."

"Stow it, Arthur." Audrey was in no mood for brotherly criticism.

"Never mind," piped up Twit. "Maybe Young Whortle and Sammy will get better."

"I wouldn't bet on it," said Audrey. "They can't say I didn't try and warn them, can they?"

"Aye." Twit laughed. "But you made a right pig's ear of it."

Audrey could never be angry with Twit and she sighed loudly. "Oh, you're right, both of you. What a fool I must have looked to them." She laughed at the thought of it. "Oh, well, what shall we do now?"

"There's the Hall to see," Twit said. "They've been at it all night–me dad's gone to see it already."

"The Hall?" asked Audrey mildly. "What's that?"

"Oh, you'll see soon enough." Twit chuckled, leading them away from the edge of the ditch and into the field.

* * *

Jenkin held tightly to the cornstalk. He could see Todkin a little farther away and behind he heard Figgy humming to himself. Jenkin waved at Todkin and a little paw was raised in answer.

"Jenkin," a familiar voice called up to him. He looked down and on the ground below, Alison Sedge was peering up at him with a paw shielding her eyes from the sun.

"What you wantin'?" he shouted down to her.

"To talk to 'ee," she answered. "Come down–me neck's startin' to ache."

"Darn her," grumbled Jenkin as he nimbly descended the stalk. It was the only free day he had had for weeks. His father had told him to celebrate the Green Mouse's bounty in the field and he was only too happy to do so. He did not want to waste his time with Alison Sedge.

She waited patiently at the base of the stalk for him and twisted her hair coyly. Suddenly Jenkin was at her side. "Mornin'," she said.

"Don't tell me that's all you wanted to say, Alison Sedge," he puffed.

"No, just bein' p'lite that's all," she told him sniffily. "'Ere, what you got that feather in your hair for, Jenkin Nettle?" She reached over to pull it out. "Let me put it in mine–suit me better."

He stepped quickly aside. "You go pick yourself another flower," he said, irritated. "This is my good-luck charm, this is."

"Luck is it?" she asked in surprise. "What does your dad say to that?"

"Nothin', cause I ain't told him and don't you either." He licked his sore lip and Alison had enough tact to change the subject.

"What I really come to tell 'ee is about the ratwoman and the girl that came with her."

"Oh yes?" Jenkin tried to disguise his interest.

"Had a right old dingdong, they just did. There was that Mrs. Akky Yakky a-makin' a potion to heal Young Whortle and Skinny Samuel when that girl comes bargin' up and rants on about it bein' poison."

"Was it?"

"No, she's barmy." Alison sniggered. "That rat up an' drank some an' she didn't snuff it. Made that town mouse look real daft, she did."

Jenkin looked past her, and curious, Alison turned around. Toward them came Arthur, Twit, and Audrey. "Well, here she is herself," said Jenkin. "Shall I ask her if she is potty for you?"

"Pah," said Alison, tossing her head. "I ain't stayin' to talk to no loony. I'm goin' to meet Hodge–see if he wants to come to the meadow with me."

"Suit yourself." Jenkin grinned as she hastily departed.

Arthur and Audrey had never been in a cornfield before. They gazed about them with great interest. It was like a thick, dense wood of stalks. If the fieldmice had not made pathways they would have had to struggle and fight their way through like explorers in a jungle. They craned their necks to see the tops of the stems where the young ears waved gently in the breeze. Bright red poppies were tangled in the field and Audrey gaped in wonder at the gorgeous flaming flowers. It was a more beautiful place than she had expected.

"Look," said Twit presently, "there's Jenkin. Hoy there, Jolly Jenkin!"

"How do," he said shyly with his eyes on the ground. "Where you goin' then, Twit?"

"Arthur and Audrey ain't seen the Hall yet," Twit replied. "I was jus' takin' 'em there. You on sentry, Jenkin?"

"Sentry?" asked Arthur.

"We don't leave the field unguarded once the Hall's been done," said Twit. "There's a great ring of lads circling the Hall keepin' a look out for enemies."

"Where?" put in Audrey. "I haven't seen anyone so far."

"Hah, miss." Jenkin laughed. "You ain't been lookin' proper." He pointed upward. "How's things, Figgy?"

"Fine so far!" came an answering call from above.

"There's someone up there!" gasped Arthur. "He's at the very top of the stalk."

"Where else would you sentry from?" asked Jenkin, highly amused.

"I'd love to do that," Arthur said as he stared upward.

"Have a go, then," urged Jenkin.

"Old Arthur won't make it," tittered Twit, "not with his tummy."

"Huh!" snorted Arthur, stepping up to the nearest stalk. He hesitated. Now that he had to climb it, the stalk did seem very high.

"Go on, then," encouraged Jenkin, "ignore Twit."

Arthur frowned and breathed deeply. Then, with a loud grunt, he jumped up and grasped the stem with his paws. He dangled in the air like a caught fish, winning another giggle from Twit. Arthur tried to climb, passing paw over paw. The stalk wobbled and swayed treacherously.

"Wrap your tail around it," advised Jenkin.

Arthur tried, but once his tail had gripped the stalk it refused to budge anymore.

"I'm stuck," he cried, and with a thud he fell to the ground.

Twit rolled around, his sides aching. Even Audrey laughed and Arthur glared at them both–after he had shaken some of the dust out of his fur.

"Shall we show you how it's done?" offered Jenkin. "Twit?"

Twit wiped the tears from his eyes and stood beneath the stalk Arthur had tried to climb. "Ready?" he asked Jenkin.

Jenkin, standing under another stalk, nodded. "First to the top," he said. "Say when, miss."

Audrey counted them down. "Three, two, one–go."

The fieldmice shot up the corn as if they had wings. Their legs and paws were a blur and their tails spiraled around the stems faster than anything she had seen. It was Jenkin who won–just a second before Twit.

"Beat you at last." He waved triumphantly.

"I be out of practice," panted Twit, "this time next week I'll leave you standin'."

Arthur regarded them enviously, wishing he could do half as well. Jenkin slid down quickly, eyed Audrey bashfully, then said to Arthur, "Don't worry–you'll soon learn. Come see me after you've been to the Hall if you're willin' an' we'll get you up a stalk afore the end of the day."

"If only I could," Arthur sighed in disbelief.

"Anyway, you best get goin'," said Jenkin, "soonest there, sooner you can come back." He looked up, Twit was still enjoying being at the top of the corn. "Been a long time since he sat up on sentry," murmured Jenkin. "Thought he were dead, you know–we all did. He's a good bloke, but a bit simple."

"He doesn't get into fights," remarked Audrey sternly, "and I bet he's done more in his life than you ever will."

"Never said he hadn't!" Jenkin refused to be provoked. "All I'm sayin' is, there's some in Fennywolde who don't respect the Scuttles–say Twit's a dimmy and more besides. Not me–I like him. I reckon he's too good-natured, though. Folk take advantage and think he's daft. That's all."

"I think," said Arthur breaking in, "that one day Twit might get pressed too hard, and he may surprise a few around here if that kind nature of his snaps."

Twit slid down the stalk. "Oooh, that did me good," he said, beaming from ear to ear. "Ain't nothin' like it for blowin' the cobwebs away. You ready to see the Hall now? Come on, then."

They left Jenkin behind and he flashed up his stalk and resumed his sentry duty.

Deeper into the field went the three friends until the dense corn around them began to thin out more considerably and appeared to form a corridor, the ceiling of which was made by twisting together the ears of corn from opposite "walls." It began to look very grand and imposing.

"This be the main way to the Hall," Twit informed them in a hushed, reverent tone. "This be what they all were doin' last night."

"It's very clever," remarked Arthur.

Twit chuckled. "Just you wait."

"What's that ahead?" asked Audrey as they turned a corner.

"The great doors," Twit answered.

At the end of the corridor there were two large doors made completely from tightly woven corn stems. They reached up as high as the growing corn itself, and on either side of them were two fieldmice who carried themselves importantly–they were the door guards.

"Mornin', Twit," greeted one of them.

"Hello, Grommel, how've you been keepin'? Your back still playin' you up?"

"Somethin' chronic, Twit lad. These your town friends?"

"Right enough. This here's Audrey Brown and this be her brother, Arthur. I be takin' 'em to see the Hall."

"Then pass, friends," said the door guard, and he stood aside, pushing open one of the large doors.

Audrey and Arthur stepped through and blinked.

The Hall of Corn was immense. It was wide and long, and clumps of corn had been left standing at regular intervals, giving the impression of mighty pillars–but the Hall was open to the sky. At the far end, on a wickerwork throne, sat Mr. Woodruffe–able at last to take up his plaited scepter and govern the Hall as every King of the Field had done since the time of Fenny.

Many fieldmice were bustling about, building large spherical structures halfway up the corn stems.

"What are they doing?" asked Arthur.

"They be our summer quarters," replied Twit gleefully. "You never slept till you spent a night in a fieldmouse's nest–not on the ground, but halfway in the sky," he added dreamily.

It certainly was very grand. Audrey was overcome by the industriousness of the Fennywolders. All this had taken only one night to accomplish. She was amazed.

"There's me dad," said Twit suddenly, and he ran over to where Elijah Scuttle was working. He had built a good large nest for him and Mrs. Scuttle and was in the process of completing a slightly smaller one.

"How do, Willum," he nodded to his son. "Thought 'ee an' Master Brown could share a nest."

"Terrific!" said Arthur.

"Don't be doin' it too high, though, Dad." Twit laughed. "Old Arthur can't climb too good."

"Now, now, Willum," chided his father softly. "You knows I do make your mam a straw ladder every year–I'll do 'un for Master Brown too."

Mr. Scuttle was a pleasant fieldmouse. He looked like an older version of his son, except there were creamy whiskers fringing his chops and on his shoulders there were two white scars where no fur would grow. He did, however, have the same mischievous twinkle in his eye.

"And what about you, missey?" Elijah addressed Audrey. "I'm not sure if you want to sleep with your ratty friend."

"Oh no, Mr. Scuttle," gasped Audrey, horrified, until she realized he was teasing her. He grinned and said, "I'll make 'ee a real pirty nest for one, so she can't squeeze in."

"Thank you," said Audrey, greatly relieved. The thought of having to share a nest with Madame Akkikuyu was too terrible even to joke about.

"Look," began Arthur. "I better go back and find that Jenkin chap–I'm not going to be the only boy using a ladder–what would everyone say?"

"I'll come with you, Arthur," said Twit. "I got me some practicin' to do." So the two boys went off, laughing and jostling each other.

Audrey decided not to join them. "Is there anything I can do, Mr. Scuttle?" she asked.

Elijah looked surprised, then pleased. "Aye, missey," he said delighted. "See you over there." He pointed to a pile of moss and soft grass picked early that morning by a robust group of mousewives. "That there," he continued, "is what we do line our nests with–featherin', we calls it. Makes 'em real comfy and soft it do–you could fetch some if you're willin'."

"Certainly," said Audrey. She made her way over to the heap of feathering–although she could see no feathers in it whatsoever.

She passed beneath half-made nests where husbands not as deft as Mr. Scuttle cursed as the weave fell apart. She wanted to learn more of the families who shouted cheerfully to one another from nest to nest and drew the very young children up on straw ropes. Some stout wives who refused to be parted from the bed linen were taking sheets and pillows into the nests with them. Audrey walked by one group of children who were all sitting down, listening with eyes agog and breaths held to an old mouse brindled white with age telling them stories. It was Old Todmore–the storyteller of the field, and today he had a new tale to tell. Most of the children had been in bed the night before so had missed the excitement of Madame Akkikuyu and the owl and were now listening to the story, thrilled and captivated.

"Well, there's poor Young Whortle Nep with this great deadly owl about to chew off his head when crashin' through the meader comes the answer to our prayers–Madame Ak . . . Akky . . .?" Old Todmore was finding it difficult to get his tongue around the fortune-teller's name.

"Stop a-doin' that Abel Madder!" he said, vexed. "Now where was I? Oh, aye, well, crashin' through the meader comes the answer to our prayers–Madame Ratlady."

Audrey did not know whether to be amused or alarmed at how the fieldmice considered Madame Akkikuyu to be their savior. She wondered how those two young mice were faring after drinking that potion.

Finally she reached the heap of feathering and gathered some spongy moss in her arms. Three other girl mice were there doing the same. They smiled at her nervously.

"Hello," said Audrey.

They nodded their heads in reply.

"I'm Audrey Brown," she persisted.

One of the girls who had a mass of coarse, straight red hair said, "You be Twit's friend."

"That's right."

"Saw you last night with another towny."

"That's my brother, Arthur."

"Arthur is it?" cooed one of the others.

"Aye, Dimsel, and only a brother," said the first.

"Tush you," cried the one called Dimsel, nudging her friend.

The girl who had not yet spoken pushed the others aside and said, "How do, Audrey. I be Lily Clover. This one with the nose of a Hogpry be Iris Crowfoot."

"Hogpry yourself," shoved Iris.

"And this be Dimsel Bottom, she's mad keen on your Arthur."

"Oh, Lily!"

"It's true, ain't it?"

"Well!"

Audrey laughed. She liked these three and she wished Dimsel the best of luck concerning her brother. For a while they chatted amiably, then Iris said, "We best be goin', our mams'll take on so if we don't 'ave the featherin' done soon."

As they left Lily turned and asked Audrey, "You met Alison Sedge yet?"

"No–I don't think so."

"Well you just mind when you do–got claws has our Alison." Lily cast a lazy, lingering eye over Audrey's ribbon and lace before she said, "Aye, you watch out, me dear." And with that she left.

Audrey wandered back to Mr. Scuttle. He had started work on her nest now and he called down to her.

"Leave it down there, missey, if'n you're not sure of your stalk paws yet."

Audrey waved to him, then fetched some more.

The morning turned into lunchtime and merry wives brought out cheese and hot fresh bread for their hardworking husbands.

Gladwin Scuttle appeared with her arms laden and Arthur and Twit were following eagerly. They sat down and munched happily, Mr. Scuttle swilling down the bread, which stuck in his throat, with some blackberry ferment and telling his wife how he was progressing. It was hot work and he was glad of the rest. He sat with his back to a stalk, his ears beetroot red.

Mrs. Scuttle passed a critical eye over her bedroom for the summer and nodded satisfactorily, then told her husband to help some of the others she had seen whose attempts at nest building were pitiful.

"Ah," said Elijah, "Josiah Down won't never learn if'n I always do it fer 'im. Never has patience with the framework, that's what does it."

"Well," tutted Gladwin, "I passed Mrs. Down just now and she did ask me to mention it to you."

"Reckon I'll pop over later on," he promised.

All around, the light, happy sound of fieldmice talking,

relaxing, eating, and laughing filled the air. Audrey lay on her side and watched the inhabitants of Fennywolde content in their element. The Hall of Corn was near to completion. Nearly all the nests were finished and it was interesting to see the different styles. Some were perfectly round, others egg-shaped; there were small ones and those large enough to need supporting by many stalks. Yes, the Hall was a marvelous place and Audrey could not wait to sleep in her nest and see the stars shining through the small entrance.

The midday sun glittered on the dust from the straw, which swirled in a fine mist over their heads. It made everything look hazy and unreal.

Twit saw her gazing around and said, "You should see it when the corn is really ripe, then it looks as if the entire Hall is made of gold."

"It is marvelous," she sighed. "Grand yet simple as well." She wondered if the fieldmice would decorate the Hall properly with garlands of flowers and chains of daisies. In a small way it reminded her of the chamber of spring and summer that she had entered in Deptford when she had received her mousebrass. As she thought of it an idea came to her.

Just then their lunch was disturbed by a cheer from some of the families and calls of "Hooray."

Audrey strained to see. There was Jenkin coming through the doors and with him was Young Whortle.

The families rushed up to him to see if he was really all right. But apart from some nasty bruises and a bandage over his shoulder he seemed fine.

"It was that potion," he said. "Didn't taste too good but made me sit up and take notice. Sammy's gettin' better too–that ratlady reckons he'll be up an' about in a few days."

The crowd murmured in wonder and praised Madame Akkikuyu's skill in healing.

"Where be she now?" asked one of them.

"Why she's with my mam a-bottlin' that stuff to keep for next time someone gets ill," replied Young Whortle.

"That's a turn-up for the books," whistled Arthur when all the commotion had died down. "Who'd have thought that goo actually worked?"

"Well, I didn't, for one," said Audrey. "I look an even bigger idiot now, don't I? Oh, well, rather that than have one of those two get poisoned."

Lunch was over and Elijah climbed up to the nest again, taking some feathering with him. Mrs. Scuttle tidied up and went to the still pool to wash the bowls. Twit scurried up and helped his father.

Arthur was eating the last bit of cheese absently. Then forgetting to wipe his whiskers, as usual, he pulled Audrey to one side and told her.

"Look, Twit's been telling me about Jenkin–you really mustn't tease him anymore about those bruises, you know."

"Why ever not?" demanded his sister curiously.

"Because his dad gave them to him. Apparently, Mr. Nettle often hits Jenkin–thinks it's good for him."

"Oh," stammered Audrey, "I feel terrible now. Why doesn't his mother do something?"

"Because she's dead–died when he was born, apparently, and no one else likes to interfere with Mr. Nettle–he's the mousebrass maker, you see."

"Poor Jenkin."

"Yes–so just be a bit nicer next time, eh?"

"Of course, Arthur."

"Well," Arthur said, changing the subject, "this afternoon I'm going to crack climbing one of those dratted stalks if it kills me. What are you going to do?"

"Oh, I've had an idea to make something for the Hall."

Arthur regarded her doubtfully. "What sort of 'something'?" he asked.

"A corn dolly. You know, like the ones at home in the chambers of summer in the Spring Ceremony. I'm surprised they haven't already got some here."

"Maybe they don't know how–I didn't know you did, either."

Audrey shrugged. "Easy. I watched the Raddle sisters once."

Arthur considered the idea for a moment, then said, "Yes, that sounds nice, you could present it to Mr. Woodruffe when you've finished and let him decide where to hang it." He looked around to see if any crumbs had fallen on the floor but was disappointed, so he went off to talk to Jenkin again about his climbing.

Audrey picked up some thin straws and began to plait them together.

It was more difficult than she had thought. The plaits were impossible to keep even and free from ugly gaps. However, eventually Audrey became more adept with the straw and her confidence grew.

She intended to make something simple to begin with–a bell shape perhaps, but as the straw flicked between her fingers her ambitions for it soared.

Audrey decided that the figure of a girl would be best, with corn ears for arms and a dress of bunched stalks.

The afternoon wore on. The dolly grew larger under her fingers, far larger than she had intended. Some mouse children who had been running around playing chase stopped and watched her. They had never seen anything like it before and Audrey talked to them happily as she made it.

Alison Sedge wandered into the Hall. Hodge had walked with her to the meadow, but she was in such a sulk that he had left her and gone to join Todkin on sentry.

Alison was thinking about Jenkin and the look that he had on his face when he saw that town mouse. It was uncomfortably hot and Alison was in a bad mood with the world. She decided to go to the still pool to bathe and admire her reflection.

She had just been gathering some wild rosemary to rinse her hair with when she decided to see how the Hall was coming along and if her father had finished her own nest.

It was as she crossed the Hall that she noticed a small crowd of children near the Scuttles' nests. And there, in the center of all the attention, was that town mouse! Curious and irritated, Alison tossed her head and strode nearer.

The dolly was now taller than Audrey, its head was a loop of plaited straw and she was busily straightening it as at the moment the whole thing had an amusing drunken air about it.

The children were watching everything Audrey did keenly. Alison quietly drew close and observed the scene acidly. She looked at the town mouse's silver bells tinkling on her tail and noted with envy the lace dress. Alison glanced down at her own simple frock, which seemed shabbier by comparison, and pursed her full lips.

The dolly was getting better every minute and Alison saw the admiring looks Audrey was getting from the boys who went by. Young Whortle was leaning out of the large Nep family nest positively ogling.

Alison regarded Audrey coldly, then a slow smile curled over her mouth and she spun on her heel and ran out of the Hall.

There, the dolly was finished. Audrey was very pleased with the final result, even though it was much larger than she had anticipated. The plaiting had worked well and only the Raddle sisters would be able to criticize it–but they were not there.

"What's it for?" ventured one of the children shyly.

"It's a decoration," said Audrey. "Will you help me take it to Mr. Woodruffe?"

Eagerly, small paws helped her lift the corn dolly and carry it to the wicker throne. Mr. Woodruffe watched them approach with a puzzled look on his face.

Audrey and the children put the corn dolly down and curtsyed and bowed before him.

"Can I do something for you, lass?" he asked.

"Please, sir," she began, "I have made this corn dolly to decorate your Hall."

The King of the Field laid his staff of office on his knee and leaned forward to inspect the dolly.

"It is most . . . unusual," he remarked jovially. "I wonder, could you teach our young ones to make such things?"

"Why yes, sir, they seem to enjoy watching me making this."

"Very well," declared Mr. Woodruffe, "you, Miss Brown, shall . . ."

A sudden commotion interrupted him. The doors of the Hall were thrust aside and Isaac Nettle stormed in.

He rushed over to the throne with a face as black as thunder and no one stood in his way–they had seen that mood before.

Isaac pointed a shaking finger at the King of the Field and cried, "What heresy is this? What sin have thee welcomed, Woodruffe?" He flung his arms open wide and yelled to the sky. "Forgive thy subject, Almighty, that he should have fallen into such folly."

"Isaac!" muttered Mr. Woodruffe sternly. "What's all this about?"

Mr. Nettle glared around at Audrey. "Pagan idolatry! Brought hither by this unclean creature."

Audrey was astounded at his passion. She had never seen anyone so angry before and some of the children began to cry.

"It's only a decoration," she protested.

"Silence, fiend of the deep cold," ranted Isaac. "Thy craft speaks for itself. It is a blasphemous effigy and mocks the design of the Green Mouse. Oh, Great One, do not let us pay for the misguided deeds of the ignorant. She is the scum of the vile cities, the cream of the sinners–not one of your true servants. Punish us not for her wrongdoing."

"Now look here!" fumed Audrey, her astonishment boiling to anger. But he would not listen to her.

"Shun the image maker," he cried to the mice who were gathering to see what was going on. "See how she wears her vanities!" he flicked her ribbon with contempt.

"Don't you touch me!" she shouted, outraged.

By now everyone in the Hall was watching them. Twit dropped his feathering and slid down the stalk.

"Beware the maker of dolls. Repent ye or the vengeance of the Green shall smite ye down." Isaac moved nearer to the corn dolly and raised his fists to smash it.

"Don't you dare!" cried Audrey, pushing herself between him and the figure of straw.

"Away, profane one!" roared Isaac, shoving her roughly. Audrey stumbled and fell backward.

Twit reached Isaac before he had a chance to smash the dolly and stood glaring up at him, his eyes smoldering with a frightening fire that none had seen before.

"Get thee gone," warned Mr. Nettle harshly.

Twit was breathing hard. No one had ever known this mood in the little fieldmouse and the crowd gasped and wondered at the outcome. Twit's teeth flashed as he bared them and put up his fist.

"You oughtn't to have done that," he shouted, trembling with emotion. "Try it again an' I'll do fer you."

Isaac stared at Twit and bawled, "See how the heathens taint your subjects, Lord. Out of my way, simpleton."

Twit stood his ground and an alarming, unpleasant growl came from his throat.

Arthur and Jenkin came running into the Hall. Word had spread around the sentries about what was happening.

They saw Isaac raise his hard paw to Twit. "Father!" shouted Jenkin. "No, you mustn't."

Arthur sped over to Audrey and helped her up while Jenkin swung on his father's arm.

"Nettle!" bellowed Mr. Woodruffe. "That is enough. I will not allow you to spoil the Hall of Corn."

Isaac threw him a foul glance, but he persisted.

"Listen to me. I am your king! I am the law here."

Isaac faltered and put his arm down slowly, all the while staring steadily into the level eyes of Mr. Woodruffe.

"I cannot allow this behavior," continued the King of the Field.

"I do but honor the Green and keep His laws."

"Maybe, but you offend me!"

"Then I shall not enter here again," Isaac roared. He whirled around, snatched up the corn dolly and strode off crying, "This abomination has stunk before the Green Mouse long enough." And he carried it out through the doors before anyone could stop him.

"Consider yourself banished from the Hall till your temper cools," the king called after him.

All the fieldmice relaxed and muttered, shaking their heads. Then mothers came and fetched their children away from Audrey.

Elijah Scuttle came puffing up red-eared and worried for his son. Twit, though, had calmed down.

"You all right?" he asked Audrey. She nodded and thanked him. Twit let out a great sigh of relief.

"I'm so sorry," stuttered Jenkin to both of them. He was dreadfully ashamed of his father.

"Oh, Jolly Jenkin," Twit brushed the incident away as his humor returned, "thank 'ee for comin' quick–I nearly let fly then."

"Oh, dear," Audrey said to Arthur, "I seem to be getting on the wrong side of everyone here, don't I?"

He tried to reassure her. "But it wasn't your fault, I'm sorry about your corn dolly–you spent such a long time on it."

"That doesn't matter," she said, "I'm just glad no one got hurt. That could have been very nasty then. Twit really took everyone by surprise, didn't he?"

"Maybe," remarked Arthur thoughtfully, "I suppose it's this terrible heat as well." He frowned suddenly.

"What is it?" asked his sister.

"Just this," he began slowly. "How did Mr. Nettle know you were making a dolly? He passed below us in the field and he was angry before he got here."

"That is strange," agreed Audrey.

From her nest, Alison Sedge watched them with a satisfied smile on her pretty face.

CHAPTER EIGHT

THE VOICE

Arthur made it to the top of a stalk at last, to the cheers of Twit and Jenkin. He could barely see them as night was falling and already its shadows were gathering about Fennywolde.

Arthur gazed over the top of the field. The silver light of dusk played over the rippling corn ears so that it really did look like a shimmering sea and he, Arthur, was floating on it. It was a bizarre feeling. Now he began to understand the love that fieldmice have for climbing.

"Come on, Art," called up Twit. "I don't want to stay down here all night–I wants me bed."

Arthur tried to slide down as he had seen his friends do, but he scraped his paws and bloodied his heels, then landed with an undignified "bump" on the hard ground.

"Did 'ee like it?" inquired Jenkin.

"It's just wonderful up there," enthused Arthur, scrabbling off the ground. "Could I be a sentry, do you think?"

"Wait till tomorrow, Arthur." Twit yawned.

"I'd best be off now," said Jenkin. "I'd like to stay with Figgy and the others on sentry, but my dad wouldn't like that."

"Will those mice be on sentry all night?" asked Arthur, surprised.

"'Course," replied Jenkin. "No good havin' sentries if they go home at night."

"Well, shouldn't we stay?" Arthur addressed Twit.

Twit yawned again. "Oh, come on, Art," he said sleepily. "If I do sentry tonight like as not I'll drop clear off and bash me head in–I was up all hours last night a-talkin' to my folks. Let me have one good night's sleep an' we'll do a ghoster tomorrow."

"Well," Jenkin began, "if I don't go now I'll be in for it. 'Night, lads."

"Hope your dad's calmed down now," Twit ventured.

Jenkin licked his sore lip and nodded. "So do I. Oh well, I'll probably have a lot of praying to do when I get back, that's all. See you tomorrow hopefully." He ran off out of the field.

Arthur watched him go until the night swallowed him. "Will he really be okay, do you think?"

"Should be," Twit answered. "It's not him Isaac's mad at. Now, we gonna get some shut-eye tonight?" They made their way through the corridor to the great doors.

* * *

In the Hall of Corn all was calm. Nearly all the mice had gone to bed to try out their new nests and here and there orange lights showed through the openings as they settled down. Some fieldmice were talking, enjoying the refreshing change of a night spent under the sky without having to dread an owl attack. The hum of their chatter mingled with the quiet snores of sleepers, which in turn blended with the rustle of the corn.

The summer stars shone down onto Audrey's face. Her nest

was snug and warm, and the moss that lined it was soft and scented. She nuzzled down into the cool fragrant feathering, which smelled of the green earth and shady forests. It was at times like these, when the peace and beauty of Fennywolde were overpowering, that she thought it might not be so bad to spend the rest of her days there.

She closed her eyes and, breathing heavily, sunk deeper into her bed.

Suddenly the world seemed to quake. The nest shook violently from side to side. Audrey was jolted out of her short velvet sleep and hurled about. What was happening? She tried to cling onto the round walls of the nest and staggered to and fro, unable to keep her balance. The bells, which she had removed from her tail, jangled and rattled around the nest like beads in a baby's rattle.

A claw appeared over the opening and then everything went dark.

"Mouselet?" Madame Akkikuyu squeezed her huge head through the tiny hole, blocking out the light. She looked at Audrey. "Why mouselet in here?" she asked curiously. "No room for Akkikuyu to sleep–come down, mouselet, and we sleep on ground together."

"No!" answered Audrey sharply. "This is my bedroom now and it's not big enough for two."

Madame Akkikuyu insisted. "But, mouselet–little friend, Akkikuyu not like be alone in dark. Night has voices, they speak to her," the rat whimpered. "Besides, Akkikuyu not well–she need friend, need mouselet to help."

"What's wrong with you?" demanded Audrey sternly.

"Akkikuyu's ear–it aches and pounds."

"Why don't you go and make yourself some potion or other," Audrey suggested.

"Have tried, mouselet," assured the fortune-teller. "Akkikuyu has rubbed on bramble leaves and said the charm, she has made the paste of the camomile flower but still it hurts. I am frightened, mouselet."

"Look," said Audrey, too tired to continue. "Why don't you get some sleep. It might be better in the morning and you could ask Mr. Scuttle to build you a nest tomorrow next to this one."

But Madame Akkikuyu merely stared back at her with the eyes of a scolded dog, hurt and confused. "Come down," she asked one last time, "for Akkikuyu sake."

"No," Audrey said, and she hated herself immediately.

The fortune-teller looked crestfallen. She stuck out her bottom lip and said sullenly, "Akkikuyu go–she sleep on ground alone, poor Akkikuyu." She pulled her head out of the nest and began to climb down again.

Audrey leaned out and saw the diminishing bulky figure reach the ground. In the darkness of the Hall floor she could just make out the spots on the rat's red shawl and they quickly bobbed away.

"Oh, she can please herself," mumbled Audrey. "I never promised to stay with her all day and night, did I?"

She remained leaning out of her nest for some time. Fennywolde was cooling after a hot day. The wind had dropped to a whispering breeze, which brought sweet fragrances out of the meadow.

Presently the muffled sound of voices drifted up to her. It was Twit and Arthur returning at last. Their nest was above hers and slightly to the left. She waited for them to climb up.

Out of the gloom appeared two little paws and then Twit's head popped up.

"Hello, Audrey," he said, drawing level with her. "You comfy in there?"

"Yes, it's lovely, your father's very clever."

"Reckon he is–oh!" two plumper paws had emerged and grabbed Twit's tail tightly.

"Shove up!" shouted Arthur.

Twit giggled, then said good night to Audrey before vanishing into his nest.

Arthur came into view, climbing the stalk determinedly. His tongue was sticking out as it always did when he was concentrating.

"Arthur," said Audrey when it looked as if he would continue up without noticing her.

Arthur flinched in surprise. "Hello, Sis," he said, startled. "You still awake, then?"

"Yes–I had a visit from Madame Akkikuyu."

"Didn't try to get in did she?"

"Yes, but it was too small. I sent her away in a sulk and I wish I hadn't."

"Oh, blow," said Arthur. "If she goes running off at the slightest thing, well . . ."

Audrey interrupted him. "But, Arthur, she said she wasn't well and she mentioned that voice of hers again."

Arthur scoffed. "She's going batty–none of us heard that voice on the boat, did we? Yet she swore blind she had. I wouldn't worry about it, Sis, really. Now look, I'm sorry, but I've got to go–my paws are killin' me, hanging on like this. See you in the morning."

"Good night," Audrey called after him as he wriggled into the nest above. She withdrew into her own bed and sank into a deep, untroubled sleep.

* * *

Madame Akkikuyu wandered through the field miserably. Her right ear ached terribly and her best friend had not done anything to help. She kicked stones belligerently and felt sorry for herself.

She soon left the field behind and walked along the edge of

the ditch, cursing her ear and rubbing it vigorously. How it pained her. A constant dull throb pulsed inside, like the worst toothache imaginable. It was almost bad enough for her to want to run to the lonely yew tree and chew on its deadly poisonous bark.

Bit by bit the pain increased.

"Oooh," whimpered the fortune-teller despairingly.

Madame Akkikuyu sat down at the stony stretch of ditch and buried her head in her claws, moaning to herself. The pain had only begun when the sun set, and as the night became darker and cooler it grew more intense.

"Akkikuyu."

The rat looked up quickly. She could see no one–only the ghostlike moths fluttering overhead.

"Akkikuyu!" repeated the voice.

The fortune-teller wailed loudly. It was that voice again–the one that had haunted her from Greenwich.

"Leave me!" she cried.

"Akkikuyu," the voice persisted. It was stronger than it had been on those previous occasions. It was a strange, sickly sweet voice, which made her shudder.

"Listen to me," it said softly.

"No," snapped the rat. "Never, Akkikuyu not want to go round bend. Leave me."

"Listen to me, let me help you."

"No, you not real–Akkikuyu barmy, she hear voice when nobody there."

"But I am real, Akkikuyu."

"Who are you then?"

"My name is–Nicodemus," whispered the voice, "I am your friend."

"Then why you hide?" asked Akkikuyu, glaring suspiciously at the shadows, which seemed to have closed around her. She rubbed her head. She had seen something out of the corner of her eye and thought it was a spider dangling from her hair.

"I do not hide, Akkikuyu," crooned the voice of Nicodemus. "I am here."

And to her everlasting horror Madame Akkikuyu saw who it was that spoke to her.

"Aaaghh!" she screamed, getting to her feet in panic. But there was nowhere to run. On her right ear the tattooed face was moving and talking. The old ink lips were opening and closing and the drawn eyes were staring straight at her.

"Aaaghh!" she screamed again. She thought she had finally gone out of her mind. "Akkikuyu is cracked! Oh poor Akkikuyu," she sobbed.

"Listen to me, Akkikuyu," Nicodemus ordered. "Trust me, you are not mad."

"Stop, stop," whined the rat. "Stop, or Akkikuyu murder herself. This cannot be. Inky faces do not talk–they are doodles on skin, not real peoples."

The face on her ear began again. "Akkikuyu, listen, I am merely using this tattoo to talk to you. It is a channel through which you are able to hear me. I am really far, far away."

The fortune-teller ceased her sobs. "What are you?" she asked slowly.

"I am a spirit of the fields," said the tattoo, smiling. "I am the essence of the harvest, the sunlight on a distant hill, the splendor of a golden meadow, the heady perfume of the hawthorn in bloom."

"Why you speak to Akkikuyu? Spirits not supposed to talk to feather or fur."

"Because, dearest lady, I am trapped. Caught in a void–a horrible limbo where nightmare spirits of darkness dwell. I must escape. You must help me, I must return to the fields ere I perish for eternity."

"How you get trapped?" asked the fortune-teller doubtfully.

"That is a long and frightening tale, which I cannot relate.

Help me, Akkikuyu–give me sweet liberty."

She considered his entreaty, then shook her head. "No," she answered plainly. "Akkikuyu is mad–you not there–she imagine all this, so shut up."

"What proof do you need, woman?" demanded Nicodemus sternly, and in his impatience his voice faltered and became ugly. "You must release me."

"So you say," said Madame Akkikuyu, "but how is this to be? Akkikuyu have no great magicks to work for you. She know only herbs and medicines to make mouselings better."

The voice shouted, "But I can teach you, Akkikuyu. All the forces of nature are mine to command. You could learn from me secret knowledge known to none of your kind–just think of it." The voice lulled and coaxed most invitingly.

Madame Akkikuyu thought hard. A yearning awoke inside her–it seemed to be a very old feeling nudged to the surface by Nicodemus's promises. Magical power, he would give her that! The hunger for it, which welled up inside her, felt so new, yet also strangely familiar. Nicodemus's voice began again.

"You could be a queen, Akkikuyu," the tattoo went on, "mighty above all others."

Madame Akkikuyu seemed to come out of the illusions he was weaving about her.

"Tach!" she snorted. "Akkikuyu not believe in magic. Power of herb yes, and rule of fate yes, but not magic. Tricks and tomfool nonsense."

The face on her ear screwed itself up with impatience. "Do you want a demonstration? Very well. I shall show you what can be done and what powers can be yours."

"What you do?" inquired the fortune-teller expectantly.

"Look down there!" said Nicodemus. "At the bottom of the ditch!"

There, lying on the stones where Mr. Nettle had thrown it were the remains of Audrey's corn dolly.

"Go down there," instructed Nicodemus. The fortune-teller did as she was bid and made her way down the side of the ditch, hanging onto the tufts of coarse grass, which grew up its steep banks.

The dolly was in four pieces, testaments to Mr. Nettle's passion. The head and arms had been torn from the dress section.

Madame Akkikuyu tutted to see the damage. She had heard of Audrey's corn dolly from Young Whortle.

"Straw lady bust," she said aloud.

"Then join it together, Akkikuyu," said Nicodemus craftily. "Put back the head and fix in the arms."

"No," said the rat, "Straw ripped. She not go back together now."

"Then put the pieces where they belong and I shall do the rest," beamed the face.

Madame Akkikuyu arranged the arms and head around the body in their correct positions and stepped aside.

"Now," said Nicodemus, "with the bone from your hair draw a triangle around it. Good, now throw open your arms to the night and repeat after me–only make sure you do it exactly."

They began the invocation to the unseen spirits of the world.

"Come, Brud. By slaughterous cold and searing ice I call thee. Come out of the shadows, awake from your empty tomb and walk amongst us. I entreat thee, make whole again your effigy."

Madame Akkikuyu repeated all the words and watched the corn dolly in fascinated silence.

All around them the grasses and leaves began to stir and rustle, beating against each other like applause. Inside the triangle the moss that grew over the stones writhed like clusters of angry maggots and burst open new shoots like green fireworks. Everything living within that area grew and bloomed a thousand times faster than normal. Then, as Madame

Akkikuyu stared in disbelief, the severed stems of the corn dolly's grain arms twisted and coiled into the body section. The plaited head put out a tentative wiry tendril like a bather testing the water, then rooted itself onto the shoulders.

"Aha," squealed Madame Akkikuyu, "dummy repaired."

"Quite," said the tattoo matter-of-factly. "Are you convinced now, Akkikuyu?"

The rat nodded quickly, "Oh yes, Nicodemus, my friend–you real, Akkikuyu not bonkers." She hugged herself as she gazed at the completed figure of straw.

Nicodemus continued. "Would you like to see more?"

"More?" repeated the rat. "How so?"

"This has been a mere child's trick, Akkikuyu, compared with what you could achieve under my learned guidance."

"Tell me more," said the fortune-teller, eager to see other wonders. "Akkikuyu want to see more."

"Very well," the voice muttered softly, "step nearer to the straw maiden. Enough–do not touch the triangle. Now we need blood."

Madame Akkikuyu backed away. She did not like the sound of that. "Blood?" she queried cautiously. "Why for you want blood, and where from?"

"To give the doll life," announced Nicodemus. "Blood is a symbol of that. Just three drops are needed. I daresay you could nick your thumb and squeeze some out."

"Give doll life!" exclaimed the rat wondrously. "You can do such? You are very strong in magicks, field spirit. Quickly show Akkikuyu."

She took out her small knife and made a tiny cut in her thumb.

"The blood must fall on the straw," Nicodemus told her as three crimson drops were forced out onto the corn dress.

"Now stand back," commanded the voice.

Madame Akkikuyu did so and felt a thrill of fear tingle its

way along her spine and down to the tip of her tail.

"Hear me, oh, Brud!" called out Nicodemus. "Give this image life–let sap be as the blood on the straw. Pour breath into its empty breast and let stems be as sinew."

A deathly silence descended over the whole of Fennywolde. The fieldmice shifted uncomfortably in their soft nests as a shadow passed over the sky. Birds shrank into their feathers as they roosted in the tops of the elms and feared the worst. A hedgehog in his den of old, dry leaves felt the charged atmosphere and curled himself into a tight ball of spikes. Down came the shadow, thundering from the empty night on the back of the wind. The treetops swayed and the leaves whipped around. The grass in the meadow parted as the force fell upon it and traveled wildly through, flattening and battering everything in its path. It rushed toward the ditch and went howling down into it.

Madame Akkikuyu stood her ground as the unseen fury tore at her hair and pulled her shawl till it choked her.

And then all was still.

The fortune-teller lowered the claws she had raised against the ravaging gale and looked down at the dolly.

"Command it," said Nicodemus.

"I . . . I?" she stammered.

"Who else? It will obey none but you."

Madame Akkikuyu swept back the hair, which had blown over her face, and peered again at the corn dolly. "Up," she ordered meekly.

One of the grain arms gave a sudden twitch and the rat drew her breath sharply.

"Up!" she said again with more force.

The straw figure flipped itself over, rustling and crackling. It leaned on its arm and jolted itself up until it stood before her.

The fortune-teller took some steps around the dolly and waved her arms over it just in case someone was tricking her with cotton threads. But no, the corn dolly was alive!

"Instruct it to bow before you," suggested Nicodemus.

"Bow," said the rat.

With a snapping and splintering the corn dolly bent over and bowed.

"Hee hee," cackled Madame Akkikuyu, joyfully jumping up and down, her tail waving around like an angry snake. "It moves, it moves," she called. "And only for Akkikuyu, for she alone. See how it dances."

She pointed to the figure and jerkily it moved from the confines of the triangle, making odd jarring movements. Its dress swept over the stone floor like the twigs of a broom as it pranced in a peculiar waltz. The arms quivered in mockery of life and the loop head twisted from time to time as though acknowledging an invisible partner. It was a grotesque puppet and Madame Akkikuyu was its master.

The corn dolly tottered this way and that, buckling occasionally in a spasm that might have been a curtsy and shaking its dress with a dry papery sound. Madame Akkikuyu capered around with it, beckoning and following, teasing and pushing, until finally she panted, "Stop!" and the straw dancer became motionless.

"So," began Nicodemus in a pleased tone, "you must choose, will you help me?"

"Yes, yes," she crowed gladly.

"Excellent, Akkikuyu. We must prepare for the spell that will release me from this endless darkness where I am imprisoned."

She was eager to learn more and asked, "What do we need Nico? I fetch, I get."

"Hah!" The tattoo laughed. "First I must teach you, and there are many ingredients to find–some will not be easy, others will. There is a ritual involved in the breaking of my bonds, and everything must be perfect."

"Trust me, oh spirit. Akkikuyu no fluff." As she said it she thought her own voice came to her out of the past.

"Come then, let us talk away from this ditch. Only the hours of night are afforded to me. That is the only time I may speak with you, Akkikuyu, so spend your days wisely and make no exertion that may tire you out ere night falls."

She agreed and promised to rest for most of the daytime from then on. As she climbed up the bank the fortune-teller glanced back at the corn dolly and grinned as she thought of the powers that would soon be hers. What would her mousey friend have to say to this, she wondered.

CHAPTER NINE

MOLD TO MOLD

It was another baking-hot day. Audrey awoke to a blazing blue sky empty of cloud. She rubbed the sleep from her eyes and peeped out of the nest.

The Hall of Corn was glowing with light. The sun shone down on the stems, and those stout wives who had insisted on taking their sheets were shaking them vigorously outside the nests, waving them like dazzling flags of surrender.

Old Todmore passed below, swaggering on his bowed legs and nibbling a straw. He took up his usual position in the Hall and watched the world hurry by.

"Bless the Green for morns like this," he sighed, stroking his whiskers.

Tired sentries came into the Hall blinking and yawning, while those newly awake ran to take their places.

"Where's our Hodge?" a small mouse-woman asked Figgy.

"Haven't seen him," was the sleepy reply.

"Well, I'm not takin' his breakfast to him. Sentry, sentry–that's all that boy thinks about."

Arthur poked his head out of his nest. He was covered in bits of grass and moss. "Mornin', Sis!" he said brightly. "Breakfast's ready–didn't you hear Mrs. Scuttle calling?"

"No," replied Audrey, "but I'll be down in a minute." She retreated back into her nest, but after breathing the fresh air of the outside world the atmosphere in her bedroom seemed stifling. She decided that nests were lovely places to spend a night, but in the daytime they were like ovens.

As soon as she had dressed and brushed away some stray bits of straw she clambered out and descended the ladder Mr. Scuttle had made for her.

On the ground below, Gladwin Scuttle had spread a clean cloth and laid out the breakfast things. Arthur was well into his third helping when Audrey arrived.

"Mornin', missey," greeted Elijah. "And how did you sleep last night?"

"Very well, Mr. Scuttle, thank you."

Mrs. Scuttle patted the cloth by her side and said, "You sit down here, dear, and tell me what you think you'll be doing today."

"I think I'd better find Madame Akkikuyu," Audrey answered glumly. "I was a bit nasty to her last night."

"Hey, Sis," Arthur butted in, "I'm going to be a sentry today. Twit's going to present me to Mr. Woodruffe and they do a little ceremony or something," he added with his mouth full.

"That's right," agreed Elijah, "you'll be made to swear an oath of allegiance to Fennywolde for the rest of your days."

"But, Arthur," Audrey pointed out, "you can't promise that. What about Mother? You said you'd go back."

Arthur looked ashamed. "You're right. Do you know, I hadn't thought about home since I've been here–aren't I awful?"

"Never you mind," consoled Elijah. "I'll pop over an' have a word or three with Mr. Woodruffe–we'll see if'n we can't bend the rules a tiny bit." He got to his feet and set off in the direction of the throne.

The doors of the Hall opened and in came Madame Akkikuyu. She looked tired and she trudged along with heavy limbs. The families of fieldmice waved and nodded to her as though she were a dear old friend, and Mr. Nep bowed politely as she walked by.

"Here comes trouble," observed Arthur dryly. "Good morning, Madame Akkikuyu," called Audrey, trying to be as nice as possible. "Did you sleep well–how's your ear today?"

The fortune-teller gave her a weary glance and mumbled. "Akkikuyu not sleep–she busy all night finding root and herb for mousling potions." She showed them her claws, which were caked in soil and dirt. "Ear better," she added grudgingly.

"Sit down and have something to eat, Madame er . . ." offered Gladwin kindly.

Madame Akkikuyu grabbed a whole loaf and shook her head. "Akkikuyu not sit–she off to sleep."

"Oh," said Mrs. Scuttle. "Well, when my Elijah gets back I'm sure he'll make you a nest of your own."

"No," the rat declined sharply. "Akkikuyu no like mousey house. She go find place to sleep."

"Akkikuyu," said Audrey, "if you like we can go for a walk or something later."

The rat regarded Audrey for a moment and shrugged. "Maybe," she replied, and stalked away, tearing the bread into great chunks and gulping them down as she went.

"Oh, dear," said Gladwin.

"She ain't happy with us mouselets," remarked Twit lightly.

"This is all my fault," admitted Audrey. "I'm not turning out to be a very good companion for her, am I?"

Arthur munched thoughtfully on a crust. "You know," he began after a while, "Madame Akkikuyu is a lot more independent than she was when we set off–haven't you noticed? I don't think she needs you anymore, Audrey. I do believe she's settled in here better than we have."

"I ought to be relieved," sighed his sister. "It's funny, though–I feel just the opposite, as if I've betrayed her."

"Don't be soft," Arthur told her. "You came all this way, didn't you?"

"Well, let her down then," argued Audrey. "I haven't been much of a friend to her, have I? She thought we were best friends–I think I failed her in that."

"Pah!" declared Mrs. Scuttle. "Rats and mice being friends! I never heard of such a thing!"

They waited for Audrey to finish nibbling her breakfast, then Elijah came puffing back.

"It's all fixed and sorted," he informed Arthur. "We put our heads together, such as they are, an' we come up with the answer."

"So I can still be a sentry?" asked Arthur.

"Aye, lad, you can be a sentry for as long as you likes–till you goes home."

"Great!" shouted Arthur, dancing around. "When can I start?"

"Right now, if you're willin'. Mr. Woodruffe's a-waitin' on you."

So, with great excitement, they all went over to the wicker throne where the King of the Field sat with his staff of office on his knee.

"A blessed Eve to you." He smiled warmly.

They all bowed and curtsyed to him, and Audrey contrived to whisper into Mrs. Scuttle's ear, "Eve?"

"Midsummer's Eve, child," Gladwin murmured back.

"So, Master Brown, you wish to become a sentry and guard our Hall from enemies. Is this so?" said the King of the Field.

"Yes, sir," said Arthur keenly.

"Majesty!" hissed Twit.

"Yes, Majesty," corrected Arthur.

"Who presents this mouse to the King of the Field?" asked Mr. Woodruffe solemnly.

"I do, Majesty," chirped Twit. "He is a friend of mine and a braver lad you never did see." He found it hard to stifle the chuckles as he described Arthur to the king. He had to follow the correct procedure, which had been unchanged for countless years.

"Now you must swear loyalty to me, your king, and the land of Fenny."

Arthur nodded to show that he understood.

"Raise your right paw, Art," prompted Twit. "Now hold this hawthorn leaf."

"The hawthorn represents virtue and honor, Master Brown," explained Mr. Woodruffe. "But it is also the sacred tree of the Green Mouse and we shall name him as a witness. Are you ready to be sworn in?"

Arthur's lips had gone dry and he swallowed a lump in his throat. He wished his father was alive to see this. "Yes, Majesty."

"Repeat after me," commenced Mr. Woodruffe. "I, Arthur of the brown mice, visitor from the gray town, do most solemnly swear by holy leaf and in the Green's name to protect the Hall of Corn from any evil, though my life should fail in the attempt, till by His Majesty's leave I am released from service."

Arthur breathed a sigh of relief as he finished the last sentence.

Elijah nudged his wife. "That's the bit we put in," he told her proudly.

"Now, young sentry," began the king briskly, "you may go about your duty. Have you been taught all the signals and alarms yet?"

"Why, no, Your Majesty."

"See to it, William Scuttle," ordered Mr. Woodruffe with a twinkle in his eye.

They all bowed and curtsyed again and as they were leaving Twit said to Arthur, "They're real simple when you knows 'em. Blackbird cries and funny whistles–that sort of stuff. We usually use them to tell each other when it's dinnertime, though. Mind you, the most important alarm of all and one you must never use 'cept in the direst need is to yell *Fenny* at the top of your voice."

Audrey resumed her conversation with Mrs. Scuttle. "Will you be celebrating the Eve tonight at all? We do in the Skirtings."

"I remember, yes, we have a bit of a party. This afternoon all us mums and all the girls are going to make some bunting. There's a lovely group of rose trees over by the hedge and we thread the petals onto a string. It does look jolly."

"Could I come along?" asked Audrey. "I can't imagine anything more boring than watching my brother climb a stalk all day long. I haven't a clue why he wants to do it."

"Hah," said Gladwin. "You sound like you've lived in Fennywolde all your life. We can't understand why the menfolk love it either. Anyway, you'd be most welcome, dear. Oh, there'll be such a time tonight! In the excitement of William returning and the Hall-making going on, I clean forgot all about the Eve myself till Elijah asked about it last night."

The sun was climbing higher in the brilliant sky. The heat hammered down and Audrey felt dizzy.

"Is there somewhere cool I could sit, Mrs. Scuttle?" she inquired, wiping her forehead.

Gladwin tutted and scolded herself. "Why, there I go, forgetting myself again–when I first came here I was limp as a lettuce for weeks. Housemice aren't used to all this sunshine. Mind you, I can't remember it being quite so hot as this before."

She gazed around at the merry families with their plump, pleasant wives and red-eared husbands. This is what she had given up her old home and family for and she had never once regretted it. Suddenly she clicked back to the present and looked at Audrey sheepishly.

"Oh, dear," she flustered, "there's me wandering off again. You want to get cool, don't you, dear–well the best place I used to go when I felt a bit off with the heat was the still pool."

"Yes," said Audrey, "Arthur told me that's where you get all your water from."

"Now the ditch has dried up we have no choice. You should see poor Grommel trying to carry a full bucket of water with his bad back–poor thing."

Mrs. Scuttle eventually pointed to where the pool was. "Just follow the ditch and you can't miss it."

Audrey set off. She went through the great doors of the Hall and walked straight into Jenkin Nettle.

"Hello, miss." He grinned.

"Oh," muttered Audrey, blushing. "Good morning Jenkin," she added lamely.

"You looks nice this mornin', miss," he said, enjoying the situation.

Audrey giggled and thanked him. "But I always try and look this nice for Arthur." And she sauntered out of the field with Jenkin's eyes following her admiringly. The younger children were playing dust slides near the elm roots.

"You'll catch it when your mothers see you." Audrey laughed.

The grubby children considered her for a moment, wondering whether they ought to say anything in reply, but cleaner, older sisters grabbed them by the paws and dragged them away whispering at them.

"No, Josh you mustn't–you know what Mam told you 'bout that one."

Audrey was taken aback. Evidently, Mr. Nettle's outburst

yesterday had been the chief topic of Fennywolde gossip. Audrey was surprised that so many had actually believed his ridiculous accusations.

"Still," she shrugged, "it takes a long time to make friends, and time is something I'll have plenty of here."

She carried on along the ditch, past the elms and the winter quarters and an entrance where the sound of Mr. Nettle hammering on the mousebrasses rang out in time to his deep voice booming out hymns to the Green Mouse.

Soon she found that she had wandered into a patch of dismal shade and she shivered to herself. Rearing high above her was the lonely yew tree, the frightening tree of death. Its branches poked out like bony fingers and sharp claws. She hurried on, past that place–it was much too eerie and dark for her liking. No grass grew in its shadow and no birds sang in its branches.

The floor of the ditch began to get softer. Instead of dry choking dust it had become a rich brown mud, which yielded under her little pink feet like a dark fruitcake that had been cooked too quickly. The surface was crusty yet underneath it was still gooey and spongy.

It was a sign that she was not far from the pool. Soon her footprints began to fill up with water as she passed. She pushed through the trailing leaves of an ivy creeper and found herself staring into the still pool. It was as if she had crossed the threshold into another world, a cool, silent place where magic was almost visible. The harsh sunlight was filtered through the layers of bright new leaves and dappled the water with great splashes of shimmering green, which in turn were reflected back and bounced around once more. Dragonflies in their polished emerald armor flashed over the water's surface chasing gnats. Fine trails of bubbles slipped through the water then burst silently, too small to make a ripple. The still pool was a beautiful place.

Audrey stared, not even daring to breathe in case everything should disappear–so much did it look like a fairy grotto. The edge of the pool was fringed with plants: water plantains, horse-tails, and yellow rattles grew there. Behind one clump a husky voice began to speak.

"Alison Sedge–you are the loveliest thing in creation."

Audrey looked up, startled.

"You are lovelier than the flowers in your hair. Just look at you. That hair, the goddess would be proud of it."

Audrey put her paw over her mouth. She wanted to laugh. It was a girl's voice that spoke.

"Those eyes–they're luscious, they are. A boy could drown in those."

Audrey crept around the plants to see who it was–it didn't sound like any of the girls she had met the day before.

"Those lips–don't you want to eat them up, lads? A finer cherry-red pair of lips there never were, won't someone pick them?" Now there came a sound of pretend kissing.

Through the leaves Audrey saw Alison Sedge. She was gazing at herself in the water, enchanted by her own reflection. Her thick hair hung down either side of her face, nearly touching the water. This was the reason Audrey did not recognize the girl immediately. She decided that it was rude to stay there without letting the mooning fieldmouse know she was there, so she coughed politely.

Alison Sedge whipped around and stared in horror at Audrey, embarrassment, shame, and surprise all registering in her beautiful eyes.

"I'm sorry for intruding," said Audrey. "I'm Audrey Brown–a friend of Twit. I don't think we've met." And then she remembered, this was the girl who had glared at her that first night when Madame Akkikuyu chased away the owl.

Alison composed herself and groomed her ponytails back behind her ears.

"Saw you other day," she said mildly.

"Oh, when?" asked Audrey, not seeing the trap.

"When that ratwoman made you look real stupid." Alison tittered.

"Oh!" was all Audrey could find to say.

"Your brother know Dimsel's after him?" asked Alison, her subtle mind moving on to a different subject.

"Erm . . . no," replied Audrey, trying to keep up with the shifting conversation.

"Not much of a catch–either of them," remarked Alison outrageously.

Audrey choked and spluttered. How rude this girl was! She could find nothing to say in reply. When she did manage to recover her wits, Audrey caught Alison running a critical eye over her dress and collar. This was better; Alison's plain frock was no match for them. The other girl sniffed and looked away.

Oh no, thought Audrey, and she gave her tail a slight flick. The silver bells tinkled sweetly.

Alison jumped in surprise and stared at them coldly. Then she smiled and fiddled abstractedly with her mousebrass–it too tinkled: maybe not as sweetly, but it was enough to draw Audrey's eyes to it. She recognized the sign of grace and beauty and rolled her eyes heavenward.

"You not old enough to have a brass, then?" queried Alison.

"I did have one," said Audrey, "but I lost it."

"Careless," the other observed coolly.

Audrey did not feel like explaining about the altar of Jupiter to Alison, so she said nothing.

"Young Whortle's better now." Alison changed the subject again.

"Yes," said Audrey–this was another dig about her foolish display yesterday morning. Well, she thought, if that's all you can throw at me, go ahead.

"Skinny Samuel's gettin' better too," resumed Alison.

Audrey decided to join in this little game. In an innocent voice, she said, "That Jenkin's a nice boy, isn't he?"

The hit went home and Alison scowled. Through clenched teeth she managed to say, "The Nettles are all barmy. I'd have nothin' to do with 'em."

"Oh, I don't know," sighed Audrey demurely. "Jenkin's always sweet to me."

"He's like that to all the common sort," spat Alison. She didn't like it when someone got the better of her and was not used to her remarks thrown back with added sting. "I had to tell him to stop pesterin' me," she added.

"Said I looked nice this morning and always calls me 'miss.'" Audrey held out her paw to examine her nails–something she never did usually.

Alison pursed her lips, then arched her eyebrows craftily and said, "His dad's loony too–wonder how he knew 'bout your daft dolly, though?"

Audrey understood at once, and for her the game ended.

"Can be dangerous livin' in the country if'n you're not used to it," droned Alison. "And try an' take what don't belong to you."

"Oh, I'm quite safe," said Audrey defiantly and with an edge to her voice. "You see I don't scare easily–if I come across a snake I don't run away."

"Really?" Alison sounded bored and unimpressed. "You'd get bitten then."

"Oh no," Audrey assured her calmly. "You see Madame Akkikuyu and I are best friends. I'd get some of her potions and shrivel that snake up." She brought her face close to Alison's and added darkly, "Either that or I'd choke it with my bare paws just for the fun of it."

Alison backed away–she did not like the look in Audrey's

eyes. She tossed her head and said, "I can't waste my time here all day."

"Yes." Audrey smiled. "I saw you wasting your time before."

Alison huffed and flounced off.

Audrey shook her head. So that was Alison Sedge! Lily Clover was right–she did have claws; it might not be wise to get on the wrong side of her, but it was too late now.

Audrey lay back and enjoyed the tranquil magic of the pool in peace.

* * *

The morning turned to lunchtime. On sentry duty, Arthur's stomach began to growl. He looked over to Twit and signaled that he was about to climb down.

Twit waved back cheerily but made it clear that he was quite happy to stay on duty a little longer.

Arthur scrambled down the stalk and went in search of food.

A narrow path veered away from the main corridor and he wondered if it was a shortcut to the Hall. It seemed to go in the right direction, so he took it and began to whistle one of Kempe's songs.

He stopped in his tracks. Something was wrong–he could feel it. Cautiously he continued farther along the path. What was that in the way up ahead?

"Oh no," muttered Arthur under his breath. He ran over to the dark lumpy shape, which sprawled awkwardly over the ground. At his feet was the body of a mouse.

For a couple of minutes Arthur could only stand and gape, shock freezing his limbs. Then he knelt down and bravely laid his paw on the sad little body. It was stone cold. The mouse must have been lying there for hours. Gingerly, he turned the body over, and squealed in fright. It was Hodge. He recognized him at once. But it was not just that which upset him. Hodge's face was ghastly to look on. Like a mask of horror, the eyes were popping out, and the mouth was fixed in a wild and silent scream. It seemed almost as if Hodge had died of some terrible fright. But Arthur could see savage marks on his throat and his neck looked pathetically thin and squashed.

Slowly it dawned on him. Hodge had died of strangulation–someone had murdered him.

Now the cornstalks seemed to hem Arthur in and the whole place took on a sinister aspect. His skin began to crawl. He gulped and gazed around fearfully. What if the murderer was still there somewhere, hiding and watching him? What if even now it was coming to get him?

Arthur yelped as panic got the better of him. Never before had he been so frightened. "I've got to get out!" he squeaked and ran up the path again, stumbling and falling in his haste.

"FENNY! FENNY!" he cried out desperately. Voices were raised at once in answer to the urgent call. Arthur picked himself up from the ground, took no heed of his bleeding knees and ran straight into Jenkin. The fieldmouse stared at Arthur's terrified face and gasped.

"What is it?"

Arthur hid his eyes and began to shake all over.

Jenkin shook him urgently. "Tell me, Arthur, what is it?"

Arthur pointed up the path. "Hodge," he said thickly, pointing back up the path.

Jenkin dashed to see. "Don't look at him," cried Arthur after him. It was too late. Jenkin cried out in horror.

Other sentries came running. Twit was the first. He stopped in surprise when he saw Arthur's expression.

"Art?" he began curiously. "What is it? Why, you're tremblin' all over."

A group of sentries gathered around. Arthur would not let

them pass. They were all anxious to know why the major alarm had been used.

Eventually Jenkin came staggering back–his face matched Arthur's and he was weeping.

The sentries murmured and looked at one another nervously.

"It's Hodge," sobbed Jenkin. "He's dead."

The sentries opened their mouths and shook their heads in disbelief. Twit looked fearfully at Arthur, who was trying to say something.

"No!" he shouted violently. "He's been murdered!"

* * *

A grim, silent group made its way to the Hall of Corn. Mourners lined the corridor and the sound of lamentation was heard everywhere in Fennywolde.

Jenkin, Young Whortle, Todkin, and Figgy carried the body of their friend on their shoulders. A white cloth had been placed over Hodge's face by Jenkin so that no one would have to look on that grisly horror again.

Grommel and the other guards opened the great doors and let the group in. Word had spread quickly through the field, and the grief of Hodge's parents was terrible to hear and to see.

Elijah came and took Arthur to one side. Twit disappeared into his nest and brought out the flask given to him by Thomas Triton.

"Here, Art," he said gently, "drink some of this."

Mr. Woodruffe held up his staff of office and cried angrily, "What creature has done this? We must not rest till the fiend is captured. Summon everyone into the Hall at once!"

For those who had not already heard the tragic news, Jenkin placed a piece of straw between his thumbs and blew hard. A high screech echoed over Fennywolde and all who heard it clutched their mousebrasses fearfully and ran to the

Hall. Isaac Nettle dropped his hammer and abandoned the forge.

Soon everyone was there except Audrey. The Hall was buzzing with grief and anger as the mice held on to their children tightly and called for the murderer to be found.

Isaac learned from his son what had occurred and turned to the king furiously.

"See?" he raged bitterly. "Now do you see what happens when you turn your back on the Green's holy laws. He has been swift to show His anger."

"Silence, Nettle!" stormed Mr. Woodruffe. "I will not have you say such rubbish in front of Hodge's parents."

"Thee must all pray–pray hard and beg the Green's forgiveness for having allowed the heathen into our midst." He whirled around and pointed an accusing finger at Arthur. "Where is thy sister–the blasphemer?"

"Isaac!" roared the king before Arthur could answer. "I will not allow you to turn this into one of your prayer meetings! I have a search party to organize and you could attend to Hodge there."

Mr. Nettle calmed a little and regarded the body grimly. "Verily–I shall order the service."

As Mr. Woodruffe dispatched fieldmice to search the field, Arthur turned to Twit and said, "I wish I knew where Audrey was. This is another thing for Mr. Nettle to jump down her throat about. Did you see the faces of some in the crowd? They were agreeing with him!"

"Here's Akkikuyu, Arthur," Twit warned as the rat strode into the room.

"What goes on?" she asked. "Who make all the noise and hullabaloo? They wake Akkikuyu." Then she saw Hodge's body and tutted sadly. "Poor mouselet–he beyond Akkikuyu's help."

"He was strangled," said Mr. Woodruffe gently.

"Who did so?" she asked in astonishment. "I give *them* a throttling."

"We are about to try and find out," said the king gravely.

"Poor, poor mouselet," she sighed. "No more cheeses for you."

"Arthur," ventured Twit, looking at the fortune-teller, "you don't think?"

"What . . . Akkikuyu?" said Arthur. "No, she was too shocked when she saw Hodge just then. I don't think it was her. . . . Good grief, no, it couldn't possibly have been."

Alison Sedge watched everything in horror. She could not take her eyes off the body. That lifeless thing had once been a boy she had flirted with and lured into the meadow. Now the thought of it made her ill.

The painful wails of Hodge's parents were unbearable to her. She stumbled to her nest and bit her nails nervously. A dreadful thought had come to her. She recalled Audrey's words at the still pool: "I'd choke it with my bare paws just for the fun of it."

Alison was scared–should she tell someone or would the town mouse punish her? She wondered what Hodge had done to warrant his horrid reward.

The ceremony was held that afternoon in a shady area kept tidy for such purposes. As the body was lowered into the ground Mr. Nettle intoned, "Receive this innocent soul, Almighty. He is beyond our care now. Take him to thy bosom and cherish this small servant of yours. Mold to mold, body to Green."

Arthur's head felt thick and fuzzy. The search parties had found nothing unusual–only Audrey asleep by the pool. Now she stood next to him looking down into the grave.

Hodge's parents cast a hawthorn leaf and his favorite flower into the grave. Then Mr. Woodruffe led them away in silence.

“We’ll have to double the sentries,” said Jenkin as they walked away. “If some maniac is still out there we don’t want him to strike again. And don’t you go off on your own again, miss,” he said to Audrey.

“I shan’t,” she answered. It had been a nasty shock to wake to a different Fennywolde, one full of grief, anger, and fear. She could feel the whole atmosphere of the place had changed.

Gladwin Scuttle linked her arm in Elijah’s and went home. No one felt like celebrating the Eve of midsummer now, and the rose petals that had been gathered were left to rot.

Madame Akkikuyu looked back to where Isaac was filling in the grave. Night was drawing closer and she rubbed her ear thoughtfully.

CHAPTER TEN

MIDSUMMER'S EVE

Audrey stared out of her nest and up into the gathering dusk. Everyone in Fennywolde had gone to bed early, trying to blot out the tragic day with sleep. Even so, Audrey could hear the sound of weeping. She lay back on her moss bed and reflected on the death of Hodge and its implications. Was it now dangerous to walk alone in the field? Was the murderer of Hodge still at large out there? And what manner of creature was it, anyway? Some of the fieldmice had come to the conclusion that the beast had been a wandering rogue whom Hodge had surprised. But after all the searching, the general feeling was that whoever had done this atrocious deed had undoubtedly escaped and was now far away.

"Ain't been nothin' like it since that old owl was around," Old Todmore had observed gravely.

The mood of the fieldmice was one of unease. Audrey had noticed that now–more so than before–the simple country mice shied away from her and looked quickly at the ground if she smiled at them. It was almost as if they thought that she had brought this tragedy down on them. She wondered if they pointed at her in secret and muttered nonsense about jinxes and the like. It was certainly good fuel for Isaac Nettle's sermons on the importance of prayer to the Green Mouse. Audrey found all this too tiresome and worrying to dwell on, so she turned her thoughts to other things.

Was Piccadilly safe in the city? She wished he was here; he'd give Mr. Nettle something to make him sit up and scowl at. She almost laughed as she tried to imagine what Piccadilly would have said, but the smile faded on her lips with the thought that the gray mouse must surely think badly of her. She had been too horrible to him for him to think anything else.

Audrey shifted uncomfortably and tried to redirect her thoughts. An image of Jenkin sailed brightly before her eyes. It was hard to believe that he was the son of sour-faced Mr. Nettle. What a fine young mouse Jenkin was! In some ways he reminded her of Piccadilly. Audrey fell asleep with the two mice filling her thoughts.

The night stars wheeled over Fennywolde. Silvery moths flew up and rode the secret breezes. The hedgehog waddled out of a leaf pile and roamed along the ditch searching for mouth-watering delicacies. The moon rose full and bright, and somewhere in a patch of deep shade Nicodemus muttered to Madame Akkikuyu of potions and spells and their mysterious ingredients.

Audrey stirred in her sleep and gradually became aware of a faint sound pulling her awake. A distant lilting music caught her ears, and despite its faintness her heart yearned to follow it.

She opened her eyes and rubbed her brow drowsily. It was an achingly beautiful melody hovering just on the edge of being heard. Audrey tilted her head and wondered where it was coming from. It haunted and enchanted her, beckoning with sweet invisible fingers.

Audrey quickly determined to find the source of the music. She slipped out of bed and turned to look for her dress. She paused and blinked: from her bag of clean clothes and personal treasures a dim light was shining.

Apprehensively, Audrey pulled open the neck of the bag and peered inside. A creamy glow at once illuminated her face and she gasped in wonderment and surprise. She put in her paw and drew out the sprig of hawthorn blossom that Oswald had given to her, back in Deptford. Tonight it was a thing of magic. The petals of the blossom, which for many weeks now had been so dry and yellowed with decay, were as fresh as the day they had been picked–only now they shone with a clear and supernatural light of their own.

Audrey could only stare at it in amazement. Yet it seemed to be the most natural thing in the world–for tonight was the Eve of Midsummer, and almost anything was possible. A thrill of expectation ran through her body as, holding the blossom before her, she left the nest and clambered down the ladder.

In the Hall of Corn nothing stirred. The nests, which lined its long walls, were dark and their entrances gazed at her blindly. The moonlight cast weird shadows all around her, and the breeze moved them so that the black shapes waved mysteriously in the gloom.

The thought of poor Hodge and his unknown assassin crossed Audrey's mind, but she managed to suppress her fear. She just had to follow the strange music. It seemed to tug her along, and she noticed that the light of the hawthorn blossom grew brighter if she went in a certain direction. Using this as a sort of magical compass, Audrey passed out of the Hall and into the wild tangle of cornstalks. Through the field and along the ditch Audrey was led, a will other than her own driving her feet toward the source of the music.

She crossed the ditch and made for the still pool. It seemed that the tune was coming from there, and as she looked a twinkle of light glimmered from behind the surrounding hawthorn bushes.

She hesitated, breathing softly. This was it–the source of the wonderful sound. The light of the blossom in her paw welled up suddenly like a star fallen from heaven. Audrey felt a pang of fear; now she was there she wondered what lay beyond the hawthorn bushes. What would she see when she drew back the branches?

Audrey bit her lip and for a moment wanted desperately to run back to her nest, but it was too late for that now. Slowly, she pulled the branches to one side.

There in the hawthorn grotto were all the mice of Fennywolde. They were arranged in a semicircle around Mr. Woodruffe and all were silent and bowed. Audrey glanced up and saw why they were all so hushed and reverent. She fell to her knees and cried out in surprise.

Floating above Mr. Woodruffe, like a dense cloud of growing things, was the Green Mouse.

He was at the height of his midsummer power and mightier than when Audrey had seen him in the spring. His fur was lush and green as grass, and on his brow he wore the crown of wheat. Here and there, fiery mousebrasses blazed out from his coat of leaves. Indeed, Audrey could not tell where his coat ended and the hawthorn thicket took over, for little green lamps had been hung all around, and they increased the wondrous quality of the place.

The Green Mouse was smiling kindly at his subjects, his long olive green hair cascading down like a lion's mane, and sparkling mousebrasses kindling a green fire in his noble eyes.

Audrey bowed her head. When she dared to look up she found that the Green Mouse was looking straight at her.

Those eyes, which she had never forgotten, now shone on her once more. Slowly the Green Mouse beckoned to her and

timidly Audrey moved toward him. He held out his great paw and she kissed it.

"We are pleased with you, little one," came the huge voice. Audrey flushed and hung her head. "There are still dangers you must face," the Green Mouse told her. "Be brave, my brassless one. I shall take care of you while I can, for spring and summer are mine to command. Remember that the Green fails in autumn and is dead for the winter." He furrowed his immense brow and shook his great head. "Let us hope my protection will not be needed in the bleak months to come, and the summer will end as we pray it will." The Green Mouse smiled and it seemed as if it was daytime. The lamps blazed back at him and Audrey realized that they were not lamps at all but shining leaves. The more he smiled the brighter they became, and the more others began to shine. Soon the entire grotto was filled with a blinding glare of green.

"Now," the Green Mouse addressed all the Fennywolders, "be not sad in heart, for verily I know your grief. Let peace fill your troubled hearts! Forget the pain of your sorrows." He raised his paws and his voice resounded around the grotto: "Tonight is the Eve, when I am in full glory, so let my light dispel your shadows."

The fieldmice cheered and began to dance in time to the music. Audrey looked around her and noticed Arthur and Twit. She rushed over to them. They were staring at the Green Mouse in wonder.

"Oh, me," sighed Twit heavily.

"Heavens," muttered Arthur.

They welcomed Audrey and then laughed, simply because they felt so light and giddy. Twit pranced around and took hold of Audrey's paw and pulled her into the rest of the dancing mice. Shyly, Dimsel Bottom sidled up to Arthur and smiled up at him. Arthur coughed nervously but was soon dancing with her.

Audrey glanced around at the assembled mice. There were Twit's parents staring deeply into each other's eyes as they whirled about sedately. Lily Clover was locked in the embrace of Todkin, and even Samuel Gorse was there, completely recovered from his mauling by the owl. At the edge of the crowd Audrey could see Jenkin holding paws with Alison Sedge—then he kissed her!

Audrey was so surprised that she stopped dancing. "Well, I never!" she exclaimed.

Twit followed her glance, "Aye, tonight they're together. In the magic of Him all resentments are forgot."

And Audrey realized in a flood of understanding that this was how it should be. Alison and Jenkin were meant to be together.

Audrey and Twit left the dance and wandered around the pool. There they saw Isaac Nettle sitting alone with a scowl on his face. He did not seem to see them—nor indeed any of the things going on around him. He merely sat and prayed sourly.

The chatter and laughter hushed and an expectant silence fell on the fieldmice. The Green Mouse bowed his great green head and raised his paws.

"Join us, Lady!" his voice boomed. "Grace our celebration with your holy presence."

Audrey looked up, holding her breath. The Green Mouse was beseeching the White Lady of the moon to come down.

In the sky above, through the fluttering, glimmering hawthorn leaves, the silver moon shone out brightly. A slight wind sighed through the branches as a faint mist flowed down to the earth and threaded its way past the fieldmice. Those it touched gasped and felt refreshed. A rich perfume came with it, and here and there tiny moonbeams twinkled and glowed in its depths.

"Oh my," said Twit as the mist reached him, and tears rolled down his little face.

The White Lady floated around the gathering and the Green Mouse lowered his eyes.

Audrey stared at the milky mist in disbelief. Now and then the wind moved it and she saw glimpses of something within. There was a fold of dress revealed for a moment, richly encrusted with pearls, and the toe of a silken slipper. The White Lady said nothing to the fieldmice, but the mist shifted in what might have been a bow to the Green Mouse. He too bowed, then pointed to the water of the pool. The mist rose up and curled around in a wide arc, then it poured down onto the pool's surface and vanished. The Fennywolders saw only a reflection of the night sky and the creamy circle of the moon shimmering in it.

"Drink," the Green Mouse instructed them.

The fieldmice cautiously went to the water's edge and cupped their paws together.

"It's like wine," shouted Young Whortle excitedly, and all the mice gasped in wonderment as they drank the moon mead.

Twit smacked his lips thoughtfully, "You know," he declared, "that beats old Tom's rum, paws down."

Only Audrey did not drink the magical water. She sat at the edge of the pool, staring into its dark mirror and fancied she saw shapes swirling amongst the stars. Slowly the shapes turned to pictures: she saw a long dark tunnel with bright lights at the far end of it and there, running for all he was worth was a familiar gray figure–it was Piccadilly. Audrey cried out in surprise. Piccadilly was being pursued by a horde of rats! Another image took over; it was all white, a landscape of frost and ice. Stretching far and wide, the snowy wasteland moved beneath her as if she were a bird flying. Something dreadful was in the sky, but she was unable to make out what it was. A glittering spear shot down at her, and the white ground lurched below and sped up toward her. Audrey felt herself hurtling down, the ribbon was snatched out of her hair, and she hit the ground with a tremendous crash.

* * *

Another hot, beautiful day began.

Audrey found herself curled up in her nest. For a moment she stared up at the woven ceiling blankly. She was unable to remember how she had gotten there. The previous night was still so vivid in her mind that the bright sunlight confused her. The sprig of hawthorn was lying next to her—dry and brittle once more. Audrey picked it up and held it against the light, trying to remember how the blossom had looked the night before.

It was the uncomfortable heat that made Audrey finally lean out of her nest.

"It's hotter than yesterday," Arthur's voice came up to her. Audrey waved lazily down at him. The Scuttles were having their breakfast. She dressed quickly and descended the ladder, eager to discuss the marvels of the Eve.

"Wasn't it magnificent?" she cried, running to them.

Elijah Scuttle gazed at her dumbly. "What were, missey?"

"Last night, of course, Mr. Scuttle! Wasn't the Green Mouse wonderful?"

Elijah and Gladwin exchanged puzzled glances.

"The Green Mouse, dear?" asked Mrs. Scuttle.

Audrey looked surprised, then laughed. They were teasing her. "Yes," she persisted excitedly, "when the Lady came down and everyone drank the magic water."

There followed a painful, embarrassed silence broken only by Arthur coughing nervously. Twit began to giggle and tickled Audrey mischievously.

"What you on about, Aud?" The little fieldmouse chuckled happily. "You been at old Tom's rum?"

Audrey stared at them. So they weren't teasing her after all! They did not remember a thing about last night. She opened her mouth to argue but saw Arthur giving her a warning glare from behind his breakfast.

Irritated and confused, Audrey quickly drank her milk. The terrible heat did not help her growing bad temper, and she pressed her forehead with her fingers, saying thickly, "I'm sorry, it's too hot for me here. I must go to the pool–I feel dreadful." She wanted to get away from them, so she could be alone and think this through–last night seemed too real to be a dream, so why did they know nothing about it? She got up to leave.

"Poor dear," tutted Mrs. Scuttle, "it does take some getting used to."

Arthur crammed the last of his porridge into his mouth, mumbled to the others, and ran after his sister.

"Well, I never did," remarked Elijah, highly amused. "That girl do take the biscuit for fanciful ideas. Hobnobbin' with the Green Mouse an' all. You'm got some quaint friends, Willum."

But Twit was staring after the Browns with concern.

* * *

"Wait, Sis," Arthur yelled, puffing behind Audrey.

She stopped and turned to wait. When he reached her he took hold of her arm and stared hard.

"Look, are you really feeling okay?"

"Yes, Arthur," she answered simply, "it's just the heat. I can't stand it."

He scratched his head and pressed his lips together. Finally he burst out, "What was all that rubbish back there, then?"

Audrey looked at her brother for some moments and shook her head. "You really don't remember anything at all?"

Arthur pulled his "don't try that on me" face and said crossly,

"Don't be daft, there's nothing to remember. We went to bed early last night: that's all that happened–not this Green Mouse stuff."

"But he was there, Arthur," she insisted passionately. "He was there–larger than life–and so were you and everyone in Fennywolde. I'm not going bonkers, believe me."

"Oh, Sis," he sighed sadly, "how can I? If it's what you want to believe, then fine, but just do me a favor and don't mention it to anyone else. You'll end up embarrassing you, me, and the Scuttles. So just keep a lid on your fairy stories, eh?"

Audrey was too angry to say any more. She spun around and strode away. How could they all have forgotten about it? A disturbing doubt crept into her mind. What if she was going barmy after all? In this stifling weather maybe even that was possible.

She made her way as fast as she could to the still pool. With her heart in her mouth she pushed through the hawthorn and entered the dappled shade.

There was no sign or trace of anything that might reassure her and prove that the Green Mouse had been there. Audrey sat down heavily and stared at the water. She was glad that Alison Sedge was not here today.

* * *

Arthur and Twit left breakfast to go on sentry duty. Arthur was excited as he would have to stay up all night on watch.

Twit nodded to Grommel as they passed through the great doors. "How do," he said.

"Mornin', Twit," greeted Grommel as they went by. "Watch this," he called after them, and proceeded to bend down and touch his toes. "It's me back," he explained, seeing their puzzled faces. "That Madame Ratlady gave me an ointment to rub on and I feels brand new."

They congratulated him and continued on their way. "Can she get any more popular?" asked Arthur.

After a short while Twit ventured, "Arthur, what did Audrey mean before?"

Arthur shrugged. "I think Audrey had a dream, that's all. Where are we going to start today?"

But Twit would not let the matter drop. "I dunno 'bout dreams–ain't too impossible–her seein' the Green Mouse. She done so afore, you know."

"So she says, but if you expect me to believe all that claptrap . . . why, she's always making things up!"

Again Twit persisted. "And our Oswald–when I was sittin' with him, he said somethin' 'bout seein' the Green Mouse in Jupiter's chamber."

"Oh, pooh!" scorned Arthur. "Oswald wasn't well, he was saying all sorts of daft things. I'm not interested in Audrey's silly stories and I'm surprised at you–don't go encouraging her, for heaven's sake. Look, there's Jenkin. Let's go join him."

The matter seemed to be closed. Twit chewed the inside of his cheek thoughtfully, then ran after his friend. The watch began.

* * *

Madame Akkikuyu waded through the deep leaf piles near the oaks. Her bag was stuffed full with fresh herbs and wild flowers, the ingredients for a special potion. Nicodemus had instructed her to collect them the night before, but there were some things that Madame Akkikuyu had trembled at the thought of getting. Nicodemus had been very persuasive.

"Listen, Akkikuyu, and remember well," he had told her. "I shall tell you how to free me from the black limbo where I am imprisoned. There must be a great spell to unfetter me and bring me back. Look how the land needs me. It is dying,

Akkikuyu! When I am released I shall cause the rain to fall and restore the water to the thirsty land and heal its burns."

Madame Akkikuyu had thought that was a very admirable thing, so she had asked him, "Tell Akkikuyu what she must do to release you."

"There must be a potion," Nicodemus had begun quickly, "and it must be the distillation of many things–but are you ready for this, Akkikuyu?"

"Yes, Nico," she had stated firmly.

"There will be herbs and flowers, which only bloom on moonless nights," the voice on her ear had continued, "and other things that are necessary but you may find difficult to gather."

"Akkikuyu get anything," she had claimed hastily.

"Good," Nicodemus had declared, "then fetch me a frog and boil away the flesh till only the white bones are left."

"No!" the fortune-teller had cried, appalled. "Akkikuyu no kill poor froggy–she good and kind."

"Believe me, Akkikuyu," the voice had wheedled, "it is only because this is so urgent that I would ask this terrible thing of you. If this is not done then no rain will fall and all the frogs are sure to perish–better one die than all."

Madame Akkikuyu had been forced to agree with his reasoning, and Nicodemus had told her to find him a frog the very next day. She looked down at her bulging bag and grimaced; there was no frog in there yet–she still demurred at murder, and had collected all the plants instead. She wondered if Nicodemus would scold her when night fell. Everything seemed muddled when he was not there to reassure and guide her and everything seemed so much less important in the daylight.

She trudged up the dell and wandered about the roots of the oaks, wiping her face with her shawl.

"Too hot," she moaned to herself. She squinted at the tattoo on her ear, but it was still. "Hah, old Nico–he not like the heat. He not see me in daytime."

She surveyed the leafy world around her and spotted some strange chalky-looking objects scattered about the base of one of the oaks. She went over to examine them.

"Hmm," she mumbled, prodding one with her claw. It was gray and dry and broke open at her touch. "Hooty cough-ups," she remarked with disdain.

They were owl pellets, tight little bundles of bone and fur that had been swallowed greedily by the owl as he devoured his prey, only to be regurgitated later when he had been unable to digest them.

"So owly still here," muttered the fortune-teller. She looked up the tree and saw the dark hole in its trunk. "Just you stay away from my mouseys," she threatened, shaking her fists, "or Akkikuyu come pluck you again."

She thought she heard a frightened hoot in response and was satisfied. It was time to find a shady place to sleep. Her nightly lessons with Nicodemus were leaving her with no energy for the following day. Madame Akkikuyu yawned widely and lumbered off to rest.

CHAPTER ELEVEN

MAGIC AND MURDER

As the afternoon wore on, the fieldmice gathered in the Hall of Corn to discuss the unusually hot weather.

"Tain't natural," remarked Old Todmore, squinting at the sky. No rain fer weeks now. Mark my words, young 'uns, there's somethin' very wrong 'bout all this."

The ground had become like stone and here and there long cracks had begun to appear. The corn in the field looked dry and some of the stalks were withered and sickly–an omen that did not go unnoticed by the anxious mice.

Waves of disquiet now coursed through Fennywolde, building on the unease left by Hodge's death. The tired and anxious Fennywolders took to looking nervously over their shoulders at the slightest noise.

Isaac Nettle, accustomed to the great heat of his forge, peered out over the field and declared to those willing to listen, "The fires of the infernal are at work here. Repent ye and crave pardon from the Almighty Green." And Mr. Woodruffe was too tired and overheated to stop him.

Some mice swooned in the swelter and all throats were burned by the hot breeze. Many spent the day by the still pool, leaving a large space between themselves and the strange town mouse who had brought the odd weather with her.

Eventually the day burned itself out and the early stars pricked the evening sky. The fieldmice clambered into their nests, relieved that the long, uncomfortable day was over and worried about the next. They cast themselves on their beds and fell into exhausted faints rather than sleep.

In some of the little round nests, plaintive voices were raised in prayers for rain. "Please, oh Green, deliver us from the sun. Bring down the rain."

Madame Akkikuyu passed through the field with a satisfied grin on her face. She had been nosing around the top end of the ditch where the mud was still spongy, and after much searching had found a dead frog.

It was a bit old and whiffy, but Madame Akkikuyu felt very pleased with herself. She had managed to keep her promise to Nicodemus without killing anything. How clever she felt! He would be very pleased with her–no need to mention how it was acquired. She hurried along, eager to put the grisly object into her pot so that the skin could be boiled away, ready for the night's instruction.

As she was walking through the Hall of Corn, a voice called down to her from one of the nests. Hastily the fortune-teller thrust the frog into her bag and glanced upward.

Young Whortle's father came scurrying down and stood beside her.

"Forgive me, dear lady," said Mr. Nep apologetically, "but I have a . . . well . . . er . . . something to say to you."

Madame Akkikuyu narrowed her gleaming black eyes and closed her claws tightly over her bag. "Akkikuyu listen," she said at last.

Mr. Nep first looked down at his feet, then twiddled his

thumbs and wiped his face in embarrassment. Finally he blurted out, "Can you make it rain?"

It was not what Madame Akkikuyu had expected and she was dumbstruck for a few moments. But Mr. Nep babbled on.

"Oh . . . we're so desperate! You've shown yerself to be wise in the craft of healing, so some of us set to thinkin' that mebbe you had other . . . skills. There, I've said it."

The rat considered him for a while and said, "You want rain magic? Akkikuyu no witch or cloud dancer–she healer."

Mr. Nep looked aghast. "Oh, I have offended you. Please, no such insult was meant. It's just that even the pool is getting low in water now and well–we're getting very worried."

Madame Akkikuyu smiled. She liked it when the fieldmice came to her for assistance. A warm tingle shot up her tail and she puffed out her chest. She rubbed her tattooed ear thoughtfully and told Mr. Nep, "Akkikuyu try–no promise."

"Oh, thank you," he said, his face relaxing "I'll tell my Nelly, she'll be so relieved. We don't know what we'd do if it weren't fer you." Mr. Nep scampered back to his nest.

"A difficult promise to keep," came a soft whisper.

The rat jumped in surprise.

"What are you going to do about it?" her tattoo continued.

"You . . . you heard, Nico?" ventured the fortune-teller nervously.

The voice of Nicodemus mocked her. "Oh yes, I heard. You want to help these little creatures by bringing rain to them." The voice suddenly changed and became full of anger. "How dare you give such promises! Who are you to offer them the power of nature? The power of life-giving rain is not yours to give, it is the province of we land spirits."

"Akkikuyu only want to help poor mouseys," she whined.

The tattoo snarled back, "Don't bother to lie, I know you, Akkikuyu–perhaps better than you do yourself. I can see into your soul, and you wish to rule these poor fieldmice."

"No," she protested immediately, "I likes them."

"Twist and turn all you like, but you cannot escape the truth. You want them to become dependent on you–to run to you for the slightest thing until they are your subjects, enslaved to your evil will."

Madame Akkikuyu sobbed. "That false. I not like that, mouseys know–they love Akkikuyu; she their friend."

"You have no friends," snapped Nicodemus savagely. "Put your trust in me alone. The mice are using you–can you not see that? They take from you all the time, what do they give in return? Nothing."

The fortune-teller fled from the Hall. But at the edge of the ditch Madame Akkikuyu sat down and wept. "I like mouseys," she blubbered through her great salty tears.

"Then give them the rain you promised," muttered Nicodemus.

"I can't," she wailed unhappily. "Akkikuyu not powerful enough. Mouseys will laugh at me and say I cheap trickster."

"You should have thought of that before," scolded the voice.

"Nico," she began, "Nico, can you not make it rain? Only tiny bit, not much?"

"But I have already told you," said Nicodemus sternly, "until I am freed I can do nothing. My powers are useless!"

"Then Akkikuyu is washed up–mouseys not believe in her anymore."

The soft voice in her ear whispered to itself and the painted eyes closed meditatively. "There may be a way," the voice began slowly. The rat sat up, excited and eager.

"Tell me quick," she insisted. "Akkikuyu will help, best she can."

Nicodemus sounded uncertain. "Are you ready, though?" he asked doubtfully. "What is required might make you tremble."

"Akkikuyu not afraid," she affirmed, and to prove it she

flourished the dead frog from her bag. "See, I bring this, like Nico ask."

"I asked for it yesterday, Akkikuyu, yet this creature has been dead for more than three days. Do you think you can trick me?"

"No . . ." she answered feebly, letting the dried frog clatter down the steep bank and smash on the stones below.

"I must have absolute obedience, Akkikuyu," demanded the voice. "Absolute! Do you understand?"

"Yes, Nico!"

"Then swear–on your soul, to obey me in all things."

"I . . . I . . ."

"Swear!"

"Akkikuyu . . . Akkikuyu swear–on soul." She hung her head and said no more. The tattoo smiled an unpleasant, triumphant grin.

"Excellent," resumed Nicodemus, "now we may proceed. The essence of rain lies in the invocation of two elements, air and water. As I am trapped you must work the spell for me. I shall tell you what to do and let us hope some rain will fall." The voice dropped to a low whisper as Nicodemus said, "For these elements we must use symbols to call upon the necessary forces–if I was there I could do it myself."

"Symbols?" asked the fortune-teller, detecting something sinister in the whispered tone. "What symbols?"

"Something that represents the elements," said the voice. "For water a fish will be most suitable."

"And for air?"

"A bird," declared the tattoo wickedly. "At the bottom of the field in the hedge you will find a blackbird's nest. Bring the bird back here."

"Alive?" asked Akkikuyu hopefully.

Nicodemus just laughed at her.

Madame Akkikuyu set off for the hedge in misery. Would her triumph in getting the rain to fall be worth the life she was about to take? At the hedge she peered up into its dark, brambly depths. It was quite difficult to see anything in there at all at nighttime, but eventually she discovered it. Gingerly the rat squeezed through the thorns and began to climb.

The blackbird was still and silent; its feathers were fluffed out and the tiny beadlike eyes were firmly closed. Only its gentle heartbeat stirred its breast.

Madame Akkikuyu pulled herself up and looked at the bird fearfully. She thought about what she had to do and her heart beat faster. The bird looked so peaceful that tears sprang to her eyes again.

"I cannot," she whispered hoarsely.

"You must," came the voice in her ear. "One swift blow and the creature will be dead. It will feel nothing! Think of your mouse friends and the rain you can bring them."

So Madame Akkikuyu slowly raised a quivering claw and shakily drew the bone out of her hair. Then, closing her eyes tightly, she brought it crashing down on the nest.

At the ditch she lit a fire under her pot and pushed the feathery body into the bubbling water.

"And now, a fish, Akkikuyu," ordered Nicodemus, not letting her think too long about what she had done.

So the fortune-teller went to the still pool and stared long at the dark water, taking no notice of the grim reflection that gazed back at her with accusing eyes. Suddenly a string of tiny bubbles rose to the surface. With a great SPLASH she smacked her claw down and scooped out a spout of water. Within it a little fish was wriggling. As she caught it in her other claw Nicodemus said to her, "Well done–but listen, Akkikuyu, do you hear?"

The fortune-teller stood still and waited. A faint croaking was just audible amid the rustle of the hawthorn leaves.

On Nicodemus's instruction she crept around to a clump of water iris in time to see a small brown frog leap into sight and hop away from the pool.

"Catch it!" screamed Nicodemus. "We still need one and this will be fresh."

Madame Akkikuyu ran after the little frog and pounced on it.

Breathlessly she made her way back to the ditch and her bubbling pot. Hurriedly she dropped the fish into the boiling potion and repeated the spell after Nicodemus.

"Here me, folk that dwell in the spaces between the stars," he began. "I abjure all light, darken the sky, bring down the rain–in the name of Nachteg I command it, for you know who I am."

There was a silence and the rat looked up expectantly. But the tattoo said, "Now you must kiss the frog, Akkikuyu, and the spell shall be complete."

Grimly Madame Akkikuyu returned to the edge of the ditch and picked up the limp, slimy body. She gritted her teeth and kissed its head.

Nicodemus sighed and the first spots of rain pattered down.

In the Hall of Corn the fieldmice were disturbed in their sleep. They nuzzled and snuggled deep into their moss beds but could not escape the incessant drumming overhead. One by one the mice were roused from their beds and popped their heads out of their nests to see what the noise was.

"Rain!" they cried out with glee. "It's raining! Hooray!"

They abandoned their nests and danced around in the Hall with their faces upturned.

Mr. Nep gasped in wonder at the miracle, woke his wife, and went down to tell everyone. "It's the ratlady! I asked her to make it rain and she has! What a marvel she is. We must go and thank her." The fieldmice joyously trooped out of the Hall to find Madame Akkikuyu. The door guards went with them.

Sleepily, Audrey leaned out to see what the fuss was. A large drop of rain fell with a *plop* on her nose. She wiped it off and looked into the drizzling sky.

"Hello, dear," said Mrs. Scuttle, descending the ladder close by. "My, what a wonder! Everyone's saying that your ratwoman has made it rain. They've all gone to find her–imagine. Elijah and I are going to follow them–I don't think I'll sleep anymore tonight, and it will be light soon." She let the rain fall on her gladly. "Oh, it seems like years since the last drop we had. Are you coming?"

Audrey shook her head. Here was another feather for Madame Akkikuyu's cap. Wearily she sighed, "Give her my regards–but I'm going back to bed."

"Oh, well, you know best, dear."

* * *

At the ditch they found Madame Akkikuyu beaming broadly. Her potion pot was now empty and the fire was out.

"Mouseys," she said welcomingly, throwing open her claws. "Akkikuyu bring rain as promise."

"Astounding," cried Mr. Nep, shaking her vigorously by the claw. "Truly wondrous–well done." Everyone joined in to praise her, until Madame Akkikuyu flushed with pleasure.

But the celebrations were short-lived. The rain suddenly stopped.

"Won't be no more rain out of that sky," said Old Todmore, examining the heavens.

He was right. The magic rain shower had finished, and Madame Akkikuyu shook her head in dismay–it certainly wasn't worth the murders she had committed that night.

"That spot o' water won't have done much good at all," observed one mouse sorrowfully. "Ground's too dry to soak it up. It's not long afore sunrise an' all that rain'll steam off soon. Bah–darned waste o' time."

The Fennywolders tutted sadly. All their high hopes had been dashed. Now they felt more flat and miserable than ever. All agreed, however, that Madame Akkikuyu had done her best, better than any of them could have done, but this didn't get them anywhere.

Madame Akkikuyu glanced at the tattoo on her ear, but Nicodemus was silent–it was too near daybreak for him. She wondered if he had known how short the shower would be. She left the mice and sat by herself on the steep bank and cried regretfully.

* * *

Young Whortle was making his way through the field when dawn's gray light crept over Fennywolde. He was a heavy sleeper and was surprised to find himself alone in the nest that morning. He knew nothing of Madame Akkikuyu's rainmaking and none of the others had returned yet.

He had gone through the great door wondering where Grommel and the other guard had gotten to.

"Funny," he said to himself, "where they all gone, then?" He put his paws behind his back and began to hum a jolly tune. He felt much better now and his shoulders only gave him an occasional twinge. Secretly he hoped that he would have scars like Mr. Scuttle, as proof of his bravery.

A mist was rising as the meager rainfall turned to vapor. It was thick and white, and soon, without realizing, Young Whortle wandered out of the main corridor.

"Oh, curse this fog," he muttered crossly. "I wish Sammy was here with me." He rubbed his shoulders for they had begun to ache in the damp mist. He looked up suddenly. He ought to be out of the field by now, but the white, swirling mist billowed around him. He was hopelessly lost.

Something moved in the corner of his eye. He turned quickly and the mist pressed around closely. "Hello?" he called brightly, "someone there, then?" There was no reply, only the rustle of the cornstalks. Young Whortle shrugged and put the movement down to the swirling of the mist. He set off again in no particular direction, knowing that sooner or later he'd come across some familiar landmark. The mist grew thicker and flowed over his plump face.

"This is a daft nuisance," he muttered and began to whistle a tune that Hodge had taught him. The tune died on his lips as he remembered his dear friend. He had been found murdered in this very field.... Something rustled behind him–and it wasn't just the cornstalks. Young Whortle walked a little faster. He wanted to stop and take a look. But what if it was something horrible waiting for him, with long sharp teeth and pointed claws? Young Whortle shivered. He knew he was giving in to panic.

The rustling sounded again–only this time it was on his left. He yelped and stared wildly around him. Suddenly he broke into a wild, panic-stricken run, deeper and deeper into the field, not caring where he went just so long as he was away from the horror that lurked in the suffocating mist.

He crashed headlong through the dense stalks, squealing out loud. Sharp stones bit into his pink feet till they bled, and coarse leaves razored through his paws. "Oh no," he whimpered as he felt his breath rattle in his chest, "I can't go on much farther."

His legs crumpled beneath him and Young Whortle lay panting on the hard ground. He was a small, frightened animal, totally alone in a turgid sea of mist. He had never felt so forlorn. Even when the owl was after him at least he had known what he was up against. But this was different. Here the danger hid out of sight, waiting to strike when its victim least expected.

He strained his ears for some minutes but could hear nothing.

"Wait till I tell Sammy this," he told himself in a voice louder than he had intended. "He won't half laugh! 'Things you get yourself into, Warty, 'he'll say."

Young Whortle got to his feet, his legs still a bit wobbly. He scratched the top of his head and tugged the little tuft of hair that grew there. Then he froze.

Thin, long fingers appeared out of the mist and came for him. As he yelled for his life he felt something tighten around his neck.

"FENNY!" he screamed desperately, "FEN–"

Only the cornstalks rustled in reply.

* * *

Arthur looked up. He was sure he had heard something. He and Twit were the only sentries left on duty–the others having gone to see Madame Akkikuyu with the rest of the fieldmice.

Arthur looked across at his friend, who was swaying happily on a corn ear. "Did you hear that, Twit?" he shouted.

The fieldmouse gazed over with a blank look. "What be the matter, Art?" he called back.

"I'm not sure . . . but I think I heard the alarm."

Arthur tried to pierce the low mist with his eyes. He felt ill at ease. Something dreadful was happening down there–he was certain of it.

"I'm going to raise the alarm myself," he told Twit decisively. "I don't like that mist down there–it could hide anything. It's creepy." He cupped his paws around his mouth, keeping a tight hold on the stalk with his legs and tail, and called out "FENNY!" as loud as he could. Twice he repeated the cry, then both he and Twit climbed down.

"Should we wait fer the others?" asked Twit anxiously. Now he was on the ground, the mist was up to his chest and writhed over him like a living thing. In the dark places of the field the mist looked deeper.

"No time," said Arthur firmly, "come on."

They left the corridor path and plunged into the wild places of the field.

"Is it Hodge's murderer, do you think?" asked Twit quietly.

"Might be," answered Arthur gravely. "We should have brought a stick or something just in case."

"Here," Twit pressed a stout staff into Arthur's chubby paw. "Thought they might come in handy," he explained.

"Good thinking," praised Arthur, greatly cheered. "The two of us should be able to handle whoever it is."

"Or whatever," added Twit timidly.

Arthur gulped. "We," he said, trying to sound brave, "we've fought off a band of bloodthirsty rats before now."

"Yes, but there was five of us then and only three of them," observed Twit glumly. Arthur brandished his stick before him like a sword, cutting through the dense mist only to have the gaps fill up again thicker than before.

"We'll be all right," he said aloud, but his feigned confidence fooled no one. "Just don't think of anything frightening, Twit. What would old Triton say if he could hear us, eh? Something like 'lily-livered landlubbers' I bet. And what about Kempe? Why don't we sing one of his bawdy songs to make us feel better and get rid of all this gloom?" Arthur cleared his throat. "Rosie, poor Rosie . . . why aren't you singing, Twit? Twit?"

Arthur spun around, but his friend was gone. Only the mist met his gaze and closed in on him. From far away–or so it seemed, he heard the little fieldmouse call his name anxiously.

Twit had stumbled over a stone and in that instant had lost his friend. The mist poured in around him and he was alone.

"Arthur!" he shouted meekly. "Where are you, Arthur?" But

the fog swallowed his tiny voice greedily. His cries dwindled to murmurs and then into silence. Twit was afraid. The stick he held trembled in his paws as he tried to make his way through the corn. He was totally lost. For all he knew he was going around in futile circles. Then he began to hear the noises.

The fieldmouse paused and waved the stick about him in a frenzy. "There . . . there's five of us here, matey, so clear off sharp!"

The stems crackled and snapped to his right. He ducked and darted off to the left. Now it was in front of him, rustling and scraping, coming ever closer. It was going to get him–to murder him as it had done with Hodge. Twit turned to flee again, but the noise seemed to be all around him now. His courage left him and he stood still and howled sadly, "Please, no!" but the thick milky mist muffled his voice.

Long twiglike fingers emerged out of the fog like ghosts. Twit tried to fend them off, but it was all in vain. A plaited loop was pulled over his ears and caught him around the neck.

"EEEK! HELP! FENNY!" he squawked as the loop began to tighten and strangle him.

"Help . . . Fenny . . . Help . . ." Twit choked on each word and scrabbled at his throat. It was no use. The loop continued to throttle him and Twit fell senseless to the ground.

"Twit!" bawled Arthur, smashing through the stalks. "Twit!" He thrashed the air with his stick but could see no one. The fiend had slipped silently away.

"Twit," moaned Arthur as he knelt by his friend's side. "Oh, Twit, don't be dead." He cradled his friend's head in his paws and listened for a heartbeat.

A faint murmur fluttered in Twit's chest, and Arthur wept. Slowly, the mist began to disperse.

Gradually Twit came to. His breathing was labored and he touched his neck tenderly. There were big black bruises forming all around his throat. He grinned at Arthur shakily.

"Reckoned I were a goner then, Art," he croaked.

"You'll be fine now," assured Arthur. "We ought to get out of here while we can. Look, the mist's thinning." He helped Twit to his feet and they staggered off.

"Did you see who it was?" asked Arthur curiously.

Twit shook his head slowly. "No, Art . . . but it were uncanny. All I saw was something that looked . . . looked as if it were made totally out of straw."

CHAPTER TWELVE

HUNTERS IN THE NIGHT

When Arthur and Twit hobbled into the Hall of Corn, they found a throng of mice waiting for them. The Fennywolders had heard Arthur's alarm call but had had no idea where to go, so they had assembled in the Hall and waited.

Arthur breathlessly explained what had happened to him and Twit, and Mrs. Scuttle hurried over to help her son.

The fieldmice shook their heads, stunned that this could happen again. Mr. Woodruffe stepped onto the throne and raised his staff for silence.

"Now we know," he declared, "the creature–whatever it is, is still at large. We must search the field once more."

As the fieldmice went to find weapons, Mr. Nep came rushing out of his nest with a pale, frightened face. "My son," he cried, "my son has gone."

"Has anyone seen Young Whortle?" asked Mr. Woodruffe grimly. All the fieldmice shook their heads, and a chill entered the Hall. "Then we must look for him also," he said, "and let us hope he has only gone exploring again."

A large party of strong husbands set off through the field, wielding sticks and cudgels. Arthur was too tired to join them—he had been up all night and desperately wanted some sleep. He even declined the offer of breakfast.

A group of wives who had been left behind chatted together dismally and clutched at their mousebrasses. All were fearful.

Suddenly one small child asked its mother, "Are we all going to die, Mam?" Nobody answered. But the tension was broken and a hysterical mousewife burst out, "Who is doing these things? What have we done to deserve this?"

Just then, Mr. Nettle came into the Hall followed by Jenkin. "Perhaps the villain is amongst us!" he shouted above the hubbub.

This was too much for the worried mice. A ripple ran through them, and they looked at their neighbors suspiciously. Why, it might be any one of them.

"What do you mean, Nettle?" asked Mr. Woodruffe sternly.

"All I say is that though ye search ye will find nought. Maybe the foul one is one of our folk, playacting behind a fair mask."

The crowd stirred uneasily and murmured to one another.

"Now just wait a moment," said Mr. Woodruffe. He feared that something nasty could happen if Isaac was allowed to go any farther. He did not want the fieldmice to be at odds with one another. "You're talking out of your hat, Nettle," he said. "We were all at the ditch with Madame Akkykookoo when this happened, so it can't be any of us."

The crowd sighed with relief.

Isaac Nettle shook his head and gazed upward. "Were we all present, I wonder?" he said loudly.

Everyone followed his glance and the murmurs began again. There, climbing out of her nest, was Audrey.

"I think perhaps one was not with us," uttered Isaac darkly.

Arthur sprang forward in spite of his fatigue. He saw what Mr. Nettle was driving at. "Rubbish!" he growled angrily. "Not even you believe that."

Mr. Nettle's face was stony, and the crowd's mutterings grew louder.

Jenkin stepped up to his father. "Dad," he pleaded, "you know Miss Brown's not to blame."

Isaac turned on his son and struck him violently across the face. "What dost thou know of yon painted sinner?" he bellowed, but Jenkin merely glared back at him with a face full of anger, then turned and walked away.

Isaac strode after his son.

"Listen to me all of you!" boomed Mr. Woodruffe, commanding their attention again.

"If there are any among you who are foolish enough to listen to old Nettle's rantings then I warn you now. There are stiff penalties for those who disobey the King of the Field. Let none of you lay a paw on our guests from the town. Now go about your business or wait for your husbands to return; only clear the Hall."

The crowd shuffled away grumbling and whispering.

Audrey had watched all this with curiosity. She had not the faintest idea of what was going on, but caught several hostile glances aimed at her from the crowd. The fieldmice moved away from her when she passed them, as though terrified of what she might do to them. She quickly made her way to the throne and asked Arthur, "What's going on? What's happened?" Quickly Arthur told her about the creature that had tried to choke Twit.

"Arthur," she said when she had made sure that Twit was all right, "I don't like it here–these mice don't like me. They think I'm some sort of devil–and quite frankly they give me the shivers too. You wouldn't believe some of the stares they were giving me then. I felt as if they would tear me apart given half a chance."

Mr. Woodruffe put his arm around her shoulder. "Now lass, don't you fret none. They're a friendly lot in Fennywolde, really. It's just that right now they're scared, what with the weather and Hodge's murder and now poor Twit this morning. They need to feel safe, and if that means they have to stick the blame on some outsider, then that's what they'll try and do. Don't worry, though, I'll not let them–I've a cooler head than most, but it's a tricky job with old Isaac sticking his tuppence in. He knows how to get them riled, he do, and it's a shame, but he don't like you, and once he's got somethin' in his mulish head that's that."

Audrey was not comforted. The day was another scorcher, but she stayed away from the still pool for fear of confrontations. Instead, she helped Mrs. Scuttle with small tasks and jobs that did not really need to be done, but it kept her busy and out of folks' way.

Arthur and Twit slept all day, so Audrey had no one of her own age to talk to. She felt bored and lonely, and the Hall of Corn began to feel like a jail. Once she spotted Iris Crowfoot carrying a bowl of water for her mother. Audrey waved, but Mrs. Crowfoot scolded her daughter for daring to smile back. How could anyone think that she was connected with the murder of Hodge? It was too ridiculous for words! Audrey would have laughed at their silliness if she was not so worried and afraid.

* * *

Alison Sedge sat in the meadow weaving a necklace of forget-me-nots. As she worked, she mulled over her suspicions. She hated Audrey with all her heart. She wished that Mr. Nettle had struck her instead of Jenkin–Alison would like to see Audrey's lip swell up like a blackberry. That would spoil her fairy looks! She cursed the ill fortune which had brought the town mouse to her field–just when she was having a bit of fun with the boys too. It had been a good start to the summer, she had been admired by everyone, and had flirted with everyone.

Suddenly Alison shuddered. A horrible thought occurred to her. One of her suitors now lay under the earth: if she had been nicer to him on that fateful day would Hodge still be alive now? Young Whortle was missing as well–she hoped he was safe. If things got any worse there would be no boys left for her to flirt with.

The meadow grass rustled close by. Alison sprang to her feet and backed away nervously.

"Who's there?" she asked.

"Oh, is that you, Alison Sedge?" It was Jenkin's voice and he sounded none too happy at meeting her.

Quickly Alison sat down again and struck her most casual and alluring pose. "Over here, Jolly Jenkin," she invited huskily.

He came into sight through the silvery flowering grasses, and Alison beckoned him over. His eye was purple and the lip was bleeding again.

"Oh, Jenkin," she cried in alarm. "You look awful, this is a real baddun this time. You rest there," she added kindly. "I'll go fetch some water to bathe that eye in."

But Jenkin wouldn't have it. "I'll be aright in a bit," he explained.

"Is it very sore?" she asked. His eye was an angry bluey purple and she could actually see the lip throbbing. Alison wanted to throw her arms about him and make it all better. This was what she wanted, and at that moment she realized that all her flirting had simply been a waste of time. Time that should have been spent with Jenkin.

"Oh, Jenkin," she said, moving closer, "Your dad's horrible

to you–p'raps it's time you left him an' built a nest of your own in the Hall."

With his good eye Jenkin regarded Alison coolly. Her creamy hair brushed against his arm and her breath smelled of wild strawberries. There had been a time–not long ago, when he had prayed for her to be near him like this, but not now. He stood up and moved away.

"Were my fault these," he said, meaning his bruises. "I oughtn't a mentioned Miss Brown–my dad don't like her."

Alison was slightly vexed. He had interrupted her just as she was about to kiss him. "I don't like her either," she snapped. "She ain't right in the head an' I think she's got somethin' to do with Hodge."

"Pah," snorted Jenkin, "you'm just jealous. Not even my dad really believed that rubbish, he just said it to make her look bad."

"But, Jenkin," protested Alison. "She told me, she said that she'd choke anyone what got in her way."

"Shut it, Alison, don't bother." Jenkin turned and looked away. "Y'see," he confessed shyly, "I likes Miss Brown a heck of a lot and nothing you can say will change that."

He left Alison on her own. She twisted her fingers around the necklace she had just made and tore it off. In a cascade of tiny blue petals Alison Sedge wept bitterly to herself.

* * *

Audrey lay in her nest staring at the starry sky. Everyone had gone to bed–everyone except for Arthur and the other night sentries. Twit was not allowed to join them till he was fully recovered. His throat was still sore and his voice was hoarse and croaky.

Audrey wondered how much longer she could go on living in Fennywolde if the hostile atmosphere continued. Her job as companion to Madame Akkikuyu was more or less over now–she had only seen the rat briefly that day at lunch, but she was so popular with everyone that they had only said a few words before someone grabbed the rat and invited her to join them.

There was one thing that really puzzled Audrey. Madame Akkikuyu looked different. For some time she had not been able to put her finger on what it was. Then she realized. The fortune-teller was no longer black–her fur was changing color! Now she was a sleek chestnut and it seemed to get lighter with every day. It was most peculiar, but the Fennywolders believed that it was the country air and sunshine that was the cause.

Madame Akkikuyu certainly looked very different from the pathetic creature Audrey had seen in the Starwife's chamber. She had grown strong and if not fat, then well padded.

Her thoughts were interrupted by a small, polite voice whispering under the nest entrance.

"Miss Brown," it said.

"Who is it?" she whispered back.

"It's me–Jenkin."

"Oh," Audrey was surprised, "what do you want?"

"To talk to you–meet me down here when you're ready."

Quickly she pulled on her clothes and tied up her hair with her best ribbon. What could Jenkin want at this time of night? It had to be very important. She climbed down the ladder and stood before him. Even in the pale moonlight she could see the marks left by his father's hard paw.

His eyes lit up when he saw her. "You always do look nice," he said.

"Thank you." She blushed. "What is it you want?"

Jenkin looked around furtively. "I can't tell 'ee here," he said shyly. "Can we go somewhere a bit privatelike?"

"Yes, all right," she consented, extremely curious. Jenkin led her out of the Hall of Corn by a small side entrance, taking care that the sentries did not see them.

"Why all this secrecy?" she asked him.

"My dad's forbid me to see you," came the reply in a hushed voice. "He says you're a town heathen who don't know good from bad."

Audrey felt that there was quite a lot she could say about Mr. Nettle, but for once, she held her tongue and let Jenkin continue.

"He tells me you ain't worth a crumb, that you're wicked all through an' that since you've come here we ain't had nothin' but misery an' death."

This was quite enough! Audrey felt herself near to exploding. "If that's all you've got to tell me I might as well go back now. I've got a brother who can tell me all that and more besides, thank you very much. In fact, if I don't go now you'll find yourself with another black eye."

To her astonishment he laughed. Not an unkind, mocking laugh, but a gentle good-humored chuckle. "Reckon you could do it too," he said. "But don't go yet–not till I've had my say. Look, we're all right here now. There ain't no one to listen."

The moonlight fell on his fine hair, and for the first time Audrey noticed that he had combed it. He swallowed hard and began.

"I told you what my dad thinks," he lumbered on awkwardly, "cos that don't matter to me no more. I'm never goin' back to him or our winter quarters–I've left."

"Good for you, Jenkin," said Audrey, not yet seeing what he was driving at. Was that berrybrew she could smell on his breath?

"Tomorrow I shall start a-buildin' a nest around the Hall," he told her proudly, the stars sparkling in his round, excited eyes. "What I'm sayin', Miss Brown–Audrey is . . . well, I'd like you to share that nest with me. Cos I loves you and wants . . . to wed you. . . ." He stared at her hopefully, then uttered something under his breath, "Darn I forgot!" and quickly he knelt down on one knee. "You don't have to answer straight away like–think it over."

Audrey was bewildered. A proposal of marriage was the last thing she had expected, and it took some time for it to properly sink in.

"You really want to marry me?" she sounded shocked and slightly amused.

"More than anything–that's the Green honest truth." He watched her intently with wide, trusting eyes like a baby.

Audrey's heart went out to him. The plain truth was that she did not love him, but a strong desire to see Piccadilly again grew in her.

She knelt down beside Jenkin and took his paw in hers. "Oh, Jenkin," she said slowly, "I'm sorry, I don't want to hurt your feelings, but I can't accept. I'm extremely flattered, but no–you see, I now know that I love another. I never realized it before."

Jenkin hung his head. Audrey felt so sorry for him, but she remembered the Eve of Midsummer and knew that Alison was meant for him.

"There is someone who cares for you very much," she said, trying to break through his barrier of sullen silence.

"Who's that, then?" he asked miserably.

"Alison Sedge," Audrey replied, and she squeezed his paw tightly.

"Tuh," sniffed Jenkin, "she don't care for no one but herself," he answered thickly.

"Was she always like that?"

"No–there was a time when me an' Alison went around together quite a bit, but then she got her mousebrass an' everything changed."

"Then it can change again, Jenkin," urged Audrey. "Forget about me–I'm just getting in the way of the two of you. I know that you and she are meant for each other. Truly."

There was such a ring of certainty in her voice that Jenkin looked up at her and for a second caught a flash of green fire flicker in her eyes.

He gasped and Audrey kissed his cheek. "You just wait," she said, "you'll be the one giving her the runaround, only don't make her suffer too much–I've already made that mistake."

"Have I made a fool of myself?" asked Jenkin bashfully.

Audrey smiled. "Not at all. It's nice to know that not everyone in Fennywolde thinks I'm a monster." But as she said it the hairs on the back of her neck tingled.

Suddenly the cornstalks were thrust aside and something crashed toward them.

Audrey could not believe her eyes and Jenkin fell back in fear. The corn dolly she had made was lurching toward them! No longer was it the trim, neat figure she had woven but a mass of tangled, twisted stems–bent with hatred and evil spells. The arms, which had been pretty corn ears, had grown long and wild with spiky fingers, which clutched at the air greedily and waved around full of menace.

The nightmare figure staggered toward them, its twiggy fingers outstretched, ready to catch them.

Jenkin acted quickly.

He grabbed Audrey's paw and dragged her away just in time. "Come on!" he yelled.

Audrey snapped out of her trance and they stumbled off through the field, the figure pursuing them closely. It scraped its untidy skirt over the stony ground and flayed the air with its thin arms, groping for them. Its plaited loop head twisted from side to side, seeming to sense rather than see where it was going.

Jenkin and Audrey ran in blind terror with the papery crackling sound rustling close behind. Audrey slipped and quick straw fingers grasped at her heels. "Aaarh!" she squealed as they dragged her back and the figure loomed over her, lowering its plaited loop purposefully.

Jenkin beat the straw with his fists and the fingers released Audrey and grabbed him. The loop slipped over his head, but he ducked and nipped off with Audrey.

"Not far to go till we're out of the field," he called to her, "then we should be able to go faster."

Audrey leaped over stones and dodged the stalks that blocked her path. Her tail bells jangled wildly as the clutching fingers searched for her hungrily.

"Quick, Audrey, hurry!" Jenkin had reached the edge of the field and turned around to help her.

She glanced over her shoulder and cried out. The corn dolly bore down on her, sweeping over the stony ground at a terrific speed. It raised its spindly arms and brought them knifing down.

Audrey felt herself yanked backward. Jenkin had hold of her and he carried her clear of the field.

"Look Jenkin," she gasped, "it isn't following us."

Jenkin put her down and stared back. The corn dolly remained within the confines of the field, its arms upraised.

"Why isn't it chasing us?" asked Jenkin nervously.

"Maybe it can only live in the field," suggested Audrey. "Perhaps it needs to be amongst the growing corn to come alive."

"It's horrible," said Jenkin shivering. He frowned; the thing seemed to be waiting for something to happen. It reared back the loop head as though sensing another presence. Jenkin moved his eyes from the straw figure, up to the tops of the dark elms and out into the starry sky. . . .

"Get down," he yelled, and roughly pushed Audrey to the ground. It was too late to save himself.

A pale, silent ghost slipped out of the night sky and snatched

him up. Jenkin squeaked in pain as Mahooot scooped him up in his vicious talons. He saw the ground disappear below him and heard the owl cackle to itself wickedly.

"Foood, foood, lovely mooouses."

Audrey saw the owl swoop into the darkness over the meadow and heard Jenkin's frightened voice fade away.

Then Audrey screamed.

The corn dolly rustled its pleasure and slunk back into the shadowy cover of the field.

On sentry, Arthur recognized his sister's voice and soon everyone in Fennywolde was awake and lighting torches. They ran in a blazing line to see why she was making that fearful noise.

Audrey was on her knees when they found her, staring across the meadow with big dark eyes that were dreadful to look on. Arthur shook her to stop the piercing screams.

"What is it, Aud?" he asked wildly.

Without seeing him she pointed out into the sky and said weakly, "The owl! The owl has got Jenkin."

The fieldmice cried out in dismay, but from their midst, one figure stepped forward into the circle of torchlight. It was Jenkin's father. None dared look at him. His face trembled with emotion and his lips turned white.

"Jenkin lad," he said, sounding as if he had been stabbed. He turned on Audrey and his eyes burned at her accusingly. He raised a quivering finger and pointed. "You have done this, you!"

Before she could reply, out of the crowd stepped Madame Akkikuyu. The rat took a torch from one of the fieldmice and held it above her head.

"So," she shouted and all looked to her. "Mousey boy got by owly. What you do?"

"What can we do?" asked Arthur bitterly.

"Go fight the mangy bird!" she cried, whirling the torch around. "Come, mouseys, we go to save him!"

The fieldmice cheered her as she led them down the banks of the ditch like a general. Mr. Nettle followed like a sleepwalker.

Arthur and Audrey were joined by the Scuttles. "Arthur," Audrey whispered to her brother, "Jenkin and I were chased out here by a terrible thing! It was . . . it was my own corn dolly, Arthur! It must have killed Hodge! It tried to kill us too! What can I do?"

Arthur gulped. There was no use doubting her. Twit had been attacked by something made of straw that morning. "Look," he said, "don't mention this to anyone yet–you're in enough trouble already. What do you think they'll do if they find out your figure has come to life and murders people?"

They hurried after the lights of the rescue party. Twit took Audrey's paw and patted it.

In the empty glade near the field only one mouse was left. It was Alison Sedge. She watched the torchlight dwindle in the distance and shook her head. Her sobs were silent and her heart broken. She ripped off her mousebrass and flung it away.

* * *

Madame Akkikuyu led the fieldmice through the dark meadow. She whooped and shouted challenges to the owl, and the fieldmice took heart at her courage. They came to the oak trees and the rat thrust her torch into the earth.

"Stay here, mouseys," she told them. "I go to hooty!"

"Find my boy!" begged Mr. Nettle.

"Kill the owl," chanted the fieldmice, and Arthur and Twit were alarmed to hear them. They spoke not as individuals but as a great, many-headed creature with a hundred fiery eyes eager for blood. Only Twit's parents and Mr. Woodruffe did not join in. They hung back and put their paws to their mouths fearfully.

Madame Akkikuyu began to climb the tree. It was easy for her. Her claws sank into the soft bark and she ascended swiftly.

"I get you, hooty," she snarled angrily. "I tell you leave my mouseys be."

She pulled herself up to the hole in the trunk and announced herself.

"Hooty. Akkikuyu here again."

"Whooo?" came a hollow voice.

"Akkikuyu–the owl rider and neck plucker. I have mattress need stuffing!" She laughed and pulled the bone from her hair.

Sounds of agitated scrabbling issued from the black recess. Mahooot was trapped and he knew it.

"Ha!" bawled Akkikuyu, springing across the threshold and stabbing the bone in front of her.

Mahooot had been lying in wait for her, intending to bite her head off as soon as it poked through the hole in the tree trunk. He darted forward, but she brought the bone crashing down on his open beak. It crunched and chipped, and Mahooot hooted in agony.

In a foul temper he shot out a deadly talon and snapped it tight around the fortune-teller's neck. She wailed in surprise and dropped the bone as he dragged her into the darkness.

"Not so fast, hooty," she yelled, and kicked the owl in the stomach.

"Oooof!" moaned Mahooot as the air rushed out of him and he collapsed, wheezing, on the floor.

Madame Akkikuyu shrieked with laughter and disentangled herself from his clutches.

She retrieved her bone and brought it smashing down on the talon that had gripped her. The sharp claws splintered into a thousand bits.

Mahooot roared in his pain and Madame Akkikuyu crowed with delight. Then she dealt the other foot a devastating blow and danced about.

The owl lunged at her in a mad rage. He knocked her off balance, so that she stumbled and fell backward. Then Mahooot beat her down with his powerful wings until she was overwhelmed by his feathery bulk. His body crushed her and he bent his flat head to nip with his damaged beak. He pulled out a quantity of her thick hair until Madame Akkikuyu squawked shrilly. That was it! This owl was getting above itself.

"Enough hooty," she said, spitting feathers out of her mouth.

Mahooot cackled and continued to squash her. She thrashed her tail from left to right, so he bit it and the blood oozed out. Madame Akkikuyu gnashed her teeth. He had gone too far.

"Dooown, yooou doxsie!" he hooted, reveling in her suffering. "Mahooot is yooour dooom!"

Madame Akkikuyu blew a muffled raspberry underneath him and managed to pull an arm loose. With one swipe she punched Mahooot savagely under his beak. He staggered backward and she was free.

Nimbly she stepped out of the dark hole and ran along the branch outside.

"Nyer, nyer," she taunted him, waggling her bottom at the hole. "Come out, hooty, Akkikuyu thrash you good an' proper."

In a cloud of soft white feathers Mahooot left the hole. He spread out his enormous wings and reared himself up to a towering height.

"Die!" he boomed in a chilling voice.

"Oho," chuckled the fortune-teller, "not yet owly, Akkikuyu not ready to snuff candle–you play her game now." She slipped her claw swiftly into the bag slung over her shoulder and pulled out a small cloth pouch.

Mahooot made a ravaging dive at her. The rat flung the

pouch at him and a poisonous concoction exploded in his face.

She smartly stepped to one side as Mahooot floundered past. His eyes were stinging and he could not see. The smell of burned feathers fouled the air.

"Ooow!" he screeched in panic as he fumbled along the branch on his broken talons. "Mahooot is blind, ooow."

Madame Akkikuyu poked and teased him mischievously, until he could bear this monstrous ratwoman no longer. The owl flapped his wings and rose shakily into the air.

The fortune-teller let him go unmolested.

Mahooot spiraled around, unable to see where he was going. Then, with a dull thud, which smashed more of his beak, he flew into a tree trunk. Mahooot fell to the ground, bouncing off the branches.

"A fine sight to see," said a voice in the fortune-teller's ear. "What a heroine you are. The darling of Fennywolde."

"Nico," she welcomed, "I thought you not come tonight."

"I have been busy elsewhere," said Nicodemus, "but come, we must talk, you and I, for it is time you learned of the spell that will release me."

"Wait," said Madame Akkikuyu as she remembered Jenkin, "I have mousey to find."

"The lad is dead!" said Nicodemus coldly. "Now step into the owl's hole, Akkikuyu, and I shall tell you what must be done."

* * *

As Mahooot came crashing down out of the high branches the fieldmice who were waiting below cheered wildly and rushed forward.

"Stop, wait!" ordered Mr. Woodruffe, but they surged past him like a river and began to hurl stones at the dazed owl and beat it with their sticks.

"This is obscene," shouted the King of the Field. But they did not hear him. They only heard the gasps and cries of Mahooot as they tore at him. "They've gone mad," said Arthur, appalled.

Mr. Woodruffe turned and hid his head in disgust, then threw down his staff of office. "They will not listen to me anymore and I want nothing more to do with them. They are not mice tonight–they are the nastiest kind of rats."

"It's far worse than it ever was at home," said Audrey. They walked away with Mr. and Mrs. Scuttle. Fennywolde had become an evil place to live.

* * *

In the owl's nest Madame Akkikuyu listened as Nicodemus began.

"It is a mighty spell which we dare to attempt, Akkikuyu," he said. "Are you brave enough for it?"

"Yes, Nico."

"Then this is what we need. You must build a fire and feed it with the herbs I shall tell you to gather. Around this fire you must say the words of release and cast into the flame a mousebrass."

"A mousebrass, Nico–why so?"

"All this shall become clear to you, yet it must be a special mousebrass, it must be made in hatred and be a sign of destruction and death."

"Where I get such a dangler?"

"That also I shall tell you. All has been arranged. Wheels have been set in motion, Akkikuyu, and the time for the ritual is soon. At the time of the ceremony, however, I must be protected from the heat of the fire for I shall be vulnerable for a while. I must project my essence to a place of safety. Look in your bag–there you will find a vessel suitable for me."

Akkikuyu rummaged around inside her bag until she found what Nicodemus meant.

"You mean this, great one," she muttered, reluctantly taking out her most prized possession. The moonlight curved lovingly over the smooth glass ball that the fortune-teller had brought with her from Deptford.

"Excellent," he crooned delightedly. "That is most suitable! Have it with you at the fire's edge–only remember, Akkikuyu, that once the spell is complete you must smash your prize to release me. I do not want to spend another age imprisoned in there."

"I promise, Nico," she said with regret as she stroked her beautiful crystal ball.

"And one more thing, Akkikuyu. There must be an exchange of souls or the spell will be useless."

The fortune-teller trembled. "Souls? What am I to do this time?"

"There must be a sacrifice to the flame," Nicodemus whispered. "My essence will cross over to your world, and a soul must cross back in return. We must cast into the fire one who is not protected by a mousebrass."

"Who you think of?" she asked warily.

The reply was snarled back at her: "The one who has abandoned you, Akkikuyu, the one who spurned your friendship and tried to make a fool of you in front of everyone."

"No," cried the rat in dismay.

"Yes!" hissed Nicodemus. "She is unfettered by the Greenlaws and bound to no one. It must be her. You are sworn to obey me–throw Audrey Brown into the fire!"

"Mouselet!" Akkikuyu wailed miserably.

CHAPTER THIRTEEN

A WITCH AND A FOOL

The sun rose over Fennywolde to announce yet another feverish day.

Twit rose and leaned out of his and Arthur's nest. The Hall of Corn was unusually quiet–but not calm. He could almost feel dark forces surging through the field like evil water, and a half-forgotten memory awakened in him.

"Blow me," he said to himself.

Behind him, in the sweet mossy darkness, Arthur's drowsy voice mumbled, "What is it?"

The fieldmouse scratched his head and said, "I just remembered somethin', Art."

"If it's about last night I don't want to know," came the weary reply.

"Well it has somethin' to do wi' last night," admitted the fieldmouse, "but really I was just thinkin' of those bats back in Deptford."

"Oh, Orfeo, and . . . who was it?"

"Eldritch."

"That's right–what made you think of them?"

"Well, when they took me a-flyin' through the roof an' into the sky, they showed me some wild critters–they were 'orrible and mindless. I only just recalled that Orfeo askin' me if there were any of the–how did he put it–any of this 'untame breed' in my field. I said as I didn't know of any."

"So?" Arthur was baffled. "What made you think of that now?"

Twit turned a worried face to his friend, "Don't you see, Art? The bats knew. They was warnin' me!"

"What, against wild cats here?"

"No," said Twit gravely, "against my own folk here. Last night, Art, they weren't mice–Mr. Woodruffe said so, they were just like that 'untame breed' in the city. Horrid beasts with no thought 'cept killin'. I'm afeared for Fennywolde. What'll happen next?"

* * *

Madame Akkikuyu looked down into the ditch and prepared herself. Her task today was not pleasant, but she had sworn on her soul to obey Nicodemus. She mopped her brow with a corner of her shawl and set her jaw determinedly. She hated the idea of what she had to do, but Nicodemus would not be pleased with her if she failed him today.

She marched from the edge and strode to the elm trees where she hoped to find Mr. Nettle. A mousebrass was needed and he was the only one who could make it. Her problem would be persuading him.

Isaac Nettle, grim and steely eyed, was hammering a piece of metal in his forge. The ruddy glow of the forge fire shone on his fur and glinted off his drooping whiskers. But that was the only light in the gloomy place. Even in Isaac's heart there was darkness. Only grief and loss filled him. He pushed himself into his work passionately, smiting the red-hot metal with his hammer, trying to blot out his sorrow with the effort. Fiery sparks flew and scorched his skin, but he was thankful for them. He wanted to feel pain and be punished: for Jenkin, the shining joy of his sour life, was gone, plucked out of existence.

The ringing of his hammer was so loud that he did not hear the knocking at the door. He continued to beat the yellow metal till it was flattened, then, with a pair of tongs, he plunged it into a bucket of cold water. It was only when the steam had cleared that he noticed the ratwoman standing quietly by the door.

Madame Akkikuyu nodded at him. "Morning," she said.

Isaac grunted. He did not want to talk to anyone this day–or any other for that matter. He turned back to the fire and raked the embers together.

"I say morning," the fortune-teller repeated.

Isaac looked at her with unfriendly eyes. "Leave me!" he growled.

She shook her head. "You lose boy last night. You need talk–get it off bosom, Akkikuyu good listener, she hear your woe."

For a moment his face was impassive, but suddenly he broke down. Like a wall of glass his defenses shattered. Mr. Nettle wept openly.

"Jenkin, Jenkin, I've lost you, my son. I loved you and I never told you–not once."

Madame Akkikuyu took Mr. Nettle in her arms and patted him gently on the back. "There, there," she soothed, "that right, let it out. Tell Akkikuyu."

"Oh, Meg!" he cried. "Look after our boy, he's with you now."

"Meg?" asked Akkikuyu, "She your wife, yes?"

Isaac nodded feebly. "Meg died when Jenkin was born. I always blamed him for that–I loved her so. And now I've lost him too. I don't know what I'm going to do. I'm so sorry, lad, if you can hear me. Forgive your father!"

"Shhh," hushed Akkikuyu, pushing him gently onto a stool, "in the great beyond all things are forgiven–he knows now."

Mr. Nettle calmed down. When his last sniffs were over he thanked the rat shyly. "Verily, thou art a messenger from the Green, come in my darkest hour. And last night also–you did what no other dared, you tried to save my son. I thank thee for that. Truly thou art blessed!"

Madame Akkikuyu shrugged off these compliments. "Yes, I try, but was too late. What a shame your boy out last night. Why he not here safe with you?"

Isaac's face tightened and he became stern and grim once more. "It was the town mouse!" he spat bitterly. "It was she who lured my son away." He had forgotten now that it was his beatings that had driven Jenkin away from him.

"Aaahh, yes," muttered the fortune-teller, "Miss Audrey! Tell me Nettley, why did your boy meet her last night outside the field? And why she not there when Hodge was found, and where is the other boy?"

Mr. Nettle rose and scowled. "It is she!" he declared. "Ever since she came here there has been nought but pain and death! She has brought it!"

"Quite so," agreed Akkikuyu. "And tell me this! That mousey is of age, so why she no wear a mousey dangler?"

Mr. Nettle looked at her wildly. He had never noticed that, and he the mousebrass maker. "She should have one," he gasped. "Every mouse receives a brass when they come of age."

Madame Akkikuyu rushed in with her explanation. "Maybe Green Mouse think she not worthy of such a gift."

"My Lord!" Isaac exclaimed, staggering back. "Where were my wits? Why had I not thought of this? She must be evil indeed for the mighty Green to deem her unfit for a mousebrass. What manner of creature can she be?"

"A witch!" snapped Akkikuyu. "Why else your corn wither

in the ground and mouseys die young? What black powers she brung to your fair field, Nettley?"

Isaac was incensed. "What can we do? We must confront her and cast her out."

"No," said the rat hastily. "We must pray to the Green, see what he thinks." She narrowed her eyes and peered at Isaac through their narrow black slits. "Maybe," she began, as though working out a plan, "maybe you should make a special mousey dangler that will bring ruin on the mouselet. Make it with curses and surely the Green will hear you."

Isaac looked doubtful. He took his position as mousebrass maker extremely seriously. He considered the suggestion but declined.

"I will not presume upon my Lord," he explained. "I will not anger him by making a brass of my own design. I must know it to be his will."

Madame Akkikuyu sighed, but there was one more trick up Nicodemus's sleeve. He had been prepared for Isaac's piety and had instructed her to take him to the owl tree and wait there.

"Nettley," she said, "it hot in here, I go for walk. Come join me, leave your danglers and talk with Akkikuyu."

Isaac was unwilling: others in Fennywolde might see him and he did not want that. As if she understood this, Madame Akkikuyu added, "We not go to Hall, we walk in meadow!" Mr. Nettle agreed and he followed her out of the forge.

As they walked Madame Akkikuyu pointed out plants and reeled off their good–or bad–qualities. Mr. Nettle tried to listen and pay attention, but his mind was elsewhere. Inside, he was seething. The thought of Audrey Brown, that odious town mouse who had wrought so much grief and harm, inflamed him and his fingers itched for his hammer. What could be done with her? Her crimes were too great to go unpunished. If she was a witch then there was only one way to deal with her. He wondered if the Fennywolders would agree with him.

When Mr. Nettle next looked up they had left the meadow and he drew a sharp breath. Madame Akkikuyu had steered him toward the oaks and the sight of them brought the pain of his loss back to him.

"Why are we here?" he questioned her with a faltering voice.

"Oh, me!" said Akkikuyu, trying to sound shocked that she could have been so thoughtless and unsympathetic. "Silly Akkikuyu–her head not screwed on today. Come Nettley, we go from here." She moved back a few paces and observed Isaac keenly. He seemed to have seen something near one of the roots and he made no attempt to follow her.

"Look!" he said, "There's a shining thing over yonder. What can it be?"

Akkikuyu squinted in the direction he was pointing. The fierce light of the sun was reflecting off something down there. Isaac walked up to the great root cautiously.

"Oh no, Nico," she breathed to herself, "not this–he suffer enough."

When Mr. Nettle reached the great root he fell to his knees and shrieked. Madame Akkikuyu ran over to him and looked over his quaking shoulder.

There on the dusty ground was an owl pellet, one of those tight little bundles of fur and bones. Sticking out of it was Jenkin's mousebrass.

The sign of life blazed in the sunlight as Mr. Nettle wrested it free of the pellet. Then he turned his face on the fortune-teller and cried, "I shall make that brass, and may eternal damnation fall on that town mouse. For every stroke of the hammer shall be a curse and malediction–may she suffer for the agony she has given to me and my son."

Madame Akkikuyu smiled soberly–Nicodemus would be pleased.

* * *

The morning passed and the afternoon crept up. The rings of Mr. Nettle's hammer sang over Fennywolde.

The atmosphere in the Hall of Corn was terrible. Arguments broke out for the slightest reason. Old Todmore yelled at the children who were pestering him for a story and told them he had better things to do. One of the young boys kicked his stick and ran away.

"Come back 'ere, Abel Madder," fumed Old Todmore, "I'll clout you one!"

Dimsel Bottom and Lily Clover were seen quarreling and they had to be separated when plump Dimsel flew at her friend in a shocking fit of rage.

Josiah Down kicked the family nest to pieces while his wife called him a no-good cheddar head.

All this was watched in fearful silence by the Scuttles and their guests. They kept well away from the rest of the fieldmice and looked at one another in disbelief. What was happening to everybody?

Audrey decided to go to bed early that night. She sat in her hot nest with her knees tucked tight up under her chin. She was frightened. Several times that day she had heard her name mentioned in high, disapproving voices, and when Mr. Nep went by he actually spat on the ground when he saw her.

* * *

Alison Sedge was restless. She did not want to go to bed. All day she had lain in the shade by the still pool, thinking of Jenkin. She remembered their happy days together before she had received her mousebrass, but that was gone now and good riddance. She wore no flowers around her neck anymore and had not once gazed at her reflection. Her hair was forgotten and neglected in two untidy plaits. She had not eaten all day.

Twilight came. Reluctantly, Alison picked herself up and ducked under the hawthorn branches. She passed over the ditch and entered the field. The corn was silent. No wind rustled its ears or rattled its stalks. Their long black shadows fell on Alison like the bars of a prison. She became increasingly uneasy. The field was an eerie place. She had never noticed how impenetrable those dark shadows were before. Alison gulped nervously as she remembered the murderer that hid in here, throttling unwary mice who wandered around alone. How could she be so stupid?

A noise startled her. The corn moved behind and a crackling rustle moved toward her.

Alison did not wait to look. She ran deeper into the field toward the Hall of Corn, but the rustling grew louder. It was ahead of her now and she could see dim shapes before her. Alison wheeled around and sped back toward the ditch, missing the path in her haste.

Suddenly she tripped and stumbled. She put out her arms to save herself but landed on something soft.

Panting heavily, Alison lifted her face–and stared into the blank eyes of Young Whortle. She had fallen on top of his discarded body. Alison leaped up and screamed at the top of her voice.

In the Hall of Corn the fieldmice were once more disturbed by the alarm call. What could be the cause this time?

They lit their torches and fled out of the great doors.

"What is it?" asked Audrey as Twit slid down past her nest.

"Another alarm," he answered, "we must all go–come on, Aud!"

They followed the other mice. Arthur had been on duty and slid down a cornstalk as they ran by. "Wait for me!" he puffed.

The fieldmice ran along the ditch, fearing the worst. Had another tragedy occurred? Then, crashing out of the field came

Alison Sedge. She ran to her mother's arms and squealed.

"It's Young Whortle–he's dead. I found his body in there."

Mr. and Mrs. Nep held onto each other for support. "Where is he?" cried Mr. Nep, preparing to enter the field.

"No, don't go in there," shouted Alison, "there's something after me–it nearly got me."

The fieldmice made angry noises and lifted their torches high above their heads. "We must find it!" they declared. "We must put an end to this murder!"

Before any of them could move, there came a splintering and rustling sound. Out of the field, silhouetted against the sky, was the evil corn dolly.

Its looped head jerked from side to side as if it were sniffing the air. Then it began to advance stiffly toward them.

The fieldmice gasped and staggered back in horror.

"It's that doll thing!" some of them muttered. "How is it moving like that? It is bewitched."

Isaac Nettle came out of his quarters and beheld the scene with a mixture of horror and satisfaction. The straw figure was truly an abomination, yet surely now there would be no doubt that the town mouse was to blame for everything. Here was the proof of her witchcraft.

The corn demon marched awkwardly on and the mice fell back before it. Its wild arms were raised and its twiggy fingers twitched eagerly.

From the dark shadows near the ditch Madame Akkikuyu observed the scene with interest. "See how I let the mice do our work for us," whispered Nicodemus. "We shall see what they do with Miss Brown."

The demon struck out with its arms and caught hold of Dimsel Bottom. She squeaked with fright as it drew her near its lowered head.

Isaac raced up to the thing and dealt it a savage blow with his hammer. The corn dolly buckled as the hammer plunged into the straw, but it reared itself up again immediately and with one powerful arm swept Mr. Nettle off his feet and flung him to the ground.

"Save us, Green Mouse!" he wailed.

The thing was unstoppable. It placed its head over Dimsel's and the plait began to tighten. Arthur rushed out and pulled the hideous thing off and Dimsel sped away.

The fieldmice were driven back, terribly afraid. "Where is that town mouse?"some began to ask, and the call was taken up by all of them. "Where is the town mouse? Where is the town mouse?"

At the rear, Audrey held Twit's paw in terror. Out of the crowd Mr. Nep saw her and cried, "There she is. Bring her forward."

Feverish paws grabbed Audrey and pulled her away from Twit and the Scuttles. Through the mass she was dragged and shoved until she was pushed out in front of her creation.

Audrey could not escape. She tried to turn back, but angry paws and bodies barred her way. Arthur tried to help her, but found that his arms had been grabbed and the mice were holding on to him fiercely.

The corn dolly swept up to Audrey and lowered its head again. Audrey screamed, "Stop. Stop."

The figure jerked up quickly and lowered its arms. Then, to her everlasting horror, it bowed before her and fell lifeless to the ground.

The crowd stared at it with wide eyes and then Mr. Nep said, "It obeyed her."

"Witch," hissed the mob, "witch, witch, witch!" They circled around Audrey menacingly.

Try as he might, Arthur could not struggle free, and at the back, Twit could not break through the crowd.

Isaac Nettle came striding forward booming, "The town mouse is a witch. She has insulted the Green Mouse by weaving idols, and conjured spirits to give life to her hellish work. Three of our folk have died because of her. What do we do with a witch?"

"Burn her," cried the crowd.

"No," whimpered Audrey as they tied her paws behind her back. "I'm not a witch!"

But her voice was drowned out by the cries of the angry mice.

Isaac picked up the motionless corn dolly and cast it down into the ditch. Then he hurled a blazing torch after it and the figure immediately burst into flames. The loop head blackened and withered into a wisp of oily smoke.

The fieldmice pushed Audrey to the edge of the ditch and the glowing ashes rose up and curled around her ankles.

"Burn, burn!" they repeated excitedly. Two strong husbands lifted her up and swung her out over the flames.

Madame Akkikuyu covered her face with her claws and trembled. Nicodemus laughed triumphantly. All was going wonderfully.

"STOP THIS!" Mr. Woodruffe wrestled forward angrily. "You must all stop this!" He pulled Audrey out of the mice's paws and she clung tightly to him.

Isaac thundered in and whirled Mr. Woodruffe around. "Go back to your nest, Woodruffe. You are not our king now. Let us do what must be done. The witch must die!"

"But you can't burn her, Isaac. It's unspeakable!" He appealed to the crowd, "Surely you cannot have sunk so low to allow this. Never has a mouse been burned in Fennywolde. As for you, Nettle, I'm surprised. This has the smack of paganism in it."

The fieldmice looked anxiously at their leader. Mr. Woodruffe was right, they had never burned a mouse before. "But what are we to do with her?" asked a frightened Mrs. Nep.

Isaac snarled and yanked Audrey from Mr. Woodruffe's grip.

"Then she shall hang!" he proclaimed. "Let her choke, just as her creature choked Hodge and Young Whortle." He signaled to the crowd and they swarmed along the ditch, with him at their head and Audrey stumbling at his side.

"We've got to do something," said Arthur when his captors released him. "Will they really hang her, Mr. Scuttle?"

"'Fraid so, lad," he answered in dismay. Gladwin wrung her paws together.

"We're not done yet, boy," said Mr. Woodruffe. "Come on!" They ran after the angry crowd and pushed their way through.

Twit remained behind. He had never felt so useless in all his life. He was too small to do anything useful. He wished that Thomas Triton was there–he would have shown these mice a thing or two with his sword. But the midshipmouse was not there and there were far too many fieldmice to fight against anyway. This needed a cool head and lots of wits. Twit, the simple country mouse, had neither. He was the one with "no cheese upstairs," the butt of every joke. Now the life of a friend was in danger and he could think of nothing to help.

Suddenly he gasped. "Could I?" he asked himself. "Would it work?" There was only one way to find out. He rushed forward.

At the yew tree a tight circle of mice had formed. In the center were Mr. Nettle and Audrey. Her wide eyes were rolling in terror and their whites were showing. A straw rope had been slung over the "hanging branch" and a noose had been tied in one end.

Mr. Woodruffe barged in followed by Arthur. "This must not happen!" he cried. "Execution must only be as a result of a trial and only then if the accused is found guilty."

"We know she'm guilty," yelled Mr. Nep. The crowd roared their agreement.

"This is against the Greenlaws!" continued Mr. Woodruffe.

Isaac held out a trembling paw. "Thou knowest full well the respect and honor I hold for the mighty Green. I would not do this thing if the law did not permit. It is you who have forgotten the law, Woodruffe. Did not Fenny himself declare that all witches must be put to death?" The mob roared again and waved their torches. "Bind their paws so they may not interfere!" commanded Isaac.

Both Arthur's and Mr. Woodruffe's paws were tightly bound and strong arms were clenched about their necks.

"No, no," wailed Arthur. "My sister's not a witch–believe me."

Madame Akkikuyu left her place of shadow and moved toward the yew. "Quickly, Akkikuyu," said Nicodemus. "I must see! The girl must not die by hanging, she must be alive when the flame takes her. If you can cut her down before she is dead we may still be able to perform the spell. But hurry, and keep away from those torches, the heat of them is agony for me." The fortune-teller hurried forward, a confusion of loyalties whirling around her jumbled head.

Mr. Nettle put the noose around Audrey's neck and pulled the knot down tightly. Then he took hold of the other end and began to draw it down. Arthur closed his eyes.

Yelps and squeals broke out of the crowd and the mice jumped as something bit and clawed its way through. It was Twit. He didn't care how he got past. He ran into the ring, and before anyone could stop him he had slipped the rope from Audrey's throat.

"Leave her be!" roared Isaac, looming over him with his paw raised.

A smoldering green fire seemed to issue from Twit's eyes and Isaac faltered. "I come to claim her!" Twit shouted at the top of his voice. "I claim her in the name of the Green."

"How dare you blaspheme!" growled Mr. Nettle. "She is for the noose."

"Do you forget your own laws, Nettle?" Twit barked back at him.

"What laws?"

"The law of the gallows," snarled Twit.

"The gallows law," repeated everyone in astonishment–surely Twit was not that stupid.

Mr. Woodruffe reminded Isaac as he stood, searching his memory. "The gallows law runs thus," he said. "Any may invoke the law of the gallows–if a willing spouse can be found beneath the hanging tree then the accused, whatever the crime, will be reprieved."

"A spouse!" mocked Isaac. "Who would marry a witch?"

"I will," said Twit proudly. "I invoke the law and offer my paw in marriage to Audrey Brown."

The crowd rippled in discontent and Nicodemus hissed in Madame Akkikuyu's ear.

"No! The girl must not marry–it will bind her up in the Greenlaws and she shall be useless to me. Stop this now."

The fortune-teller entered the circle, but instead of obeying Nicodemus she said, "Mousey must marry–follow the law of your Green. Join the two before you feel his anger." In the center of all the fieldmice the tattoo dared not move on her ear, but it glared at her venomously.

"Imbecile!" it whispered harshly.

Isaac stared at the rat in disbelief. He had made a brass for the destruction of Audrey at her request. Why was she changing sides now? "But she is to blame!" he said blankly. "Are you telling me now that she must go free?"

"She must, it is the law!" demanded Twit. "I call on the Green Mouse to witness all that goes on here. He shall know who disobeys him."

The crowd murmured. There was no getting away from it. If Twit married Audrey then she could not be hanged.

"No," cried Mr. Nep as he sensed their doubt. "We cannot let her go unpunished. My son is dead."

It was Isaac who answered him. "Silence, Nep. The way has been shown, though it grieves me no less than you. We must obey the law or we ourselves are guilty. But hear me, tomorrow we shall drive Twit and the witch to our borders and banish them. Then if any find them crossing our lands they have the right to do with them as they see fit. They are outcasts." He turned back to Twit and Audrey.

"Now, take the witch's paw in yours, William Scuttle," said Mr. Nettle.

Twit looked at her. She was much calmer now and she stared back at him with gratitude. "Do you mean to go through with it?" she asked him.

"If'n I don't marry 'ee, Aud, they'll lynch yer," he replied.

"I don't know what to say," Audrey mumbled.

"Just say 'yes' an' save yer neck," advised Twit.

"Kneel ye," ordered Isaac, "and humble thyselves before the Green Mouse." Audrey felt someone cut the ropes that bit into her wrists and she dropped to her knees beside Twit.

"Dost thou, William Scuttle, take unto thyself this mouse, Audrey Brown? To cherish through the winter and revel with in the summer? Forswearing all others until the grass grows green over you both?"

"I does," said Twit.

"Who blesses the husband?" asked Isaac. It was usual at mouse weddings for both the bride and groom to receive a blessing. This could not come from their families. It was usually friends who performed the task, but at this torchlit marriage everyone wondered who would dare bless the union of a witch and a fool.

"I do," said a solemn voice, and Mr. Woodruffe shook off his guards. He wriggled his paws free of the ropes and stood before Twit.

"May the Green bless and protect you," he said with feeling, and he placed his right paw on Twit's shoulder.

"Thank 'ee," replied Twit gratefully.

Then it was Audrey's turn.

"Dost thou, Audrey Brown," intoned Isaac bitterly, "take unto thyself this mouse, William Scuttle? To cherish through the winter and revel with in the summer? Forswearing all others until the grass grows green over you both?"

Audrey tearfully thought of Piccadilly. Sobbing she uttered, "I do."

"Who blesses the wife?" Isaac looked around. No one said anything. He smiled. There might be a hanging yet, for no marriage was complete without the two blessings, and he who blessed the groom could not bless the bride as well.

Arthur gazed at the fieldmice pleadingly. "Please, someone, anyone, don't let Audrey die." But the mice shuffled their feet and hung their heads.

Isaac chuckled and was about to pronounce the ceremony void when a figure stepped up to Audrey.

"I bless mouselet!" declared Madame Akkikuyu. Isaac glared at her, but the fortune-teller came and knelt before her friend and said tenderly, "May his mighty Greenness bless and protect you for always, and may you forgive Akkikuyu. Remember that she love you and want you to be happy in summer light–it's all I ever wanted, my mouselet." She leaned over to kiss Audrey's forehead.

"Thank you." She wept.

A big tear streaked down Akkikuyu's nose. "Ach! I always blub at weddings."

Isaac concluded the ceremony.

"May the Mighty Green join these two together, through winter, harvest, youth, and age. Let no creature come between them for now they are under the Green's great mantle." He sucked his teeth and said, "Rise, Scuttle and Scuttle."

"You better be gone before midday tomorrow," shouted Mr. Nep, "or I swear I'll hurl you both into the fire myself. The crowd began to disperse, and drift back into the field.

Twit's parents rushed forward and hugged their son and

daughter-in-law. Gladwin was tearful, but Elijah was proud. "There's another Mr. and Mrs. Scuttle around here now." He beamed.

"Not for long, though, Dad," said Twit. "Aud may be my wife, but I don't 'spect her to stay wi' me." He turned to the new Mrs. Scuttle and said softly, "'S all right, Aud. I know you aren't keen on me in that way, so p'raps it's best if'n you go home tomorrow, eh?"

"What about you, Twit?" Audrey asked. "And I can't go home anyway–what about Oswald and the Starwife's bargain?"

"Let's go and have something to eat," suggested Arthur, "then we can decide what to do."

Under the yew tree Madame Akkikuyu stood alone, sniveling into her shawl and drying her eyes.

"You fool," rebuked Nicodemus. "You interfering cretin! We might have had the girl if you had not blessed her. My plans are ruined now–Audrey Brown has been tied to the Greenlaws, the spell cannot work."

"Mouselet name Scuttle now," checked Akkikuyu sadly, "and I glad you not use her–she my friend. Akkikuyu not have many friends, mouselet only one."

The tattoo writhed with frustration. "Curse you–you Moroccan ditch drab. The spell I have prepared needs a female sacrifice, one who is of age but has no mousebrass. Am I to be marooned in the abyss till the end of time?"

Madame Akkikuyu stared out along the bank. There sat Alison Sedge, miserable and dejected. She had longed for Audrey's death and now her enemy lived and was married. With Jenkin dead, Alison knew she would never marry.

Akkikuyu frowned as Alison stood up. No mousebrass hung from her neck.

"Nico," she whispered. "Akkikuyu find another."

The tattoo stared out and grinned. "Excellent. We shall perform the ritual tonight. Prepare the girl for sacrifice."

CHAPTER FOURTEEN

THE SACRIFICE

Alison Sedge kicked the tufts of dry, scruffy grass and turned to follow the others back into the field.

"Hoy, mousey, wait for I."

The rat's voice startled her. Crossly she waited for Madame Akkikuyu to come out from under the yew tree.

"What you want?" asked Alison rudely. She did not like Madame Akkikuyu–she blamed her for bringing Audrey to Fennywolde in the first place.

The fortune-teller approached, smiling sweetly. "Let me help poor mousey," she said. "Ah, but mousey has lost pretty dangler. Where it go?"

"I got rid of it!" snapped Alison. What business was it of the rat, anyway? "What do you mean you could help me?" she added in a sullen tone.

Madame Akkikuyu walked around the girl and sprinkled fragments of yellow leaves over her. In a secret, low whisper she said, "I have spells, mousey, bring disaster on your enemies."

The mouse regarded her through the screen of fluttering

leaves. What was she up to? wondered Alison. "What enemies?" she asked stubbornly.

The rat moved closer. "Those who rob you of suitors–those who get in your way, sweet mousey. Jumped-up girls not as pretty as you."

"You mean that town mouse?" she interrupted. "Yes, I don't like her, but if you hadn't blessed the marriage back then she'd have danced the gallows jig. What are you going on about now, you barmy so-and-so?"

"Akkikuyu stop hanging, yes, because that too quick and easy for her. She too evil! She put spell on Jenky boy to make him fall for her. She led him into open and let Mahooot make him owl bait."

Alison exploded with rage. "Is this true? I ought to go and tear her apart! All that butter-wouldn't-melt routine. I hate her. I knew my Jenkin didn't really fancy her. Tell me what I can do."

The fortune-teller grinned. Alison Sedge had been an easy fish to catch. It would be easy throwing her on the fire–how could she loathe her mouselet so much?

"Akkikuyu will cast spell. You help, go get wood for bonfire." Alison hurriedly ran to collect some sticks.

"Well, Nico," the rat began, "what you think?"

"She is perfect, Akkikuyu," gloated the voice, "did you feel her spite and anger? They are strong, raw emotions. Her life essence will be most eagerly received by the gatekeepers of the abyss. Tonight I shall be free again."

Akkikuyu cleared a space on the high bank. She gathered some stones and arranged them in a circle, leaving it incomplete so that she could enter. She waited for Alison to return, then, once all the wood they needed was within, she sealed the ring with them inside. "Now, mousey," she said, "we must not break through the stones till spell complete." She began to build the bonfire. From her bag she pulled out the skull of the frog she had killed and placed it at the heart of the framework. Then around it she sprinkled the magical herbs and flowers that she had carefully gathered at night. At last the fortune-teller announced that all was ready. She stood back and admired her handiwork with Alison. It was a tall pyramid of dry branches and twigs, a satisfying result to her labors.

"Light it," urged Alison, "cast your spell."

Nicodemus chuckled to himself. "Give her the crystal," he muttered to Akkikuyu.

The rat brought from her bag the glass globe and caressed it lovingly with her claws. "Stand there and hold this!" she told Alison.

Alison took the smooth globe in her palms and gazed at it wondrously. What a marvelous mysterious object! How lovely it was with those swirls of color in its center.

"What is it?" she gasped.

"It is my delight–my peace," Akkikuyu replied sadly, "and soon it must smash."

"Will you light the fire now?" asked Alison. She was feeling impatient and wanted to get on with the ceremony.

Akkikuyu nodded. "Yes, I light fire, but first my Nico must be safe from heat."

"Nico?" asked Alison suspiciously. "Who is Nico?" She stared around her, trying to see who Akkikuyu was talking about.

"I AM NICODEMUS!" cried the tattoo triumphantly. Alison whirled around, then stepped back in alarm.

"The face! The face on your ear–it moved, it spoke!" she spluttered aghast.

Nicodemus mocked her: "I move–I speak. Hah hah hah."

Alison had had enough. She turned and tried to run from the circle of stones, but a wall of invisible force prevented her escape. She howled in dismay, but Nicodemus laughed all the more.

"Mousey not leave now ring complete," tutted Akkikuyu.

"You not listen, mousey. Now, Nico we must begin, yes?"

"Truly," said the voice, still chuckling as Alison twisted and turned around the circle in vain. "I shall project my essence into the heart of your crystal, there shall I be safe from the heat of the fire. I hope that I shall still be able to talk to you, but my powers will be much weakened by the glass." The tattoo screwed up its ugly face and became quite still.

A black cloud moved over the stars. Alison stared at the crystal in her paws and saw a pinprick of cold blue light glimmer there. Slowly it began to pulse. The light grew and filled the globe until the crystal shone like a star fallen to earth. The glass became freezing to the touch, yet Alison could not let go. Breathlessly and with great difficulty the voice spoke again, it was nearer, yet somehow it echoed hollowly. "Quickly, Akkikuyu," it said with an effort, an edge of fear creeping into it, "light the fire now! The spell must be completed soon, or the keepers of the gate will draw me back and bind me ever stronger. I have but a little time here unless the exchange is made." Akkikuyu lit the bonfire.

The wood was so dry that it kindled easily, and soon the flames leaped up greedily. The heat singed her whiskers and scorched Alison's face, but the crystal remained icy to the touch.

"Aaagghh," said the voice, "even here I feel the fire! You must hurry. Throw in the mousebrass, Akkikuyu."

The fortune-teller fished out the brass that Isaac had made for her. It was a twisted, ugly thing, made in a spirit of hatred and vengeance. She cast it into the white-hot heart of the crackling flame.

"Hear me, Arash and Iriel," cried Nicodemus. "I send you a soul in my stead. A female unprotected by the Greenlaws. Accept her and let me go free."

A deep rumble boomed in the night. Thunder was approaching. On the horizon, fingers of lightning zigzagged down between heaven and earth. A freezing gale blew up, but protected by the circle of stones, the bonfire remained unaffected. Madame Akkikuyu threw some powders into the blaze and a ball of blue flame burst into the darkening sky.

"Prepare the vessel, Rameth, so I might live again." Nicodemus screamed above the clamoring storm.

Akkikuyu hurled more powder into the flame. A blue column of smoke shot up into the air. The fortune-teller was frightened. She had not expected anything like this at all. If it carried on, the fieldmice would come soon to see what was going on. She winced and clutched her stomach. Something was happening to her . . . something dreadful . . . A terrible pain ripped at her insides. She doubled over in agony, and as she did so, she caught sight of her own body, and cried out in horror.

Her fur was changing color. Instead of being a sleek coat of black, it was now a bright marmalade orange with dark stripes. The secret, closed doors of her mind were forced open and she bellowed with fear as she remembered the past, and saw through Nicodemus's disguise.

Nicodemus laughed amid the thunder and as he did so his voice changed–it became deeper, more sinister, and absolutely evil. He crowed his triumph with insane jubilation.

"Yes, Akkikuyu," sneered the great deceiver, "it is I, your master returned. JUPITER has come back from eternity."

"No!" she yammered plaintively. "You Nicodemus, spirit of field–Jupiter dead."

"Hah hah–I am the father of lies, Akkikuyu, you know that. You have helped to release me, I shall not forget. I intend to reward you with the highest honor that is mine to give."

"What honor?" she asked in horror.

"You have opened the door of death, Akkikuyu," he congratulated her, "but my old body has been destroyed. *You* shall be the new host for my dark spirit."

"Nooo!" Akkikuyu tore at her hair and tried to flee, but like

Alison she could not break out of the stone circle.

"You cannot escape," tutted Jupiter. "Do you not listen? Continue with the spell!"

"Never," she cried, and slumped to the ground in a desperate heap, cringing from that terrible snarling voice. But unseen forces gripped her and the rat was dragged to her feet. Her claws were forced into her bag and a will outside her own guided them to the next ingredient. The powders were thrown into the flame.

"Hear me, Ozulmunn–bind her to me."

Akkikuyu's eyes stung and their black orbs trembled. A thin film of gold closed over them until only narrow slits were left. Her ears were pulled out of shape and she felt her tail grow thick, stripey fur. Jupiter's evil spells were changing her into a cat!

She threw open her mouth to scream but all that came out was a pitiful *meow*. Madame Akkikuyu clapped her ginger claws over her mouth to stop the terrible noise.

"Now, Akkikuyu, throw the girl into the fire, then smash the globe!" commanded Jupiter.

The rat's feet dragged themselves toward Alison.

The mouse had witnessed everything with incredulous despair. She cried for pity as the striped ginger rat lurched toward her. But there was nowhere to escape.

"Throw her in, Akkikuyu!" Jupiter ordered severely.

Madame Akkikuyu blinked her tawny eyes and took hold of the mouse.

"Please, please!" begged Alison as the rat pulled her toward the flames.

The lightning flashed and crackled overhead. Thunder shook the ground, and Jupiter laughed.

"Please don't throw me in," pleaded Alison. "Please, have pity on me!"

With her golden eyes it seemed to Akkikuyu that for a

moment Audrey stood before her. "Mouselet," she said, "go, run free."

"I can't," Alison wailed.

Jupiter heard them and scoffed. "You, girl, have no choice. You have an appointment with the keepers of the gates of hell. Dispatch her, Akkikuyu."

Madame Akkikuyu thought of the eternal torment that lay before her should Jupiter take possession of her body. She let go of Alison and shouted, "Mouselet, my friend! It is I who have choice. I will not serve you again! Akkikuyu is free!" With one terrific leap, Madame Akkikuyu cast herself into the middle of the fire.

The rat's ginger fur became black once more. . . . As the blaze roared up, Akkikuyu's voice was heard one last time from the heart of the flames, "Akkikuyu tried so hard, mouselet. . . " and with that she died.

A bolt of lightning struck the circle and blasted the stones apart. Alison dropped the crystal and fled through the gap, escaping into the field.

The bonfire spluttered, the flames leaped higher, and the tumult of the storm drowned out Jupiter's voice calling from the glowing crystal.

"The sacrifice has been made and They are satisfied. Release me child, release me. I am Jupiter, Lord of all Darkness! I command you to break open the globe!" Without his tattooed eyes he could not see that there was no one to hear him.

Bright, fiendish sparks shot out of the fire and fell within the cornfield.

Before long, the corn was ablaze.

The terrible spirit within the globe called out in pain as the fierce heat scorched the glass. The bonfire toppled over and fell with a flurry of burning ashes on top of the crystal. Jupiter's furious cries were muffled.

* * *

In the Hall of Corn, the Scuttles, Arthur, and Mr. Woodruffe had decided that Audrey and Twit should go back to Deptford to tell the Starwife what had happened.

The rest of the fieldmice were mumbling and talking to each other in low voices. Some of them were repenting their hasty actions while others were sorry the town mouse had got off so lightly.

Suddenly a cry made everyone turn around. All the sentries were in the Hall; none had seen Alison Sedge crashing through the field. She burst into the Hall of Corn and shouted, "It's the ratwoman–she's working for a devil, *she* is behind all this."

But before anyone could question her farther, another voice yelled out, "FIRE!"

All heads turned again. The sky was aglow and black plumes of smoke blew toward the Hall. Hot ash started to rain down and the Fennywolders squeaked in panic.

"To the still pool!" declared Mr. Woodruffe, jumping onto the throne. "Fly as fast as you can. Save yourselves."

The fieldmice streamed out of the great doors and through the corridor. They were met by the ravaging fire devouring the corn at a terrifying rate.

The Fennywolders could not escape that way–they were beaten back into the Hall of Corn by the blaze, and with a splintering *whoosh* the great doors collapsed behind them.

"We're trapped!" cried the mice.

It was getting difficult to breathe, as the air was sucked up by the flames.

One of the nests caught fire and began to burn furiously.

"Over here," bawled Arthur, "it hasn't reached here yet." Everyone ran to the Scuttles' area, and Twit guided them out through a narrow channel of choking smoke. It was so thick and hot that it burned the eyes and filled the lungs. Old

Todmore coughed and spluttered in the blackness.

"Where we goin', you daft lad? I can't see," he wheezed.

"I knows this way in me sleep," Twit called back to him.

The ears of corn above burst and spat down fiery missiles.

"Come on," shouted Arthur, trying to sound calm, "nearly there."

The babies gagged and cried, turning their tiny pink faces away from the glaring flames. Elijah and Gladwin clutched each other's paws tightly as they crouched beneath blazing arches.

The heat was furnace-hot and the tips of tails sizzled, while delicate ears roasted.

A few times Twit hesitated, doubting the way. His whiskers smoked, but the noise of the inferno, coupled with the lightning, confused him.

"This way," he decided, crossing his fingers. He dived through a wall of smoke and found himself in the glade. "C'mon," he shouted.

Soon everyone was there and they hurried over to the hawthorn bushes and dived into the pool.

"Hang on," said Arthur. "Where's Audrey?"

"Not with me, Arthur," said Gladwin, getting worried.

"I think she was with Mr. Woodruffe," Elijah muttered.

"But I haven't seen him either," Arthur cried.

"Then she must be still in there," said Twit, looking back at the field. The fire was out of control.

"Nothing could live in that," murmured Arthur grimly.

"Oh, Aud," said Twit.

When the fieldmice had left the Hall, Audrey and Mr. Woodruffe heard a faint cry. They hurried back and found Isaac Nettle lying on the ground. He had been overcome by the smoke.

"Get on yer feet, Nettle," snapped Mr. Woodruffe. He pulled the mouse up and slapped his face firmly.

"Let me be," whined Isaac miserably. He sagged down again. "Let me rest."

"Oh no, Nettle, you've done too much harm this night to fizzle out now, you old goat," said Mr. Woodruffe, hauling him away.

"Will he be all right?" asked Audrey anxiously as she looked desperately around at the burning Hall.

"Aye, lass, if we can get him out in time. Now come on, Nettle, use yer legs."

"No," cried Isaac suddenly. "The brass, my son's brass, it was in my paw. Where's it gone?"

"It must be back there," said Audrey.

"Leave it, Nettle."

"I must have it, I must. Jenkin, my lad!" He struggled wildly with them.

"If you go back in you'll suffocate," shouted Mr. Woodruffe. "Stay here! I'll go."

"No," yelled Audrey.

Mr. Woodruffe charged through the thick, clinging smoke and searched for Jenkin's mousebrass.

There came a fierce roar as a line of burning nests crashed down behind. They formed a fence of fire between him and the others. He was trapped.

"Mr. Woodruffe!" called Audrey.

"Go child, while you can," he yelled. "You can't save me. Take Nettle out of here."

More nests tumbled between them and Audrey fled tearfully away.

Mr. Woodruffe made it across to his wicker throne and sat on it just as the blazing walls caved in on him. The king died with his field.

Audrey tugged furiously at Isaac, who was singing in a mad voice. The way was practically impassable now. Terrifying sheets of fire raged on either side of the path.

"Glory to the Green," raved Mr. Nettle insanely. "See his blossoms grow."

It took all of Audrey's failing strength to make him follow her, and the ground scorched her feet badly as she dragged him to safety.

"Please, this way, Mr. Nettle," she implored.

"What flowers are these?" Isaac asked, staring up at blazing cornstalks. "Come, Jenkin, see this fair garden. What wonders have we here?"

"Please, Mr. Nettle," she cried, yanking at his paw. The flames swallowed the path behind them.

"With red roses and orange blossom–how bright they are," marveled Isaac. He coughed painfully.

Audrey pushed him farther along. Her hair smoldered and she discarded her lace collar so she could breathe.

They came to the end of their journey. A massive wall of flames reared up before them. Audrey sobbed: they could go no farther. They were cut off.

"Praise be to Him who makes the flowers," ranted Isaac.

Audrey fell to her knees. The fire roared on every side and blazed overhead. She looked around dizzily and gave up. Audrey fainted.

"Blessed be the new leaves of the hawthorn," rejoiced Mr. Nettle.

Thunder split the sky and the clouds were rent apart. Heavy rain teemed down with torrential force. The pool filled and flooded into the ditch while the blazing field hissed and seethed.

* * *

Audrey opened her eyes. There was a low, rough ceiling over her head and she was in a small bare room. It was the Scuttles' winter quarters.

"Hello, Aud!" Twit was sitting by her side.

She smiled at him. "How did I get here?" she asked. "There was fire everywhere. I thought I was done for–what happened to Mr. Nettle?"

"He's sleepin'. We found him an' you when the rain put the fire out. We all thought you were dead, but you were only in a swoon. You was lucky this time, Aud."

"Yes." She pulled her fingers through her singed hair and remembered. "Mr. Woodruffe, did you find him?"

Twit looked at the floor sadly. "He didn't make it, Aud. And we found somethin' else." The little fieldmouse fidgeted with his toes.

"What else?"

The fieldmouse raised a pale face. "Akkikuyu's dead–she burned in her own bonfire."

Audrey shook her head. "Poor Akkikuyu–are you sure?"

He nodded hurriedly. "Ain't no doubt there."

Audrey burst into tears. She had started out hating the rat but had grown fond of her funny ways. The memory of last night's wedding ceremony and Akkikuyu's blessing flooded back. "Oh, Akkikuyu, I'm sorry," she wept.

Twit patted her hand. "Leastways you're free of that bargain now Aud. You can go home. Oswald is safe."

"Yes," she sniffed, "the bargain is over." She stared at Twit and said, "But you're my husband now, Twit. I can't leave you."

Twit reassured her, "Now don't be daft, Aud," he said, "we both know I only married yer to stop yer gettin' hanged. I told 'ee you don't have to stay. Go back to Deptford–it's where you belong."

"And you?"

Twit shrugged. "A fieldmouse belongs in a field," he told her. "I'll stick around, providing my banishment's been lifted, and help with the clearing up. A nasty mess–very nasty."

"You know," whispered Audrey, "you're not as cheeseless

as folk make out, William Scuttle. You're a very wise mouse, indeed. I'll miss you." She kissed him.

"Aw," he puffed, turning bright red and twisting his tail in his paws. "I reckons I'll come back one day to see me wife an' have a chinwag with old Thomas over a bowl of rum."

Gladwin Scuttle bustled in. Her hair was tied up in a scarf and she wore a white apron. "Oh, you're awake, Audrey," she said. "Well, that is a relief. I'm just on my way to help with the cleanup. Half the tunnels are flooded by the rains and it's still pouring. No, don't you get up, young lady. You stay there for at least a week. You hear me?"

Audrey laughed.

It took nearly a week for the cleanup to end. The tunnels had been flooded with sooty water and this left everything grimy and unpleasant. One of the first things the fieldmice did was start redecorating. They stained the walls with berry juice and decked flowers everywhere. The drab years had passed and in his sickroom, Isaac Nettle, recovering from his madness, accepted the way of things. He even strung nutshells together and painted them bright colors. He was a changed mouse. Many of the children were ill with smoke sickness and Samuel Gorse left his room to visit them and cheer their spirits by acting out, with Todkin and Figgy's help, the story of Mahooot the owl. Figgy played the part of Young Whortle, who was sorely missed by them all.

Arthur arranged the burials of Mr. Woodruffe, Young Whortle, and Madame Akkikuyu's remains.

It was the first time Audrey was allowed out of doors and she was stunned at what was left of the field.

All was charred and ugly. The corn had disappeared, leaving unlovely, spiky stubble poking out of the ground. Rain puddles were coated with ash, and everything was drab and dismal. It seemed that the whole world had turned dark and gray.

The King of the Field was buried on a drizzling morning near the rose trees. The fieldmice raised a mound over him, and Isaac carved a beautiful crown of hawthorn leaves from a single piece of wood. Into it he inscribed the words: "We have lost our king whose light shone on our darkness."

He laid the monument on the top of the mound, and fresh flowers were placed there every day.

Young Whortle was laid to rest next to Hodge. Mr. and Mrs. Nep mourned the loss of their son for the rest of their lives.

The Fennywolders could not decide where to put Madame Akkikuyu. Some thought that she ought not to be buried at all, but be thrown to the birds. Most fieldmice, though, remembered her eagerness to please and the bravery she showed with Mahooot. So it was decided to lay her to rest under the hawthorn around the still pool. There it was hoped she would find peace at last. Audrey, swallowing back her tears, insisted that the remains of the fortune-teller be placed in a patch of ground that the sunlight touched. So the branches were cut back, and as the earth was piled over her grave the sun appeared in the wet sky and a pale, slender ray shone down upon the last resting place of the fortune-teller.

"It's all she ever wanted," wept Audrey.

The still pool became known as "the witch's water," and in years to come, youngsters would go there to cast offerings into it and beg for wishes. And sometimes, on certain summer evenings, when the last flickering beams of the setting sun touched a particular spot—wishes did indeed come true.

In Fennywolde the cleanup finished, and Audrey began to think of going home.

Arthur was upset at the thought of leaving. He had gained everyone's respect, and now they knew that Audrey was innocent the mice had warmed to her too. A veil seemed to have been lifted, and they became the good-natured creatures they had always been.

Finally the day dawned when it was time to leave. Audrey kissed Elijah and Gladwin good-bye.

"Tell my sister to stop poking her nose in where it's not wanted–she did that when she was a child, you know."

"Fare'ee well, lass," said Elijah.

It was time to say good-bye to Twit. "I'll miss you, William," she said thickly, her eyes brimming with tears. "I'll never forget you."

"See you, Aud," he replied brightly, but the twinkle had left his eye forever. "Say hello to Oswald for me, an' thank Thomas for his rum. Take care now."

"I will. Good-bye." She kissed her husband for the last time.

Arthur said his farewells briskly. "Cheerio," he said, waving to everyone who had come out to see them off. Dimsel Bottom slunk away and stared after him sorrowfully.

Brother and sister set off. Twit raised his paw, but his voice croaked hoarsely, "'Bye!" He tried to wipe the tears from his eyes, but they would not stop. "I did love 'ee, Aud," he whispered.

Arthur Brown and Audrey Scuttle became two specks on the horizon, making for the river. When the farewell cries of the country mice had finally dwindled into nothingness, the two town mice looked back for their friends, but they had already traveled too far. All they could see as they gazed back toward the cornfield were the elms rising high above the ditch and the yew tree spreading darkly behind them. This picture stayed in their minds long after. But although they both vowed to return one day, neither ever saw the land of Fenny again.

CHAPTER FIFTEEN

SUMMER'S END

It was the last day of summer. The breeze was fresh and cool, the sun was a pale disk in the sky. The leaves of the elms were past their best and had that tired, old look, which suggests the coming of autumn. Some of them were already curling up and turning gold.

Alison Sedge sat on the edge of the ditch, lost in thought. She no longer took great care of her appearance. Her hair needed brushing and she let it fall in tangled, untidy knots over her face. Her dress was shabby–but why should she care? In her mind she was with Jenkin. They laughed together and smiled at each other in a dreamworld she greatly cherished. Alison lived for such dreams now. She no longer tossed her head or flashed her eyes, and she never listened to compliments from boys. In fact, such compliments had ceased. Alison did not bother about that, for in her mind's eye she was the way Jenkin liked her.

She turned the black thing over in her paws. She had found it buried in a pile of ashes and cinders. Her find was scorched, blackened, and pitted but not broken. She raised the crystal of Madame Akkikuyu up to the sun, but it was too black and opaque to allow her to see within.

It was some months now since the town mice had left Fennywolde and returned to Deptford. Alison had kept out of their way. How fickle everyone was to begin liking that horrid girl after everything she had done. But no, it was the ratwoman who had caused all the evil wasn't it? Alison was confused. Her thoughts were really too full of Jenkin to dwell on other subjects for long. But there was something about this globe–it had something to do with . . . oh, she could not remember anymore.

"Curse you, Audrey," she spat, and discarded the black sooty ball. It began to roll down the steep bank. . . .

Alison struggled to her feet and walked away. She was oblivious of the light noise behind her, and did not hear the glass crack and then smash on the sharp stones at the bottom of the ditch.

Unwittingly, Alison had completed the spell that had caused so much suffering. While she dreamed of a time long before, when she and Jolly Jenkin had been happy together, a hideous great shadow rose up from the ditch behind her.

Jupiter soared into the sky–free at last from the crystal prison.

AFTERWORD

BY PETER GLASSMAN

Power-hungry rats, nature-loving mice, mystical bats . . . In *The Dark Portal*, Robin Jarvis delights readers with not just one, but three unforgettable animal societies. By creating characters with human motivations and personalities flavored by their essentially animal natures, he offers a strikingly original, totally absorbing fantasy world.

Of course, tales about animals who act like people have been told as long as people have gathered to listen to stories; Aesop's fables, some of the oldest stories in western culture, are filled with such animals, as are many tales from African, Asian, Inuit, American Indian, and Aboriginal cultures.

In the nineteenth century, when literature for young people blossomed in Great Britain, many books included animal characters who could talk—such as those in *Alice's Adventures in Wonderland*—but none featured animals subsisting in their very own societies. Then, with the dawning of the twentieth century, came the debut of the Peter Rabbit books by Beatrix Potter. Although without distinct societies or customs, the animals in these stories wore clothes and misbehaved like adventurous children (and suffered the consequences!). Soon after, Kenneth Grahame's *The Wind in the Willows* was published, and the animal fantasy novel truly came into its own; for in this story, Rat, Mole, and their friends lived quite apart from human society (although people resided nearby).

After the publication of *The Wind in the Willows*, animal fantasy books became more popular. In the early 1920s, Hugh Lofting introduced the Doctor Doolittle books, while A. A. Milne created the Winnie-the-Pooh stories, and Felix Salten wrote *Bambi*. The following decades saw the publication of such classics as Walter Brooks's Freddy the Pig books, George Selden's *The Cricket in Times Square* and its many sequels, the Newbery Medal–winning *Mrs. Frisby and the Rats of NIMH*, and James and Deborah Howe's *Bunnicula*. And, of course, there was the phenomenal success of Richard Adams's *Watership Down*.

In *Watership Down*, Adams re-ignited interest in what Kenneth Grahame had created nearly seventy years earlier—a fantasy story in which animal communities had their own distinct rules, customs, and lore based on their animal nature, yet tinged with human qualities. In the wake of this surprise best-seller, many authors wrote animal fantasies aimed at the adult market, but few met with much success.

Then in 1986, a novel by British radio performer and writer Brian Jacques was published, in both Great Britain and America. Almost overnight, on both sides of the Atlantic, readers young and old were caught up in the saga of *Redwall*. Its heroic animal characters gave fresh life to what had been thought a dead literary form—the swashbuckler—and its success helped revive American publishers' enthusiasm for animal fantasy. In the past, more attention had been given to humorous tales like *The Cricket in Times Square* and *Bunnicula*, but *Redwall* had shown readers' appetites for serious adventure stories featuring animal protagonists.

In 1989, Robin Jarvis's *The Dark Portal*, an animal fantasy unlike any other, was published in Great Britain. With its sinister characters of Jupiter and the rats who scurry to serve him (as well as their evil plotting against one another), the novel has a tinge of the occult darkness found in the writing of such masters as Edgar Allen Poe, H. P. Lovecraft, and M. R. James. But countering this blackness are the farseeing bats, who possess mystical visions of the future, and the loving mouse communities, who cherish their mouse brasses and their belief in the living spirit of spring, the Green Mouse. This careful blend of good and evil, combined with compelling mythology and powerful rituals, made *The Dark Portal* and its two sequels—*The Crystal Prison* and *The Final Reckoning*—best-sellers in Great Britain.

The summer it was first published, I was lucky enough to come upon *The Dark Portal* during a trip to London. Over the following years, every so often I would run into another person who had read and admired this series. When S. E. Hinton (the award-winning author of *The Outsiders, Tex, Rumble Fish,* and *That Was Then, This is Now*) asked me if I had ever heard of the Deptford Mice books, I told her how much I had enjoyed them, then asked her how she came to know about them. She replied that her son had discovered the books when they were in Britain and that they had quickly become his favorites at the time. And she, like all who knew them, couldn't understand why they weren't available in the United States.

Well, finally, they are. At the dawn of this new century, the Deptford Mice books are here for us to share and enjoy. Thank the Green!

Peter Glassman is the owner of Books of Wonder, the New York City bookstore and publisher specializing in both new and old imaginative books for children.

ROBIN JARVIS was born in Liverpool, England, and studied graphic design in college. He worked in television and advertising before becoming a full-time author and illustrator. It was while working at a company that made characters for TV programs and advertising that he began making sketches of mice. From these drawings, the idea for the Deptford Mice was born. ***The Dark Portal***, short-listed for the 1989 Smarties Book Prize in England, was followed by two more titles in the series: ***The Crystal Prison*** and ***The Final Reckoning***. Mr. Jarvis currently lives in Greenwich, London.

LOOK FOR THE OTHER BOOKS IN

THE DEPTFORD MICE TRILOGY

BOOK ONE

THE DARK PORTAL

In the sewers of Deptford, there lurks a dark presence that fills the tunnels with fear. The rats worship it in the blackness and name it "Jupiter, Lord of All." Into this twilight realm wanders a small and frightened mouse–the unwitting trigger of a chain of events that hurtles the Deptford Mice into a world of heroic adventure and terror.

BOOK THREE

THE FINAL RECKONING

The ghostly spirit of Jupiter has returned, bent on revenge. Struggling to survive in an eternal world of ice and snow, the Deptford Mice are worried: the mystical bats have fled from the attic, and underground a new rat army is growing. With food short and no sign of spring, the mice know that desperation is close at hand. And few, it seems, might live to tell the tale.